Through the Storm

Water Princess Series
Book 1

J.A. Guynn

Acknowledgements

Thank you to my wife for her continued support and encouragement. Without you, this story would not exist.

Thank you to Rick Brasseaux for spending time and effort as a beta-reader. Rick, you recommended little details that made a big difference in the story, not to mention pointing out I changed the spelling of the main character's name and didn't realize it.

ISBN: 979-8-9856947-6-5

Library of Congress Control Number: 2025909295

Cover Design: 100covers.com

Editor: Charlie Knight at cknightwrites.com

Proofreader: Mark Schultz, the Hyper-Speller at www.wordrefiner.com

Publisher: 3220 Group, LLC. Alvin, TX

Prologue

Screams echoed off the royal bedchamber's walls, undampened by the tapestries hung around the room. Tindra, the Queen of Croy, panted, trying to catch her breath from her latest outburst. Sweat flowed across her tawny skin, soaking the rug beneath her. Her left hand gripped King Fitzeirick's tight enough to grind his knuckles together. The stump where her right hand had been pressed hard into his thigh.

"I can't," she gasped, collapsing against her husband's chest, "keep this up." Her firesything talent did nothing to help her. Given how little her straining now affected the candles around the room, her exhaustion was obvious.

With the labor dragging on more than a day, Fitzeirick wished his wife were a stonesyth so she could draw stamina from the floor like he could. *Or if I could transfer some of my energy to her.* "You're doing fine," he said. "Just remember to breathe."

Bera, Tindra's handmaid, offered her a cup of water. "Drink, m'lady. All is well."

Tindra gulped down a mouthful as Bera wiped the queen's brow.

"I can see the top of the baby's head," Abi, the royal herbalist, said, looking up from her position between the queen's knees. "Another push should do. Bera, stand ready."

The handmaid gave the cup to Fitzeirick, moved to Abi's side, and grabbed a soft, knit, drying cloth.

Tindra drew a deep breath as weary muscles clenched. The grunt forcing its way through her clenched teeth rose to another scream as her body pushed. "Congratulations, my Queen, you have a daught— Oh. Oh, my."

"What?" Fitzeirick shouted. "What's wrong?"

"There's another hand," Abi said.

"My daughter has three hands?" Tindra asked, leaning forward to see.

"No, you have another babe!" Abi said. "Bera, cut the cord and clean her. My Queen, your work is not done."

Twins! The thought brought goosebumps to Fitzeirick's arms.

The guttural sound coming from his wife broke the king from his shock. Everything seemed to happen faster this time. Soon, he cradled his son, and Tindra held their daughter. The babies' cries brought smiles and tears all around.

"Congratulations, your majesties. They both look healthy," Abi said. "My Queen, they should eat soon. I'll help you get settled while the king spreads the good news."

Tindra nodded and leaned forward. Fitzeirick hesitated before handing his son to Bera. Once he was certain she wouldn't drop him, he lifted his wife off the floor. Abi took their daughter and cradled her while Fitzeirick carried his wife to their bed.

After one more long look at their newborn twins nursing, Fitzeirick left to make the proclamation.

At dawn, after the first full moon of the twins fifth year, a procession led them to their roan—the test to determine what their sything talents were. Captain Agrim and Sergeants Sibbi and Svan, dressed in gleaming, tan, leather armor, led the way out of the capital's southern gate.

Princess Meyla, wearing a simple, unbleached, linen dress, followed the men who were both guardians and playmates. Loosely braided, chestnut hair brushed the tops of her shoulders with each step, and her bright, brown eyes looked everywhere, gazing at the people lining the streets to watch them pass.

Prince Regin trailed behind his sister, wearing a short-sleeved shirt and loose pants made from the same cloth as Meyla's dress. His hair and eyes were lighter than hers, closer in color to his mother's. The young boy kept his eyes forward, doing his best to imitate the guards ahead of him.

Behind their children, King Fitzeirick and Queen Tindra walked hand in hand, beaming with pride. Tindra predicted her daughter would be a strong firesyth and her son would be a stonesyth like his father. Fitzeirick had noticed different tendencies in his children, but Tindra insisted he was mistaken.

Roi and Grima, the royal advisor and his wife, followed their rulers. Einns, Grima's son, stayed in the castle, manning the kitchen—his favorite place—to prepare a special breakfast for the royal twins. Roi had escorted Fitzeirick to his own roan where it was determined he was a stonesyth.

When Fitzeirick was his children's age, he lived in the far eastern lands of Croy with his mother, Sar'sa. She was a war trophy for Eirick, his father, from when he took those lands from Varia. Though Jarl Eirick cared about his bastard son, his duties as leader of Croy kept him in the capital that day. Fitzeirick was thrilled to be with his children today and wondered if his father ever regretted not being there for him nearly thirty years ago.

Three more guards, their armor matching those leading, brought up the rear. Onlookers bowed and shouted their greetings and support as the royal family passed.

Tradition and an abundance of caution dictated the trial be held well away from any structures, lest an exceptionally strong but untrained child damage something important. In a clearing off the road but in sight of the wall surrounding Croy's capital, three people waited in a loose circle. Bera rested her foot on a stone ball; Botulf, the capital's master blacksmith, stood near a small fire; Abi sat near a wooden block a few steps away.

The procession stopped at the edge of the road. Before the twins scampered ahead, Fitzeirick put his hands on their shoulders and kneeled as they turned to look at their father. Tindra stood next to him, resting her hand on his arm.

"Remember," Fitzeirick said, looking from daughter to son, "go to each element and try to feel what's in front of you. There's no hurry, so don't rush."

"Focus, breathe, and take your time," Tindra said.

The children nodded, turned, and scampered toward the challenges. Dew from the ankle-high grass wet the bottom of their clothes as they made their way to the clearing.

Fitzeirick stood.

Tindra took his hand.

Everyone else spread out to watch as the test began.

Regin, being about half a hand taller than his sister, reached the stone before her. As he stooped to put his hand on the orb, Meyla rested her hands on her hips and tapped her foot.

Tindra squeezed her husband's hand as the stone opened for their son. Regin took a piece of honeybread out of the ball, turned to his parents, and smiled before biting into the treat. Fitzeirick noticed it took more effort than he expected for his son to work the stone open.

Meyla brushed her fingers on the rock and nothing happened. As her brother tried to open the wooden box, she pressed hard against the ball, but it didn't open. She hit it with her fist as Regin abandoned the wooden box, unable to open it.

The fire bent to the boy's will before his sister reached toward the wooden box. Tindra gasped as he pulled a strip of meat out of the flames.

Her shock turned unpleasant when the wood moved as soon as Meyla's fingers contacted it. "My daughter *cannot* be a woodsyth!"

I tried to warn her, Fitzeirick thought, putting his arm across his wife's shoulders.

Chapter 1

Regin," I said, "watch where you're going."

Ink sloshed, threatening to spill each time the wagon jostled.

"Yes, Princess," he said, before sticking his tongue out at me.

I snorted at my brother, dipped my quill again, and returned to my journal. Fortunately, we'd had good weather for the trip—a few clouds hung in the sky, but none threatened rain, so I didn't have to keep my book in my travel sack.

I'm nearing the end of the exhausting ride home from Varia. Still, it was nice to spend time with my grandparents at Dauphi and the eastern keep is surrounded by so many interesting plants and deep forest. But best of all was speeding across Lake Lusebel in the boat Kurt's men built for my fifteenth birthday. Cousin Jonus and my brother would rather spend their days playing soldier or looking for other adventures, usually in the form of pursuing one of the many girls who caught Jonus's eye.

Going by the stories I'd heard, that was a habit passed down from his father. From my understanding, Uncle Crum was quite the ladies' man before he met Aunt Jesca.

That's not to say Jonus isn't attractive. He got his father's messy hair but it's the sandy color of his mother's. And his blue-green eyes are so bright, sometimes I think they glow. But he's practically family so his silver tongue doesn't work on me.

And don't get me wrong, I enjoy the thrill of a good hunt as much as anyone; stalking prey through the trees and brush, using my talent to find where the animal has disturbed the plants. It certainly gets the blood pounding in my ears but it doesn't compare to the feeling of being out on the water. The wind in my hair, surrounded by a peaceful expanse.

Considering I could catch a meal with a hook and line, if Uncle Crum and Aunt Jesca hadn't insisted I spent time with them, I'd have only come ashore to cook. Not that learning new woodsything skills from Aunt Jesca wasn't fun. To be honest, I like her more than Mother.

"I see the southern gate, sis," my brother said, pointing.

I waved to Fargrim, the closest rider to me. He nodded, put his heels to his horse's flank, and rode ahead to announce our arrival.

Instead of watching them, I looked back at the cart carrying my boat. It was light enough for one horse to pull, but two traveled faster, and Uncle Crum insisted on making sure we got home quickly.

It wouldn't have bothered me to take our time traveling back through my father's homeland. On the trip to the eastern pass into Varia, we spent a good portion of a day visiting the memorial to those who died when Satra invaded. Father raised the stone himself, putting the names Sar'sa, our grandmother, and Aesa, his first love, on the first stele. Since then, nine more blocks had been pulled to the surface. Each was marked with the names of Croians taken by the once barbaric nation on Croy's southern border. It made the history my brother and I had learned about our nation feel real. I couldn't help but shed tears.

The people who settled these lands after the war ended—a mix of Croian, Varian, and Satran—are hard-working and welcoming. Most who moved here worked for years repairing the damage done by Satra's invasion.

After establishing himself as Croy's king, my father made Satra pay for their crimes. He led the army that conquered the nation and kept it under Croian rule longer than my brother and I had been alive.

Angering Father is not a good strategy.

Capping the jar of ink, I wiped my quill on the cloth in the back of my leather-bound journal and put everything into the pack resting between my feet. Thundering hoofbeats announced approaching riders. Bolverk led the group of mounted warriors.

"Well met!" my brother and I called out together.

The men saluted when they got close. "Princess Meyla. Prince Regin. Well met and welcome home. Your parents are eager to see you."

I bet Mother couldn't care less if I came back. Pasting a smile on my face, I returned their salutes. "Lead the way."

Chapter 2

After days of traveling on soft roads, the sharp clap of hooves on stone stabbed my ears as the horses pulling our wagon stepped onto the street inside the southern gate. Thundering hoof strikes were soon drowned out by well-wishers welcoming us home.

Bolverk led us on a meandering path through the city, avoiding crowded squares and spaces too small for our wagons to pass through. It wasn't until we approached our castle that I could ignore the noise and take in the once-familiar sights and smells of home.

Father and Mother waited outside the entrance to our courtyard. They wore matching dark green outfits, nearly blending into the ivy-covered, stone wall around our home.

Like most woodsyths, I didn't care to be surrounded by stone, but this wall was a comforting sight. I supposed a stonesyth might say it grounded me. Or maybe it was the courtyard of flowers, grassy clearings, and tall trees it surrounded.

Having not seen Father in a month, I couldn't help but stare at the upside-down T-shaped scar on his cheek. His older half brother had marked him a traitor years ago. *I don't always get along with Regin, but I would never hurt him like that.*

Our parents saluted the escort as they approached, then Father waved them on, releasing the guardsmen to return to their posts.

I grabbed my bag and readied to jump once Regin stopped the wagon. As firstborn, it was my right to greet our parents before my brother, but he didn't like to follow the rules when it came to things like that. Plus, at half a head taller than me, he could run faster. As it was, we reached our parents at the same time.

I hugged my father tight, snuggling my face to his chest and smiling when he lifted me off my feet. It was our special greeting. A tradition we'd shared for as long as I could remember.

"Oh, my boy. You've grown since you left," Mother said, embracing my brother. He was tall enough to look over the top of her head now.

When Regin and I switched places, I found I was able to look Mother in the eye without craning my neck. "As have you, Meyla," she said, hugging me. "I take it the trip went well."

"Yes," I said, stepping back. I reached into my bag, grabbed a folded parchment, then made signs with my free hand. "Grandfather Mikael and Grandmother Margit asked me to bring this to you," I said, without speaking.

Mother half-grinned before taking the message from me. "Slow down. I'm well out of practice in reading Mother's hand signs."

"And I don't get it at all," Regin said.

"Me either," Father added.

I took another parchment from my bag. "And this is from King Crum to you, Father." He nodded, took it, and pointed at my boat. "Who is this for?"

"It's Meyla's new, favorite toy," Regin said. "I think she would have lived on it if Uncle Crum would've let her."

I punched his shoulder. "It was a birthday gift from Kurt. He calls it a coln."

"I told you two to stay away from Kurt and his people," Mother scolded.

"Per made me a pair of hand axes," Regin said, smiling as he reached into the wagon to get his new weapons.

"Fine looking blades," Father said, examining them before turning to me. "Did Per give you anything, Meyla?"

Regin reached back into the wagon, grabbed my new sword, and tossed it to me.

I caught it by the scabbard and drew the weapon. "A blade like Mother's."

"Careful," Mother said. "Don't cut yourself."

"I know what I'm doing, Mother," I said. "As a matter of fact, Per says I might be better than you."

Mother scoffed. "He's wrong. You don't move with a firesyth's grace. Plus, you've used a bow all your life."

"A willow bends with the wind," I said, carefully putting the blade away, "much like flame dances."

"Tindra, stop. She just got back home," Father said. "You two get your things put away and bathe before dinner is ready."

Mother glared at him. "The boat isn't staying here."

"I'll ride with it to the southern shore tomorrow and make sure it's stored correctly," I said.

"You shouldn't even have it," Mother said.

It was Father's turn to glare at her. He mouthed 'stop' before turning to me. "Why did Kurt give it to you?"

"His builders used it to test some ideas for a new kind of boat. This one's a smaller version of what's to come, and he wanted to show it to you." I stood tall and squared my shoulders as I talked. "It's amazing, Father. One person can control it. Even as small as this is, it can carry five men plus their supplies. The real one will carry twenty times that with room to spare. It's faster and turns tighter and—"

"And now she won't stop talking about it until moonrise," my brother cut me off.

Father pointed at him. "Nothing wrong with her being excited about something she enjoys."

"Yes, Father," Regin said, dipping his chin.

"But I can't spare guards to escort you to the coast tomorrow," the king continued, before scratching his chin.

"I don't need them," I said. "I can take care of it by myself."

"I know how you are with the water," Mother said. "If you go alone, you'll never come back."

I turned to say something to her, but Father cleared his throat and gave me a warning look. "I'll send some servants to move your boat into the courtyard before they put the wagon away and take the horses to the stable. I'll have Agrim find some traders taking goods to the coast in the morning and make sure they treat your boat with the best of care."

I wanted to argue but knew better, so I bowed to hide my frustration. "As you say, Father."

Chapter 3

Mother doted over Regin as we entered our castle. Before I stepped inside, I looked back at my boat one more time, wondering if I would see it again.

My brother continued talking about our month away from home, and Mother hung on every word.

Father walked next to me and put his hand on my shoulder. "It's good to have you home, my girl. It sounds like you had a good time."

"It was nice," I said, "but not as nice as Regin makes it sound."

Father chuckled. "Maybe he spent too much time around Crum."

"Jonus is just as bad," I said, smiling.

"I'm not surprised. Don't worry about your boat. I'll make sure you get a chance to use it soon. I know it's important to you."

I nodded, patted his hand, and thanked him before turning for my room.

Years ago, I had accepted a truth: Regin was Mother's favorite because he was a firesyth while I was only a woodsyth. Father had always tried to cover for her favoritism, but it was too obvious to hide when it was happening to me. It's not like she neglected me or hurt me...physically. But nothing I did was good enough for her over-critical eye. At the same time, my brother could do no wrong. "If Kurt would have given *him* the boat, it would be the greatest gift anyone ever received," I said, to my empty room, after closing the door.

Dim daylight streamed in through the windows, reminding me it would be dark before I finished bathing. I lit a candle and went about my tasks.

Looking around, I realized I didn't have anywhere to put my new sword, so I leaned it against my bow rack. *I'll have to ask Father for a shelf or something.* Before taking the time to unpack, I went around the room checking on my plants. Someone, probably Grima, had kept them watered while I was gone.

Despite our differences, one of the best things my mother did was have heated bathing pools in our rooms. They worked much like the ones in Dauphi, except the fireplace was directly under the tub instead of under our beds. The rooms there were underground, so the stone tended to be colder, and warming the bed was necessary.

Once the fire was burning, I unpacked my travel bag. My clothes went into the armoire, and I took out a dress to wear to dinner, then folded the bag and placed it in the bottom of the cabinet. My last and most important task was storing my ink and quill in the oak box under my bed, making sure to syth the compartment for my journal shut so no one could take it without me knowing.

Confident the tub had time to warm, I undressed, putting my dirty clothes in a basket and setting my boots next to my bed, then opened the tap in the wall to fill the pool. While waiting for the water to rise, I unbraided my hair. Now free, it hung past my waist. If I didn't cut it soon, I'd have to keep it up all the time or risk sitting on it.

Mother gladly cut Regin's hair and Father's, but, other than trimming the front to keep it out of my eyes, she'd always insisted on letting mine grow. I never asked why. *Maybe I should. Or maybe I'll find someone else to cut it and see what she says.* "I'm sure she wouldn't like it," I said, to the still-empty room.

I could tell the pool was full by how the water sounded when it splashed. Closing the tap, I dipped my foot into the water. *Still a touch cool, but it will warm while I soak.*

Goosebumps rose on my skin as I floated. Closing my eyes, I imagined I was back on the lake, the wind caressing my face and filling the boat's small sail. I shivered and embraced the feeling of freedom, wondering if this was how birds felt when they took flight.

My stomach growled, ripping me out of my thoughts and bringing me back to the flickering candlelight and warming air in my bathing room. Not knowing when dinner would be served but knowing I would catch some kind of criticism from my mother if I arrived late, I quickly washed myself, combed a few tangles from my wet hair, and put on the tan, linen dress I'd chosen earlier. Having spent more time in the sun recently, I noticed my skin was a shade darker than the fabric. Reaching for my boots, I hesitated before grabbing my slippers. *If I am late, maybe I can sneak in quietly enough that Mother won't notice.*

Chapter 4

I hurried through the familiar stone hallways of my home, doing my best to keep my footsteps light and quick. Father could use stonesyth tricks to soften his steps and track people through the floor. I didn't understand how, but I suspected he could track anyone from the moment they entered our castle to when they left. My grandfather was blind, but he always knew where everyone was around him. I always thought Father learned that skill from him, but both denied it.

My mother and brother were seated at the table when I entered our private dining room. Focused on doing something with candles, lanterns, and flames, they didn't notice when I took my seat. Father's chair was empty. *At least I'm not the last one here.*

Flames burst to life and others went out in a seemingly random pattern. Regin huffed with nearly every change. I quickly gave up trying to figure out the purpose, or rules, of their contest. When all the flames were out, leaving the chandelier hanging from the ceiling as the only light source, Mother whooped in victory.

"I almost had you," Regin said, slapping his hands on the table.

"I haven't taught you all my tricks," Mother said, smiling.

"What were you doing?" I asked.

They flinched and turned to look at me.

"You wouldn't understand," Regin said.

"Your sister may not be a firesyth, but she isn't slow-witted," Mother said. "Clear the table before our meal is served, and I'll try to explain it to her."

"Why should I clear the table?" he asked, a whiny edge to his voice.

"Because you lost," Mother said. "Consider it motivation to get better."

"Fine," he said, sulking. "Next time, you'll burn out and have to clear the table."

"We'll see," Mother said, smiling as she crossed her arms. As usual, she made sure her right arm sat under her left, hiding the stump where she'd lost her right hand. It was cut off fighting beside my father when he overthrew his half brother and declared himself King of Croy. Father insists she saved his life when Stina, Aunt Jesca's sister, tried to kill him.

"Light and Dark is similar to Tafl, but you don't need a board, and the rules are less rigid," Mother started explaining.

As she continued, I forced myself to hide my confusion behind a thin smile and frequent nods. I could play Tafl well enough, but this game... Regin was right. I didn't understand. Fortunately, Father came in with a couple of servers, interrupting the now-pointless, single-sided conversation.

Regin shut the door to a waist-high, wooden cabinet on the far end of the room and raced to his seat on my left. I hooked my foot behind one of the chair's legs so it wouldn't slide out easily. His light grip slipped, throwing him off balance enough to fall over backward, nearly tripping Anja, one of the Varian servant girls in our employ. She was a couple of years older than us, but my brother had started paying more attention to her lately.

From what I could tell, she wasn't interested.

Father sat, looked sideways at me, and smirked.

"Careful, Regin," Mother said.

"It wasn't my fault," he said, scrambling to his feet and blushing when he noticed Anja. "Meyla tripped me."

I frowned. "How could I? I was sitting here the entire time. If you hadn't been in such a hurry to sit before Father got to the table—"

"Then you did something with the floor," he argued.

"It's stone," I snapped. "You're the one with some stonesything talent. Plus, Father would have known if anyone sythed the floor."

"Then you did something to the chair," he said.

"I did not syth your chair."

"Quit arguing," Father admonished. "Both of you. Son, sit so we can eat. Your mother and I want to hear more about your travels."

"Yes, Father," Regin said, before yanking the chair back and nearly tripping himself again.

"Meyla, stop messing with your brother," Mother said. "You're the princess. Act like it."

"Tell him to act more like a prince," I said, crossing my arms, "and less like a fool."

Anja snickered behind me.

"I said stop it." Father's tone made it obvious he was no longer amused. "Our first meal together after a moon apart should be a happy one. Einns worked hard to make this meal special, and I for one look forward to enjoying it."

"Yes, Father," we said, together.

I let Regin tell his version of the trip, figuring Mother would just find a reason to criticize anything I said. Of course, everything he talked about was exaggerated and focused on the things he enjoyed. Mother ate up every tale.

I did everything I could to ignore him and focus on dinner. After nothing but Varian food for so long, I had looked forward to something less spicy, but Einns learned most of his cooking skills living in my mother's homeland.

"Meyla, are you feeling ill?" Father asked.

"Just tired," I said. *Of listening to my brother talk.*

"Eat," Mother said. "If you'd like, I'll teach you how to use your new sword starting tomorrow after first light. You'll need your strength."

"I'll let you know when I'm ready to try," I said. *You're just going to tell me how bad I am anyway. I could easily best two Varian recruits at once after a few lessons from Per.*

"Well, don't try to teach yourself," Mother said. "It wouldn't do for the Princess of Croy to be seen all sliced up."

"I'll be fine," I said, before biting into a piece of bread.

"It's just —"

"She said she'll be fine, Tindra," Father said, touching Mother's arm. "If she's tired, she should go rest."

"I'd like that," I said, nodding to Father. "I'm sure I'll feel better in the morning."

"If not, we'll send for Abi," Mother said.

"Sleep well, my girl," Father said. "I'd like to spend some time with you tomorrow."

I nodded again and left the table, hungry but already feeling happier.

"Mother," Regin said, as I got near the door, "Per didn't let her take the blade without making sure she would be safe with it. She's actually pretty good."

I stepped out of the room and hurried down the hall before I could hear anything Mother said.

Taking a different path to my room, I stopped by the kitchen for a small loaf of bread and a jug of water.

Moonlight lit my room enough for me to set my meager meal on my writing table and light a candle before dropping the tapestries to cover the windows. I retrieved my journal and put my feelings on the pages.

Father is trying his best, I know it, but I'm certain Mother hates me. I was so much happier away from here. It's not just being surrounded by stone. I have my plants in my room and I can wander through the courtyard and our gardens as much as I want. It's her...being away from her. Should I take her up on her offer and show her how good I am with my sword? What would she say if I bested her? What could she say? She'd never admit that I'm better than her at anything.

I wonder how she reacted to Regin telling her I was good. She probably doesn't believe him. It was nice to hear him say it though. Now, I almost feel bad for making him fall.

I sighed, put everything away, and finished my bland dinner before blowing out the candle and crawling into bed.

Chapter 5

Something touched my forehead, and then Father asked, "Meyla, are you well?"

"I'm fine," I said, blinking my eyes against the candle he held near my face. "Why?"

"You slept through breakfast. I wanted to check on you before we sent for Abi."

"I needed the rest," I said. "I feel fine."

He kissed my forehead. "If you say so. I'll wait in the hall. Get dressed, and we'll walk to the kitchen together. I'm sure we can find you something to eat."

I smiled and nodded. Once the door closed, I got out of bed and ran my fingers through my hair. *Tangles and knots.* A growling groan left my clenched teeth, and I berated myself for not braiding my hair before going to sleep. It took longer to comb through the mess than it did to braid it and change clothes. As it was, it seemed like there was more hair in the comb than there was on my head. *Maybe that's a sign I should cut it.*

As he said, Father was waiting when I opened the door.

"That took a while," he said, cocking his head. "Are you sure you're well?"

I nodded and explained about the tangles. He nodded with a smile and ran his hand across his neatly trimmed hair. "Did I ever tell you about when I cut Jesca's hair?"

By the end of the short walk to the kitchen, my sides hurt, and I had tears in my eyes from laughing at my father's tale, but his expression showed no joy. "What aren't you telling me?" I asked.

"What do you mean?" he asked, grabbing sweet rolls from a tray near the door. I noticed he took enough for both of us.

One of the cooks looked over, opened his mouth to say something, then nodded and went back to what he'd been working on.

I sniffed a nearby jug of goat milk and picked it up. "I've been laughing, but you're obviously not happy after that story. Why?"

He chewed his bottom lip for a moment, then offered me a roll. "Let's go outside and find someplace quiet to talk."

"I know the perfect spot," I said, turning on my heel.

"I figured you would."

Harsh sunlight stabbed my eyes when I stepped out of the side door leading to the closest garden. With my hands full, all I could do was squint against the glare and walk carefully to avoid tripping on anything.

"Where are we going?" Father asked from behind me.

"The fruit trees on the other side of the garden. I go there to think sometimes. It's nice to listen to the birds sing while the bees buzz from flower to flower."

"I know what you mean," Father said. "I haven't done that in a long time."

Chapter 6

Once we were well hidden in the trees, Father pulled seats from the ground with a small table to hold our meal.

He took a drink of milk and sighed. "You asked about my sadness. It comes from a troubled time in my life. I'd lost everything and wasn't sure what, if anything, I'd ever get back. Jesca was in even worse shape; she didn't know who she was. All *I* knew was she was a Varian girl who needed help."

"I didn't mean to upset you," I said. "I just didn't understand."

"You didn't know," he said, patting my knee. "You can't understand something you don't know. And this is something I don't talk about much. Don't like to think about it, to be honest."

"She always smiles when she talks about you," I said, hoping to cheer him up.

"She's a special person," he said, nodding and wiping his eyes.

"Why didn't you marry Aunt Jesca?"

He stared at me, expression blank, then chuckled. "I love her. Always will...but not like that. With everything that had happened to me and her, everything that lay ahead." He rubbed the back of his neck for a moment. "We wouldn't have made a good match."

"But she loves me," I said.

"Your mother loves you, too."

"No, she doesn't," I argued. "She hates me."

Father dropped his roll. "Oh saeta, no. My darling girl, why would you say that? Your mother doesn't hate you."

"She does." The grass near me twitched as I fought to hide my hurt. "You even have to tell her to stop being mean to me sometimes."

He nodded. "She can be overly critical, but that's because she expects your best effort."

"No matter what, she treats me like a disappointment. I can't do anything good enough for her. Even when I do my best. She demands perfection."

Father took my hand. "Your mother is a deeply loving person, but she has high expectations of her children. She sees you and your brother as reflections of herself and holds you to the same standard she holds herself to."

"But Regin can do no wrong in her eyes," I said, pulling my hand from his.

"They're both firesyths —"

"Exactly!" I shouted, jumping to my feet. "Mother hates me because I'm a woodsyth, and she's a firesyth." Fruit dropped from a nearby tree as my anger boiled.

"You have a firesyth's temper," he said, closing his eyes. "Sit, breathe, and listen."

"But—"

"Do as I said, or I will make you sit. Neither of us want that."

The ground quivered under my boots, but my shoulders slumped, and I flopped back onto the dirt seat. "Yes, Father."

"I love you more than anything, and I will never lie to you. You know this, yes?"

I nodded but didn't look at him. "Yes."

"It's understood, even expected, for there to be some amount of resentment between firesyths and woodsyths but Tindra does not hate you because of the differences in your talents. Your mother doesn't hate you at all. Quite the opposite."

Pausing, he chuckled.

"You're a smart girl, and you pay attention to everything going on around you, but you have blinders when it comes to the relationship between your mother and Regin. Yes, they have a tight bond built around their shared talent, but your mother regularly corrects his behavior."

"You said you wouldn't lie," I muttered. "He gets away with everything."

"Just because you don't see it doesn't mean it doesn't happen. You have her temper but not her talent. Had you been a firesyth, you could have lit the grass or that tree on fire when you lashed out just now. Your brother could certainly do both without much effort. Plus, you are older. Your mother is harder on you because you are next in line for the crown, and she's afraid you may never be ready."

I wiped my eyes again and looked at my father. He was smiling and held his hand out toward me. "Why would she be scared?" I asked, taking his hand. "She's taught me well. She knows I can take care of myself. I just... I don't understand what you mean."

"She'll never tell you this, so don't mention it around her, or we'll both be in trouble."

I nodded.

"When she was about your age, more than anything, she longed to be free of her parents."

"Really?" I scrunched up my face.

Father nodded. "She distanced herself from her family and ran with some dishonorable people. She was naturally gifted with grace and could take care of herself because she was quick witted, but she learned many hard lessons about life in the darker part of the Varian capital."

I furrowed my brow trying to understand. "I thought she worked for former King Ander."

He nodded. "When I met her, she did...as well as working for anyone else who would pay for her skills."

"But I'm not going to do that," I said.

"I know, but your mother sees a lot of herself in you, and it scares her, so she demands more from you. I'm not saying it's right—"

"It's not," I said.

He frowned. "Let me finish. I'm not saying it's wrong either. You're growing up and need to get ready for more responsibility. I wasn't much older than you when my father put me in charge of an entire skati."

I shivered, and he smiled.

"Don't worry—I won't do that to you. But the day is not far off when you will be involved in what it takes to rule this nation...and it's not an easy task. The simple crown I wear in public isn't heavy, but the responsibility it represents carries a lot of weight. That is another reason your mother is hard on you. No matter what she says or how she says it, never doubt her love for you."

"If you say so," I muttered.

He squeezed my hand. "I don't lie, especially not to you."

"Then how do I get her to show me she loves me?" I asked, frowning.

Father cocked his head for a moment, then nodded. "Face her on her terms. When she challenges you, overcome what she put before you. When she criticizes you, show her you are better. But when she praises you, accept it with grace and humility. I know how good you are. She wants you to be better than she was. Show her what you're made of, what you are capable of."

My frown turned into a thin grin. "I'll do my best if you think it will make a difference."

"I know it will," he said, smiling. "And I'll ask her to back down some, to let you be a young girl a little longer. Nothing wrong with some carefree fun every now and then."

I giggled. "Thank you, Father. Now, can I see my boat before it leaves?"

He shook his head. "It's already on its way south."

"Oh." My shoulders slumped again.

He squeezed my hand again. "Don't worry. The tradesmen were paid more than enough to make sure it's taken care of."

"Thank you."

He stood and pulled me into a hug. "I promise you can go to the shore soon. Maybe we'll ride down together, the four of us, and you can show me why it's special."

I squeezed him as tight as I could. "I'd like that. Kurt was eager for you to see what was coming."

He pushed me to arm's length. "Your mother was right; you shouldn't be around him too much."

I nodded. "But you are in contact with his people, which means I should be too if I'm going to rule someday."

"I deal with them to keep as much control over their activities in Croy as I can. My hope is they are gone before it's time for you to wear the crown."

"He doesn't seem so bad." I said.

"Which is what makes him dangerous. Now, I'm going to take this empty jug back to the kitchen. Why don't you find your mother and put some of what we talked about into practice?"

"Do I have to?"

He patted me on the head. "No, but it will be better if you find her than if she decides to start looking for you. Like I said, work on showing her you are responsible."

"Fine. Any idea where she might be?"

"She was going with Regin to see Thorgault. Your brother wants a vest that will hang his new axes across his chest."

I frowned. "Sounds like a strange way to carry them. Why not hang them from his belt?"

Father chuckled and nodded. "I agree, but sometimes, the boy has to learn things the hard way. Maybe you could talk to the tanner about a belt for your sword."

"I will. Oh, that reminds me—I don't have anywhere to put it."

"Once I'm done in the kitchen, I'll syth a place for you to store your sword."

I kissed his cheek. "Thank you, Father. Somewhere near my bow stand, please."

He kissed the top of my head. "Of course. Remember what we talked about. Show your mother you're better than she expects."

Sure. No problem. "I'll do my best."

Chapter 7

I ran to my room, grabbed my coin purse, and hurried out of the castle. My heart twinged when I looked at the empty space where my boat had been yesterday evening. The pang of loss did little to dampen my excitement at spending time wandering through the market square.

Instead of heading straight to Thorgault's leather shop, I took the long way around the marketplace. The crowd and sights and sounds and smells...I felt nearly as free as when I was on the water.

I picked up a wooden hairpin, wondering if using it would be quicker than constantly braiding mine. It was beautiful, made of polished maple, the dark wood from Satra instead of the lighter variety common to Croy. A twisted, fine, gold, wire inlay flowed with the curves of the woodgrain. As I reached for my purse, I heard a voice behind me.

"Oh look, it's the princess. Did the king let you out of the castle alone, or did the queen kick you out?"

I knew who it was without looking. *Runa. Great. I'd wager she's not alone.*

Thyre, Runa's mother, used to work for my parents. Mother caught her stealing a few seasons ago and banished her from the castle. Father had mercy and didn't exile her from Croy. As for Runa's father... Well, I'm not sure she ever had one.

Rumor among the servants was Thyre had moved in with a Varian merchant who left his first wife in that country and brought his daughters here searching for a more extravagant lifestyle. One thing was certain: the three girls went everywhere together, and they were troublemakers.

I put the trinket down before spinning around to find I was right. I stood face-to-face with her and her Varian friends, Zora and Idania.

"Is there something I can do for you?" I asked. Unarmed, I wasn't sure I could best her if she wanted to fight. With her two friends, I was in serious trouble.

Runa was a couple of years older than me and nearly a head taller. There was a fresh cut over her left eyebrow, and she had a thin scab on her chin. I guessed her wrinkled dress hadn't been washed in days, or she picked a horrible color of linen to wear. Her dirty, blonde hair jutted out in random directions. *Maybe I should offer to buy her a comb...or some shears.* That thought brought a smirk to my face.

"What are you smiling about?" Runa asked, poking my chest with her finger. The two Varian girls bared their teeth, like bears preparing to eat.

That doesn't look promising. I glanced to each side, checking for threats there. A crowd gathered, but no one seemed like they were about to rush me...or help me if this turned violent.

"Just enjoying some time in the market," I said, stalling and hoping she'd do something to give away her intent. *I'm pretty sure at least one of them is a stonesyth. If I have to fight, it's going to be ugly.* "It's a beautiful day. That's reason enough to be happy. Isn't it?"

She raised her left hand across her chest. Her knuckles were bruised, and her nails looked filthy with dirt or blood or...worse. "Maybe *I* don't agree. Maybe I should wipe that smile off your half-breed face, Princess."

Her elbow twitched, and I leaned back, but not fast enough to completely dodge her attack. Jagged fingernails raked across my right cheek, ripping three hot lines in my face.

Before she could draw her hand back for another strike, I grabbed my coin purse and swung it at her chin. Leather smacked against her skin and the coins inside clinked together.

Someone in the crowd shouted and it felt like the group of people closed in tighter.

Runa's head twisted to the side, and she stumbled back a step. I ducked low in case the Varian sisters tried to grab me and looked for a way out. Someone grabbed my hair just before a blow caught me in the side of my head. My ear rang, and the world went a little off-kilter. I fell to my knees.

Someone yanked my braid, twisting my head painfully.

"What's going on?"

The voice sounded familiar, but I couldn't remember his name. I tried to get up, but everything spun. Slumping forward, my hands stopped me from flopping face-first onto the smooth stones.

Something struck my back like a hammer. My legs tingled and felt like jelly.

"Break it up!" he roared.

A boot smacked into my right side, and my braid fell free. People scattered while I struggled to keep my hands and knees under me.

Rough, strong hands lifted me to my feet. My legs still didn't want to do what I told them.

"Princess Meyla?" the man questioned.

I looked up, recognized Captain Svan, and my breakfast came up as the world turned around me.

"I'm taking her to Abi's," he said, cradling me as I closed my eyes. "Dag, go tell the king and queen what happened. Tholl, Asmund, find out who attacked the princess."

"Aye, Captain," they replied in unison.

I wanted to tell him who it was, but my stomach flipped, convincing me to keep my mouth shut.

"Stone help them when Queen Tindra finds out who they are," Svan muttered, after a couple of steps.

I kept my eyes closed to keep from getting sick again.

Chapter 8

"Abi isn't here," a young man said. "She won't be back until well after moon rise."

"Princess Meyla is hurt. She needs an herbalist," Svan said. "Now."

"Oh," he said. "I... Princess... Umm... In that case, take her to the first room on the left. I'll do what I can."

Linus. I remembered Abi's apprentice's name.

The pad Svan put me on was soft. I would have gone to sleep, but Linus kept clinking bottles and jars together. Those were a minor annoyance compared to him grinding something in the mortar and pestle. That got on my nerves.

"Princess, can you hear me?" Linus asked quietly.

I nodded.

"Good. I need you to open your eyes."

"Why?" I croaked, my throat still scratchy from throwing up.

"To look at your eyes."

"I'm going to wait at the door," Svan said. "I'm guessing the king and queen are most of the way here by now. Maybe I can shield you from Tindra's wrath."

"I'd be in your debt," Linus said.

I opened my eyes and shut them again, tight, as glaring candlelight stabbed at them.

"Sorry," he said. "I know it might hurt, but I need to see your eyes."

My eyelids fluttered as I fought the instinct to keep them closed. Candlelight flashed across my vision again, turning everything red, before I felt the room spin around me.

"They look normal," Linus said. "Can you sit up?"

I shook my head and groaned.

"Fine. Can you tell me where it hurts?"

"My cheek," I mumbled.

"I see the scratches. The paste for those will be ready soon. What else?"

"Someone hit my head. Something's wrong. Everything spins when I open my eyes."

"Oh. I'm not sure about that. Abi would know what to do. Anything else?"

I nodded, and my neck ached. "They twisted my head around. My neck hurts. Kicked me in the ribs, too. My legs were all tingly, but I think they're better now."

"I'll treat your face, then see if one of Abi's books has anything about your other injuries."

"That's fine," I said. "Just want to rest."

Linus grunted before grinding the pestle again.

I recognized Mother's walk as her footsteps echoed in the hall. "Round up everyone in the market square if that's what it takes. I want names," she said firmly.

"Of course, my Queen," Svan said. "Take care of the princess, and don't give another thought to her attackers."

"And I want to know as soon as they are caught," she continued. It sounded like she was right outside the room.

"I understand," Svan said. "You'll be the first to know, my Queen."

Even if I hadn't heard her, I would have known it was Mother by the heat coming from her. "Linus, where is Abi?" she demanded.

"South of the capital, my Queen. Tending a patch of wild Lamb's Ear. Getting it ready to harvest at moonrise."

"I see." Her hot hand touched my forehead. "Can you treat the princess?"

"I have a paste for her cheek," he said, a tremble in his voice. "Her other injuries will be more challenging."

"Do not take this the wrong way, eager apprentice," Mother said, "but if you are not absolutely certain you can help my daughter, find an herbalist who can."

"I will do my best, my Queen. I promise."

She took my hand. "I don't doubt that you will. But know your limits, and don't make her worse."

"I've sworn to do no harm, Queen Tindra. If I'm not absolutely certain I can help, I will gather every herbalist in the capital...if necessary."

"Exactly," Tindra said. "Meyla, my saeta, are you awake?"

"Yes, mother."

She kissed my forehead. "Do you know who did this?"

I nodded and winced. "Runa and her two friends."

Mother's hand grew hotter. "You are certain?"

"I need to put this paste on her cheek, my Queen," Linus said.

Mother released my hand.

A grassy scent filled my nose. Out of habit, I took a deep breath and picked out the plants: marigold and coneflower with a hint of something I wasn't familiar with. Warmth spread across my cheek as the mixture soaked into my skin.

I waited to answer until Linus had finished applying his concoction.

"Chew this well before you swallow it," Linus said, pressing something against my lips. "Should ease the pain in your neck and ribs. It might help settle your stomach, too."

"Her neck?" Mother asked. "What happened to your neck"

"One of them grabbed my hair and twisted my head around." The folded, sweetgum leaf held powdered willow bark and ginger. Earthy and bitter and spicy did not make a tasty combination.

"Which side did they kick you in?" Linus asked.

"Kick... How badly are you hurt?" Mother asked.

"Svan carried me here. I couldn't stand up because everything's spinning. Breakfast came up. If I got any on Svan, please tell him I'm sorry."

"He looked clean when he got here," Linus said.

"Good," I muttered.

"Where did they kick you?" Linus asked again.

"Left side, below my breast," I said.

"Oh," he said. "I'm, uh...I'm going to press my...hand against your, um...side...uh, there. I need you to tell me...tell me if it hurts."

"Why?" I asked.

"Once I've found the...um...the, ah...the tender spot, I'll need you to take a deep breath. To see if I feel any broken bones."

"Meyla, does it hurt to breathe?" Mother asked. "Any sharp pain, like something stabbing you?"

"No, just an ache...all over."

"I'd guess she doesn't have any broken ribs, Linus," Mother said.

"I suspect you are right, my Queen, but I'd rather be thorough," he said. "If I miss something, it could make her injuries worse."

"Mother, you insisted he help me or find someone who can. Let him," I said.

"Of course. I just didn't want you to hurt any more than necessary," she said. "Please, Linus, continue working."

His hand pressed against my side nearly at my waist.

"Higher," I said. "A couple hands up."

His hand moved, but he applied the lightest pressure. At first, I wasn't sure he was still touching me.

"Close, but still higher," I said.

Mother cleared her throat. "Linus, is it safe for me to assume you've touched a woman before?"

"What?" he blurted. "I mean...um...yes, my Queen. But...it's just—"

"Stop," Mother said. "You insisted on checking for broken ribs and said you would do your best. I don't believe you are doing your best. If you are, it's not good enough. Go find a capable herbalist."

I sighed and grabbed his hand, moving it to the spot where the ache in my side felt strongest, and pressed against it. "There."

"Thank you, Princess." It was easy to hear his embarrassment. "Take a deep breath, please."

Heavy footsteps in the hall announced my father's arrival.

I did as I was asked. The ache grew, but I felt no sharp pain.

"Everything seems fine," Linus said, removing his hand. "Expect it to be bruised."

"Meyla, sweet girl, what happened?" Father asked.

"Who did this?" Regin added.

"My King," Linus said, "I'll leave you to talk with your daughter. She should be fine, but I expect Abi will want to see for herself tomorrow."

"Thank you for doing what you could for Meyla," Mother said.

Linus walked away as I explained what happened in the market. I gasped when I got to the part where I hit her with my coin purse.

"What's wrong?" Mother asked.

"I don't remember dropping it, but it's gone," I said.

"A few coins are nothing to worry about," Father said. "They can be replaced—you cannot. Do you know which one of them held you and who hit you?"

"Doesn't matter. They all took part. I'll hunt them myself and make sure they don't repeat their mistake," Regin said. "This shouldn't have happened."

"You'll do no such thing," Father said.

"But—" he argued.

"No," Father stated flatly. "When we leave, I'll send the guard after them. I'm guessing the girls are found before moonrise. You will assist your sister until she's up and around."

"Yes, Father," Regin said, his disappointment evident.

"Fitzeirick, why did you send her to the market alone?" Mother asked.

"I knew you and Regin had gone to talk with Thorgault, and Meyla wanted a belt for her new sword. I never expected her to be in harm's way," Father said.

"I told you to exile that thieving woman. Now look what's happened," Mother said. "*I* will dispense justice this time."

"And I will help," Regin said.

"Though I appreciate your offer and enthusiasm, my son...I won't need any assistance," Mother said. The heat in her words warmed the air noticeably.

"They will pay an appropriate price, my love. No blood was spilled, so temper your anger. A vengeful queen makes people nervous," Father said.

"I will temper *nothing*," Mother said. "Those wretched girls struck our daughter without provocation. I will make sure they understand their actions carry dire consequences."

"We will discuss this...later," Father said. "Regin, find Linus. We need to know how long Meyla should stay here."

"Aye," my brother said.

Father kissed my forehead. "How are you feeling?"

"I hurt, and I'm afraid to open my eyes, get dizzy, and throw up again," I said. Tears pooled in the corners of my eyes. *Those three don't deserve my tears.*

Father's rough finger brushed the wetness away. "I've had several blows to the head. This will pass with rest."

"Rest sounds good," I said. The paste on my cheek kept me from smiling when he patted my arm.

Mother took my hand in hers. "You can have all the rest you need, my dear girl. I'm proud you fought back. Next time, make sure you win."

"I'd rather there not be a next time," Father said.

"We both know there's always someone willing to hurt people," Mother said, squeezing my hand.

"True, but I didn't think our Meyla would learn that lesson yet."

"And now that she knows, I'll make sure she's better prepared," Mother said.

"I know how to fight," I said.

"You hold your own against Regin when you two tussle, but neither of you means to hurt each other," Mother said. "You need to learn how to deal with people who intend to hurt you...or worse."

"Maybe have this talk once she's out of bed," Father suggested.

"You sent for me, Sire?" Linus asked.

"Is Meyla staying here, or can she go home to rest?" Father asked. "I'm sure she'd be more comfortable in her room."

"I don't think there's anything I can do for her here that you couldn't do for her at the castle, m'lord. Expect Abi to visit tomorrow."

"If you don't mind, I will settle the payment with Abi then."

"Not at all, Sire. I'm not sure I did anything deserving of payment anyway."

"You took care of our daughter, the princess," Mother said. "I consider that a valuable service."

"If you insist, my Queen. Not to argue, that is. If you are getting ready to go, may I have leave to see to my other chores? Abi will be cross if the garden isn't tended to her exact standards."

"See to your tasks, Linus, and know your service is appreciated," Father said.

"Thank you, Sire." His shoes scraped on the floor as he backed out of the room.

"Darling, can you walk?" Father asked.

"I'm...I'm not sure."

"Then I will carry you," Father said.

Chapter 9

My heart sped up, and a warm comfort washed through me when he lifted me, cradling my hurting body against his strong chest. I wrapped my arms around his neck and pressed my head against him.

"Is Princess Meyla well, Sire?" Svan asked, when we stepped outside.

"Linus believes she will be fine," Mother said.

"Battered and bruised," Father said, "but nothing that won't heal with some rest."

"Good," the captain said. "I only regret we didn't move to break the crowd up sooner. Maybe—"

"Svan, you didn't know what was going on. Now, send your men to find Thyre's daughter, Runa, and her Varian friends. They did this."

"Aye, m'lord."

"And if you can't find them...bring me their mother," my mother ordered.

"Of course, my Queen. I'll pass word around the barracks and start the search. Harek, you find Thyre. Balli and Lini, make sure the royal family gets home without incident."

"I'll take the lead," Regin said.

Father set a slow, steady pace. Mother walked beside him, her hand resting on my ankle, until we reached my room where they couldn't pass through the door side by side.

I groaned when my back hit the bed.

"Shh. Is there anything I can do to help you get comfortable?" he asked, while taking my boots off.

"No," I croaked. "I just need to settle into a less painful position."

"I'll stay with her," Mother said. "You make sure the guard is doing their job."

"I trust them to do exactly that," Father said. "Meyla needs to sleep—leave her be. We need to discuss what happens when the girls are brought before us."

"Something unpleasant," Mother said. "But I'd rather stay here until I'm needed elsewhere."

"Our daughter is home safe and wants to sleep," Father argued.

"Father is right. I'll wait in the hall outside the door," my brother said. "Meyla, if you need anything, call out."

"I will. Thank you. All of you."

Father, then Mother, kissed my forehead. Regin patted my arm, and then they left me alone.

With the curtains covering my windows, I didn't know if it was light or dark out when I woke, but the room didn't spin when I opened my eyes. Of course, I couldn't see anything, but it didn't feel like the world was moving around me.

An uncomfortable warmth bloomed in my cheek, under the paste caked on the scratches. I tried to call for my brother, but my mouth and throat were so dry, I did little more than cough. *Let's see if I can stand.*

My bare feet hit the rough, woven rug, and I gripped the edge of my bed before deciding I was sitting up and stable. Leaning forward, still not feeling the room spin around me, I slowly rose to stand. *Good. Can I walk?*

After a couple of hesitant steps on the cold, stone floor, I felt steady on my feet, but my back was stiff, and my legs still felt a bit weak. My stomach growled. *Water...then something to eat.*

Opening the door, I stepped out and had to shield my eyes from the bright lanterns hanging on the walls. About two paces away, my brother sat on a crude, stone chair, asleep. A small, stone table next to him held a jug, a lidded pot, and two cups.

"Regin," I croaked.

He didn't move.

I stepped forward, tried to say his name louder, and got the same result. Two more steps had me standing within arm's reach. I leaned slightly and tapped my finger on the top of his bowed head.

He shook his head, looked up, blinked, then shoved me away and jumped to his feet.

A weak squeal escaped as I fell, smacking my butt hard on the floor. Pain flared in my tender back.

"Who?" He raised his fists to fight, then looked down at me. "Meyla! You're awake. It's about time you... Hey, what are you doing out of bed?"

I glared at him, acted like I was taking a drink, and pointed at the table.

He blinked again, then a look of understanding spread across his face. He poured something from the jug into one of the cups and knelt to help me drink.

Lukewarm water wet my parched mouth, and I took the cup from him and finished it myself. "So much for helping me," I said, handing him the empty container. "More, but help me up first."

"Sorry."

I frowned.

"I am. But you surprised me."

Putting his hands under my arms, he lifted me to my feet. My back didn't like moving, but I wasn't comfortable sitting sprawled out on the floor either.

"Sit," he said, pointing to the chair.

"Is it day or night?" I asked, sitting.

He raised his eyebrows while filling the cup. "It's past midday. You slept all day yesterday."

"I... What?"

He nodded and handed me more water. "Abi was here just after first light yesterday. Father wanted to wake you then, but she said to let you sleep until you woke on your own." He reached for the other cup and took the lid off the pot. "Bone broth...from last night. Want some?"

My stomach rumbled loud enough for him to hear. "Guess I'd better."

He chuckled and poured a small amount into the cup. "I'll leave this here and let Mother and Father know you're awake."

"Thank you," I said, finishing the water and then picking up the broth.

Regin left at a full run, almost smacking into the wall where the hallway turned.

Chapter 10

Though the cold broth didn't taste the best, it settled my stomach and fed my hunger. I poured another cup and had almost finished it when Mother came into view.

"Meyla, how do you feel?" she asked.

"I still hurt." I drained the cup of broth in one gulp. "Especially after my oaf of a brother knocked me to the floor."

"I said I was sorry," Regin said, behind her.

Mother frowned and glanced back at him before pressing her hand to my forehead. "You feel fevered. Father has gone to get Abi. Let's get you back to bed."

I took a deep breath. "I'd rather sit up for now."

She sighed. "Fine, but I'm getting a robe from your room."

"Something warm to eat would be better," I said, pouring another serving of broth.

"Regin, warm her cup," Mother said, turning to go into my room.

He nodded and pressed his hand against the bottom of the stone. "Sorry, sis...I should have thought to do this myself."

"No worries," I said, giving him a weak smile, "I'm sure we've all got a lot on our minds."

Closing his eyes, heat spread through the cup until it was almost too hot for me to hold. "That should do," he said, turning to leave. "I'll see if the kitchen has anything fresh."

I blew on the hot broth until Mother returned with my heaviest robe and draped it onto my lap and legs. "There. Now, if Abi says you should be in bed, you will go back to bed."

I nodded while drinking my soup.

Mother put her hand on my shoulder. "They haven't found the girls yet, and Thyre is missing too. Fitzeirick won't let me question the merchant they were living with. Sibbi tells me the man doesn't seem too concerned that his daughters are wanted...or nowhere to be found."

"You suspect he knows where they are," I said, putting the empty cup down.

"I'm sure of it."

"Then why won't Father force him to tell?"

"I don't always understand his motives," Mother said, then sighed. "But you better believe he's planning something. He's doing his best not to show it, but he's deeply upset. The longer the hunt drags on, the worse it will be for Runa and her cohorts. Are you sure you did nothing to provoke this?"

"I swear," I said.

"And Runa had never bothered you before?"

"Never. When Thyre worked here, I'm not sure she even noticed me. She never even spoke to me."

"So, why attack you now?" Mother asked, cocking her head.

"Maybe to get back at you and Father?" I suggested.

"That would make the most sense, but why now? Why wait so long?"

I shrugged.

Regin approached, carrying a small tray. "A cook warmed some goat's milk and soaked two rolls in it. Best he could do on short notice."

"That will be fine," I said, taking one of the soggy pieces of bread before he moved the pot to the floor, making room for the tray. *Warm and filling. Exactly what I need.*

"Regin, take the pot back to the kitchen and fetch another jug of water. Abi will be here soon, and I'm sure we'll need it."

"Yes, Mother, gladly."

He walked away this time.

Mother watched him until he turned the corner. "Your brother hasn't slept in his bed since we left you in your room," she said, squeezing my shoulder gently. "But I know he'd rather be with the men searching for your attackers."

"I appreciate that," I said. "I'd have done the same for him."

"I know you would, my sweet girl."

"What are you going to do to them when they are found?" I asked.

She flashed me a smile, reminding me of a cat about to make a kill. "Nothing like I want to do. Your father won't let me cut Runa's fingers off, but he did agree to let me rip out the fingernails that scratched you."

"Oh," I said, shivering. *I'm not going to ask what she has planned for Idania and Zora.*

"Painful but not permanently harmful," Mother continued. "A long-lasting reminder of her mistake."

"I can imagine," I said.

Abi and Father arrived, with Regin a few steps behind, ending the suddenly uncomfortable conversation.

"Meyla, it's good to see you up," Father said, smiling. "How are you feeling?"

"I still ache, and my cheek is a bit warm," I said. "Mother thinks I feel fevered, but I don't feel hot."

"May I take a look?" Abi asked.

I nodded, and Mother moved to make room for the herbalist to work.

"I should have put fresh paste on yesterday morning but didn't want to wake you," Abi said, gently peeling the dried mixture from my face.

I hissed as it pulled at the skin near the scratches.

"I don't like how that looks," she said, frowning before putting her bag on the floor and reaching inside.

"Those wounds look angry," Mother commented. "Did Linus do something wrong?"

"Not as such," Abi replied. "If they were deeper, I'd have stitched them closed, but in this case, all I can do is clean them and try something stronger."

I noticed Mother rubbed the stump where her right hand had been.

"Regin, dampen this," Abi said, handing a rag to my brother.

He put the jug he'd held onto the table and plunged the cloth into it, sloshing water everywhere.

"Too wet," Abi said. "Wring it out."

"Sorry," he said, spraying water from the dripping cloth when he squeezed it.

Abi sighed and took the rag from him. "Better."

The lines in my cheek stung when she touched the damp cloth to my wounds.

I hissed again, and she nodded.

"Will she have scars?" Regin asked. He sounded a bit too excited.

"Probably not," Abi said, wiping my cheek again. "A candle, please. I need to get a better look."

Father brought a candle from my room.

"Hold it here," Abi directed. "No, a little higher and closer."

It was close enough I closed my right eye and tried to ignore the warmth hitting the side of my face.

"Careful," Mother said. "Don't burn her hair."

"I won't," Father said. The candle moved back a little.

"Definitely not healing as I would expect," Abi said. "Regin, take my mortar out and pour a small amount of water into it."

"Yes, ma'am."

"How bad is it?" Mother asked.

"Nothing to worry over. We caught it early." Abi said. "I'll leave enough of this mixture with you to apply fresh pastes for four days. So long as the scratches don't look worse or ooze anything white or green, Meyla will heal within a week...ten days at most."

"What about my aches?" I asked. "My back, especially."

Abi pursed her lips for a moment. "Linus assured me your ribs are fine. Anything I give you to relieve the soreness would only make you sleepy. I could give you a rub of cat's claw and turmeric, but then you'd smell enough that some people wouldn't want you around. Honestly, there isn't much else I can do."

"She stinks already," Regin said, sticking his tongue out at me before laughing.

"Not as bad as you," I said, grinning.

"Enough," Father barked. I could tell he was trying to not smile.

"If you're feeling well enough to jest with your brother, maybe we're worried about nothing," Mother said. "Perhaps I should send Abi away and prepare your lessons."

"No," I said. "I... He started it."

Mother smiled. "Abi, what do we need to do?"

She smirked. "Let me prepare this paste, and I'll show you. Regin, can you clear the table so I have someplace to work?"

A short pillar rose from the floor next to my chair. "Will that do?" Father asked.

"A couple of hands higher would be better," Abi said.

He nodded, and the table rose.

Again, the grinding sound of stone on stone rasped at my ears as Abi worked. A minty smell floated to me before garlic punched at my nose. Soon, honey covered them both, though the garlic scent fought hard for dominance.

"A rub for my aches would smell worse than that?" I asked, nose wrinkled.

"Some people find garlic fragrant," Abi said, glancing at my mother. "I understand they eat it in some Varian dishes."

"We do," Tindra said. "Though Einns tends to avoid it, I'm surprised you weren't served any while traveling in my homeland this past month."

"Pretty sure I would remember that smell," I said.

"Me, too," Regin added.

"It's not my favorite either," Father said.

"I'll talk to Goran and see if he can make a batch of garlic bread once Meyla feels better," Mother said.

I raised my eyebrows. "I'm in no hurry."

"Me either," Regin said.

"You need to try it before you make up your mind," Mother said.

"This is ready," Abi said. "Sit still."

The scents stabbed at my nose as she spread the thick, sticky paste across my cheek.

"I can't wrap it in a bandage," she said, "so I'm going to press the cloth against it and add another layer. Who will apply this tomorrow?"

"I'll do it," Mother said, "with Regin's help."

"Watch closely," Abi said, before pressing.

I flinched.

"Hold still," Abi instructed.

I clenched my teeth and pushed against her.

"Relax your jaw," Abi said. "Don't fight me, or this won't stay on, and we'll have to wrap the bandage over your mouth."

"Then she couldn't talk," Regin said. "Do that...please."

"Only if we do the same to you," Mother said. I could hear the smile in her voice.

"What?" he blurted. "No."

"Then be nice to your sister—she's hurt," Mother said.

"I'm going to wrap all three of your mouths," Father chuckled.

Abi joined in the laughter while she applied a second coating to the bandage cloth.

"Probably best if you rest as much as you can for the next few days," the herbalist said.

"Too sore to do much," I said. Or tried to say, but the thick paste kept my right cheek from moving right, so my words were a bit slurred.

"I'll make sure she's quiet," Mother said.

"Sire!" The word echoed down the hall.

Chapter 11

"Go see who's looking for you before they stampede down the hall and knock us all over," Mother said.

"It's never easy being a king," he said, shaking his head before running away.

"There's a lesson you need to keep in your heart and mind, Meyla," Mother said.

"Sire!" The call came again before Father rounded the corner.

Hurried footsteps were coming in our direction. "Tindra!" Father called.

"What could he need me for?" Mother asked.

"Maybe they found the girls," Regin said.

"Regin, stay here and pay attention to what Abi's doing," Mother said, before hurrying away.

"I'm done here, my Queen," Abi said. "I'll scrape the rest of this paste into a jar and see myself out. Send for me if you need anything else."

"Give it to Regin, and he'll put it in his sister's room."

"I'll make sure it's taken care of," he said.

Abi nodded.

"Thank you, Abi," I said, holding out my hand.

"You're welcome, Princess," the herbalist said, taking my hand. "Remember, you need a few days of rest."

"Yes, ma'am," I said, watching the goopy, brown gunk slowly drool from the mortar into a squat, brown, glass jar.

I could tell my parents were speaking with someone just beyond the corner, but I couldn't make out what they were saying until Mother raised her voice. "You're absolutely certain?"

Abi quietly put her things away, patted my leg, and said, "If you do feel fevered, tell someone. I don't think you're going to get worse, but you could end up deathly sick if you try to hide how you feel."

"I will," I said, smiling at her.

"And I'll make sure," Regin said.

Abi walked down the hall, away from the conversation. She knew her way around our home at least as well as my family did.

"Wonder what is going on," Regin said.

"I'm not going anywhere," I said. "Sneak down there and find out."

His eyes lit up. "Good idea."

As he turned, Mother and Father came around the corner with the three guard captains following them. He stopped and turned back, acting like we were talking.

"Meyla, are you absolutely certain it was Runa, Zora, and Idaina who attacked you yesterday?" Father asked.

"Yes."

"No one else?" Mother pressed.

"Like I told you, Runa tried to slap me, but I leaned away so she just scratched me. I smacked her with my coin purse, and then they were on me. Why? Is someone claiming that isn't what happened?" I stood, and my voice rose with me. "If you found them and they are telling a different story, they're lying."

Father took a breath. "They found Runa and Thyre in the central forest not long after first light."

"When can I face them?" I asked.

Mother put her hand on my shoulder. "They're dead."

"Sounds like Runa got what she deserved," Regin said.

Mother shot him a questioning glance. "Sergeant Lopt's search party found them bound to trees with their throats cut."

"Oh," I said. An icy bolt raced down my back. "What about her two friends?"

"We don't know," Captain Agrim said. "No sign of them."

"My company is riding out to help with the search," Captain Svan said.

"Did you go back to their father and make him talk?" I asked.

"He still swears he knows nothing," Captain Sibbi said.

Father sighed. "And I'm not willing to torture a man who may have lost his daughters...regardless of who they are or what they have done."

"Any idea who killed them?" Regin asked.

"The only thing we found on their bodies was a small cache of Varian coins in Thyre's boot."

"Which seems strange, in a sense, but may mean nothing," Mother said. "Deyan's from my home country and a merchant. Who knows who he does business with? And we have enough caravans between Croy and Varia that Thyre could have gotten Varian coins from him."

"I'd heard they were mixed up with some shady Satran merchants," Regin said.

"And you didn't think to mention that before?" Mother asked.

Regin closed his eyes. "Didn't seem important until now."

"Wait," I said, sitting back down. "Do you think someone paid Runa to attack me?"

"I'm not convinced," Father said. "But we have to take that into consideration until we find out differently."

"Meaning *what*?" I asked.

"Meaning you don't leave the castle alone," Mother said.

"What about Regin?" I asked.

"It's probably best that both of you have guards around you when you leave the grounds," Father said. "At least until we figure out if there's a real threat."

"No one attacked *me*," Regin countered. "Plus, I can take care of myself."

"You're no better of a street fighter than your sister," Mother said. "It's safer to assume you could be a target too, *if* someone is looking to harm Meyla."

I rubbed my forehead, trying to understand what had happened. "I'm going to my room to tend my plants and then lay down. Do I need a guard with me for that?"

"No," Father said. "But men will be posted at every door outside and every exit from the castle grounds. No one comes in or out unchallenged."

"Already working on a schedule, Sire," Sibbi said.

"As long as guards are in place before moonrise," Tindra said.

"Of course, my Queen," Sibbi said.

"Regin, what are your plans?" Father said.

"Hadn't made any since we didn't know when Meyla was going to wake. Guess I'm going to help her until...something else comes up."

"Thanks," I said, frowning and hoping he'd pick up on my sarcasm.
He didn't.

Chapter 12

"If you want to help," I said, "tie the curtains back, then fill the watering jug."

"Sure. Be glad to," he said, hurrying past me to the closest window, "but we need to talk about what's happened."

"Why?"

"What if someone's after us...or you?"

"You don't really think—"

"That it's extremely odd that Runa attacks one of us now instead of soon after Thyre was kicked out of here. After all this time, she walks up to you for no known reason and beats you," he said.

"People carry grudges," I said, shrugging.

"But why wait until we got back from Varia?"

"Maybe she was jealous."

"Then why was Thyre killed, too?" he asked, tying the curtain back and moving to the next window.

"Wait," I said, snapping my fingers. "When she attacked me, she had some injuries on her face. It could be that she's running with some rough people. Maybe she heard about something she shouldn't have, and they were afraid she'd tell someone...like Thyre."

"That's a lot of maybes," he said. "And it still doesn't explain where Zora and Idania are or why their father isn't helping. Why isn't he worried about his daughters? Mother and Father would spare no man to find us if we went missing. He must know something."

"Or maybe he's scared," I said.

"Then why not disappear?" Regin asked. "Merchants come and go all the time. He could slip away without trying hard."

"Fine. Say you're right. Say Father's right and someone is after me or us. Why not attack while we are in Varia or traveling back from there? We passed plenty of secluded places."

He opened his mouth.

"Before you answer," I cut him off, "think about what you're going to say while you fill the watering jug." I pointed to a wooden container with a short spout.

"There's still water in the hallway," he said.

"I think you'll need longer than that to come up with a sensible answer," I said, smiling and turning away to examine my large container of angelica. *I'll need to move some to another pot soon. Maybe Regin will be nice and make me a new one.*

"We had guards for our entire trip," my brother said, pride in his voice. "That's why no one bothered us."

I tapped my finger against my chin. "Can't argue with you there. But I still don't think we're in any danger."

"Why not? She attacked you. For no reason. How can you be so calm about this?"

"You just said it," I replied, taking the full container from him. "She did it for no reason. An oak doesn't change its growth because the occasional woodpecker pokes a hole in it."

"It doesn't survive a surprise wildfire either," he said, shaking his head. "Father must think something is going on, or he wouldn't trouble the guard."

"He's doing that to keep Mother calm. The last thing he wants is to have her upset and threatening to burn everything."

He sighed. "Maybe."

"You know I'm right. I'm older and wiser than you, after all."

He scoffed. "Keep that up, and I won't help. You have light and water—what else do you need?"

I moved to examine the blackberry bush I'd planted before we left. It definitely needed water. "I could use another pot like that one," I said, pointing at the container full of angelica.

"I'd probably have to leave the courtyard to find a stone big enough," he said.

"And I need it filled with good soil."

"Did you hear me?"

I nodded.

"I can't go outside of the grounds," he said, putting his hands on his hips.

"Alone," I said. "You can't go alone. Find a guard who doesn't have anything better to do and get me what I need."

"Right," he said, snapping his fingers.

"See," I said, trying not to laugh. "Older and wiser."

He shook his head and left.

Chapter 13

I made my way around the room, noticing my butterbur plants looked off. *Need to ask Linus or Abi about them.* Soon, my back ached, and I had to sit down. I decided to use the time to record some thoughts in my journal. While writing, doubt crept into my mind. *What if Regin's right, and I'm not considering all the possibilities?*

I hadn't expected Uncle Roi and Aunt Grima to come see me and jumped when he said my name. The sudden movement hurt my back, and I groaned.

"Should we come some other time?" Roi asked, concern evident on his face.

"No, just sore," I said. "Please, come in, but you'll have to sit on the bed. And excuse me if I don't stand."

He raised two stone seats from the floor near me.

"Right. I always forget you're a stonesyth," I said.

He chuckled.

"How are you?" Grima asked.

"Well as can be expected, I suppose," I said.

"I hear you gave Runa a pretty good shot to the face," Roi said.

I gave him a summary of what happened, though I was growing tired of telling the story.

"Good thinking," he said, nodding. "Resourceful. Too bad that didn't end it right then."

"You don't have to tell me," I said, grinning.

He returned my smile.

"Do you need anything?" Grima asked.

"Regin is helping...well, as much as he ever helps."

"Young boys have different priorities," she said. "I remember Einns at that age...though most of his energy went into cooking."

"He could have done worse things," Roi said. "I could tell some stories about Fitzeirick."

"And Rorec could tell stories about you," Grima said. "As a matter of fact, I've heard a couple of them often enough I could tell them."

I'd met Roi's father some time ago. Rorec helped my father conquer Satra and was rewarded with leadership of the territory. Everyone expected Roi to take his place when he passed. I wasn't sure how I felt about that.

"Grima, do you know anything about growing butterbur?" I asked, no longer wanting to think about rulers and what may come.

She pursed her lips for a moment. "Most of the plants I grow are for weaving, but what do you need to know?"

Turning, I pointed to the pot holding my plants. "I saw spots on the underside of some of the leaves. I'm not sure what caused them."

She glanced at the plant and shrugged. "Too much water...maybe?."

"I'll ask Abi. She gave me the cutting," I said, nodding.

Grima leaned toward me and gave me a hug. "I'm glad you didn't get hurt too badly."

"Me, too," Roi added. "I'd hate to think what your mother might have done if you'd been any worse."

I told him what she wanted to do to Runa.

"Sounds exactly like Tindra," Roi said. "And I can't say I disagree with her on this."

"I wouldn't want to watch," Grima said, with a shiver, "but I think she's right. Einns was never harmed growing up, but woe be unto anyone who would have."

Roi smirked and took his wife's hand. "And you don't have a violent streak."

Grima blushed and shook her head.

He leaned over and patted my knee. "Meyla, if you need anything...send word."

"I will, Uncle, I promise."

"Heal quickly," Grima said. "I have some new fabric that would look great on you. Stop by when you can, and I'll make you a new dress."

"Thank you, I will. I promise."

She kissed me on my forehead, and Roi squeezed my hand before they left.

Forcing myself to my feet, I put my things away and lay down to rest.

Chapter 14

"Meyla, are you hungry? Einns boiled some goat for you," Regin said, waking me.

The room was dimly lit. "Huh?" I grunted and tried to stretch. My back twinged, and I groaned.

"Dinner is ready," he said. "Einns made you something soft so you wouldn't have to chew much."

"Oh," I said, sitting up as he lit a candle. "I should probably change clothes before joining everyone. I've slept in these for days."

"Mother and Father are coming here. You can stay right where you are," he said. A table sprang from the floor next to my bed, followed by three seats as he turned to leave.

I shuffled around the room, untying the curtains and lighting lanterns. *If we're eating in here, it would be nice to see each other...and our food.*

Mother led Father into my room soon after I returned to my bed. Three servants were on their heels, Regin bringing up the rear.

"How do you feel?" Mother asked, sitting directly across from me.

"Well enough to play with her plants," Regin said, as our meal was placed on the table.

Mother frowned and glanced sideways at him.

"Explains the pot full of dirt in the hallway," Father said, taking the last seat after the servers left the room.

"I feel well enough to have eaten in the dining room," I said. "And yes, some of my plants needed my attention."

"You should be resting," Mother said.

"I am," I said. "That's why I sent Regin to get the pot and more dirt."

He nodded. "Balli and Lini were eager to help when they heard it was for Meyla. I think one or both of them is sweet on you, sister."

"What?" Mother barked.

I sighed and shook my head.

"My daughter will *not* be courted by one of our guards," she said.

"I believe that is her choice," Father said.

"Can't say I'm interested in either of them anyway," I said.

"Not while Captain Svan is around," Regin teased.

"What?" Mother blurted again.

"Nothing," I said. "Regin's just trying to cause trouble."

"You best be right," Mother said, pointing at me. "Svan's too old for you anyway."

"I seem to remember your mother caught Svan's eye before we were promised," Father commented.

"We are not discussing this," Mother insisted, glaring at my father.

Regin chuckled, and I smiled

"Any word on the other two girls?" I asked, changing the subject.

"Nothing solid," Father said. "Lots of rumors, though."

"Normally, rumors are fun," Mother said, "but in this case, they aren't helping."

I nodded. "And still nothing from their father?"

"Not a word," Father said.

"Doesn't that seem strange?" Regin asked.

"Yes," Mother said. "That's why we have people watching him. If he goes to wherever the girls are hiding, we'll know."

"Do you think they're alive?" I asked.

"I think it's best to believe so until we know otherwise," Father said. "But don't worry. They can't get to you."

"I'm not worried," I said. "I don't wish them ill, but they should pay for what they did to me."

"And they will," Mother said.

"How long are you planning to keep Meyla and me restricted to the castle?" Regin asked.

"Only until we're certain neither of you are in danger," Father said.

"Why do you ask?" Mother added.

"I wanted to visit Thorgault and see how my new vest was looking," Regin said.

"Oh, and I still need a belt for my sword," I said, glancing toward where I'd left the blade and noticing two hooks on the wall cradled it above my bow stand. "Thank you, Father. That's perfect."

"Surprise," he said, grinning. "I thought you'd wake while I sythed the mounts."

"You're better than that," I said, smiling at him.

"Excuse me," Einns said from the hallway. "Is there anyone in there who would like some sweet bread and maple syrup?"

Father turned. "Yes. Come in, come in."

Our head cook entered my room. He still had a boyish look to him, even though he was more than ten years older than me...as far as I knew.

I clapped when he put a tray of warm bread dripping with sticky syrup on the table and then bowed with a flourish.

"Glad to see you up, Meyla," he said.

"Thank you, Einns. For everything," I said.

"You enjoyed the goat stew?" he asked.

"It was perfect," I said, reaching for a piece of the dessert.

He smiled wide at my praise.

"Join us," Father offered.

"Thank you, Sire, but I can't stay," Einns said. "I have another batch of bread waiting to take to my parents."

"Tell them we said hello," Father said.

Einns nodded. "Enjoy."

"Mmm," I hummed, licking some sticky sweetness off my fingers. "I will."

"We will," Regin said, reaching for a piece of bread.

Einns laughed and left us.

The sweet treat put an end to our conversation. I, for one, enjoyed the quiet.

After another piece of sweet bread and licking my fingers clean again, I yawned. "Full stomach is making me sleepy."

Father tore a piece of bread in half and offered it to Mother. She smiled and bit at it, playfully nipping his fingers. "Then it's time for us to go so you can rest," she said. She rose, grabbed Father's hand, and practically pulled him from his seat.

"I'll tell the servants to not bother you when they come to clean this up," Father said. "Sleep well, saeta."

"I'll clean up, Father," Regin said. "I still need to bring the pot in anyway."

"Thank you, brother, but that can wait," I said.

"No," he replied. "This way, you use it whenever you're ready instead of waiting on me. Who knows? I may sleep in tomorrow since I can't leave the grounds."

"Good thinking," Father said. "Goodnight to both of you."

"Goodnight," we replied together.

I watched Regin gather a load of plates. The table and seats sank back into the floor as he left.

What is he up to? While I pondered this question, he returned, hefting the stone pot through my door.

Chapter 15

"Where do you want this?" he asked.

I pointed. "There, next to the other one. And once you're done I need one more thing."

"What?" he grunted.

As soon as the pot clunked on the floor, I sat up. "I need you to tell me why you are being so helpful all of a sudden."

He put his hands on his hips. "How could you ask such a question? We always take care of each other."

"Not like this," I said. "You never do anything a servant could do for you." I pointed to the chair at my writing table. "Sit. Talk."

He held up a finger, hurried to the door and looked both ways down the hall, before closing the door and sitting in the chair. "I think there's more going on than they're telling us."

"Why?"

"The guards seem...I don't know...on edge," he said.

"Father has them on watch, day and night," I said.

He shook his head. "It's not that. They aren't talking to me and stop talking among themselves when I get near. Like they know something and are afraid I'll find out."

"I bet they don't want you telling Father they were complaining."

He frowned. "That's not what it feels like. Those men know us. Most of them have watched us since before we could walk. A few are practically family."

"Speaking of which. I'm not interested in Svan," I said, shaking my finger at Regin.

"Are you sure?" he asked, drawing out the last word. "I've seen how you look at him sometimes."

"Do I think he's handsome? Certainly. Do I enjoy being around him? Of course. He's a nice person and easy to talk to. But, like you said, he's more like family. Thinking of him romantically would be like fawning over Jonus or Linus."

"If you say so."

"I do and next time you pull something like that, I'm going to mention Anja," I said, crossing my arms.

"You wouldn't," Regin said, glaring at me.

"At least you don't deny it," I said. "I won't mention your attraction and you don't speculate who I've got eyes for. Do we have a deal?"

After chewing his lip for a moment, he nodded. "Deal."

"Glad we settled that. Now, if you don't have any actual evidence to support your suspicion, I need to rest."

He sighed. "I can't believe you don't believe me."

"It's not that — Listen, I'm not saying you're wrong because I don't know that you are. At the same time, I'm not hearing anything convincing me you're right either. None of this makes any sense. Are we missing something? Maybe, but I have no idea what."

"Well," he said. "That's better than saying you don't believe me at all. Tell you what, you rest and get better while I try to find out what's being kept from us."

"Just stay out of trouble," I said. "I'm in no shape to have your back right now."

"But you do trust me...right?" he asked, almost pleading.

"Always. If I can't trust my twin brother, who can I trust?"

"Just remember that," he said, getting to his feet. "Rest well. Meyla. I'll see you tomorrow."

"Good night, Regin."

The lanterns went out as he closed the door.

Sunlight streaming through my windows woke me. I started a fire for my bath, opened the tap to fill the tub, got undressed, and looked down at the bruise on my side; dark purple with a sickly looking green-yellow border. *Wonder if that's what my back looks like.* Knowing the water was still cool, I combed several tangles out of my hair while waiting for the water to warm.

As I stopped the flow of water, someone knocked on my door.

"I'm bathing!"

The door opened and Mother stepped into my bathing room. She grimaced. "I was going to change your bandage before breakfast."

Didn't she hear me? "Mother!" I practically squealed, turning away from her. "Is Regin with you?"

"No," she said, giggling.

My heart still pounded from near embarrassment. "Good. Well...since you're here, how's my back look?"

"Hmm...nearly as bad as your side."

I nodded. "Then it's probably a good idea for me to soak for a while. Can you bring my breakfast later?"

"Yes, my dear. I'll bring a bowl of boiled grains after we finish eating. Enjoy your bath."

"Thank you, Mother."

Chapter 16

It's strange how time passes when you're floating in a pool of hot water. On one hand, it feels like everything stops, and you've been there forever. On the other, it never feels like you have enough time to relax and fully enjoy yourself. Knowing my mother would return sooner instead of later, I cut my soak short and washed myself, all the while being careful to avoid getting the crusty bandage on my cheek wet.

My suspicion was correct. Mother entered the room not long after I had dressed and went to work combing my hair.

"I can do that for you while you eat," Mother offered, setting a bowl of boiled grains on my writing table. "Then I'll change your bandage."

"Thank you," I said. "I'd like that."

Several times, my head tilted back as my mother worked the comb through some tangles. *Let's see if I can take advantage of this.* "Would you cut my hair? It's awfully long and takes quite a bit of time and effort to comb out."

"Traditionally, Varian women don't cut their hair," Mother said, working through another knot.

"But I'm not Varian," I said, "and you cut *your* hair."

She chuckled. "I'm far from traditional, my dear girl. If you want to cut it, let me tell your father first. He's the one who wanted you to keep it long as a symbol of your Varian heritage."

"Please talk to him," I said, "but don't let him cut it. He told me what happened with Aunt Jesca."

Mother laughed. "Oh, my. I hadn't thought about that in a long time. It was so bad. Poor girl. Don't worry, saeta, I won't let him cut it."

"Thank you. Honestly, I thought you'd be upset I wanted to cut my hair."

"I thought you liked wearing it long," Mother said, caught in another tangle. "You should have said something before now. Never be afraid to talk to me about anything."

I reached back and patted her leg. "Thank you, Mother. I just didn't want to upset you."

"Over something like your hair? Never. I want you to be happy, and if a haircut helps, you have my full support. I can go get shears now if you'd like."

"Are you sure it won't upset Father?" I asked, my tangled hair yanking the comb out of her hand when I turned to look at her.

"He cut your aunt's hair because it was uncomfortable for her. He'll understand when I tell him I cut yours for the same reason."

"Yes, tell him that."

She laughed. "Plus, it would save me from combing out more bird's nests."

I chuckled at her jest and worked to pull the comb out of my hair as she left. *Had I talked to her about this before, I wouldn't have looked at that hair cuff, and Runa might not have found me.* That line of thinking smothered the happiness I'd felt about getting my hair cut.

To distract myself until Mother returned, I worked on the overgrown container of angelica, sything about half of the plants away from the rest. Mother returned when I was wrist-deep in fresh dirt, preparing to transfer the crop to the new pot Regin brought for me.

"You couldn't do that before you bathed?" she asked.

"Passing the time until you got back." I didn't turn to look at her.

"As soon as you're done, sit here. I can take care of your hair and then change your bandage," Her voice came from near my table.

I nodded and kept focusing on my plants. The roots were tangled worse than my hair. *If I damage them too much, I'll lose them all.* With my injuries, it was harder to focus and took more time and energy than usual to finish the task. After raking the dirt in place, I poured water over the plants and shuffled to the chair, ready to be off my feet.

"Tilt your head forward and hold still," Mother said. Soon, the rasping of metal scraping metal filled my ears. *Almost as irritating as a pestle grinding in a mortar.* "Should I trim it over your ears?"

"No," I said. "I don't want to look too much like Regin."

Mother chuckled, and the rasping grew louder.

"Chin up. Turn your chair and let me look at the front," she said.

A weight was literally gone from my shoulders. Cool air caressed the base of my neck. *I feel free.*

Mother stepped back and looked at me. Her eyes flicked back and forth as her mouth twisted.

I couldn't read her expression.

"Almost finished," she said, stepping toward me. "Close your eyes."

I flinched when she rested the cool shears against my forehead.

"Hold still."

"Sorry."

Three snips later, she declared my haircut was finished.

I shook my head and smiled, feeling my hair lightly brush the tops of my shoulders. "Thank you. This feels wonderful."

She smiled and kissed my forehead. "Glad to help. I'll send someone to clean the hair off the floor later. Let's change that bandage."

"Where's Regin?" I asked. "Wasn't he going to help with this?"

"Seems he's taking the idea that someone may be after you—or him—seriously. He's been sparring with the guards since first light."

I shook my head. "He tried convincing me there could be a threat to us. I'm not saying it's impossible, but it seems unlikely...at best."

"Runa's attack and murder are both disturbing for different reasons," Mother said. "It doesn't hurt to be cautious until we know there's nothing to worry about, but Regin seems to see it as a certainty. Of course, I won't discourage him from becoming a better fighter regardless of his motivation."

I chuckled. "Seems I would benefit from more fighting lessons, too."

Mother's expression changed. She had a predator's look to her. "When you are recovered, I will see you are trained properly myself."

"I've seen you and Father face off. I'm not sure I'm ready for that."

She smirked, softening her expression. "You have nothing to fear from me, sweet girl. I will start slowly...at first."

"As you say, Mother."

She nodded. "Now, let's tend to your wound."

No one would dare accuse my mother of not having grace and finesse, but she lacked Abi's gentle touch when it came to applying pastes and bandages. My cheek throbbed by the time she finished.

"What are your plans now?" Mother asked.

"I'm going outside, maybe spend some time in the garden. Anything to get out of this stone box."

"Sounds like a good idea. I'm sure you would benefit from the fresh air. Just don't leave the grounds without guards."

"I won't," I said. "What are you doing today?"

"Your father and I have meetings until at least midday. It would be nice to have lunch with you but we may be unavailable."

"If nothing else, I'll see you for dinner then. And we'll eat in the dining room."

She nodded. "As long as you feel well enough."

"I'll take it easy," I said. "May your meetings go well."

"Enjoy the garden, saeta."

Walking beside my mother, we kissed then split ways when I turned to go outside.

Chapter 17

After stepping out of the castle's shadow, I stopped and turned to face the sun. Bright light shining red through my eyelids, I stood still and reveled in the warmth.

"Excuse me, Princess," a servant said, as they passed. "Didn't recognize you with short hair. It looks good. Are you feeling well?"

I nodded. "I'm fine. Just enjoying being outside."

"Yes, m'lady, it is nice out. Have a pleasant day."

"You too," I said. "I didn't mean to be in the way."

"Pay me no mind, Your Highness."

I nodded but decided it would be best for me to be on my way.

Walking among the waist-high barley, I noticed Aslak, our head gardener, harvesting leeks. Pieces of green stalks were caught in his frizzy, red hair. I waved when he looked my direction.

He stared at me for a moment before a look of recognition brightened his eyes, one gray and the other dark green. Smiling, his thin lips pulled back from his jagged teeth, he waved back and yelled, "Good ta see ya, Meyla!"

I nodded and yelled back, "Glad to be out here!"

He winked, then went back to pulling stalks and tossing them into a nearby cart.

I continued walking, brushing my fingers against the green seed clusters and pushing my talent into the plants to check their condition and pull a little energy from each one.

A shadow passed by, and I looked up to see scattered clouds floating lazily past, like leaves in a slow river. *Doesn't look like rain.* A flight of wood pigeons entered the orchard not far from me. Their soothing calls convinced me to follow them into the rows of trees.

Placing my hand against an apple tree, I used my talent to bend a branch so I could pluck a piece of fruit, then sat against the trunk and enjoyed my snack while listening to the gray birds converse with each other.

A gentle, warm breeze rose, caressing my newly exposed neck and adding a dull roar of rustling leaves and rubbing branches to the soft bird calls. The sensations drew a smile to my face. Closing my eyes, I set my hand on a tree root and pulled a steady flow of energy, hoping it might help my body heal faster.

Something tickled my cheek. I shook my head and opened my eyes. Large raindrops plopped on the ground, splashing my foot. Thunder boomed as I jumped to my feet, and rain fell in buckets. I wanted to run, but even a jogging pace aggravated my back. By the time I got inside, water dripped from my soaked dress. The drenching made the paste on my cheek sticky again.

On my way to the kitchen to warm up, dry out, and maybe grab a snack, I ran into Regin. He looked clean and well-rested for someone who had crossed weapons with guardsmen for most of the morning.

He glanced around. "I need to tell you something. Let's get lunch and eat in your room. You need to get into some dry clothes anyway."

"What's going on?" I asked.

He held his finger to his lips. "Not here," he whispered.

Chapter 18

We grabbed a couple of pork sandwiches each, and Regin got a pitcher of tea, and then we left for my room. I made him wait in the hall while I changed. Even in dry clothes, I felt chilled, so I lit a fire in the bathing warmer while he poured tea for us. "What is so important?"

Heavy rain tapped against the windows, filling my room with a dull roar.

"We need to make plans to leave...soon."

"What?" I blurted.

"Shh. Keep your voice down."

"We can't leave," I said, "and you know it."

"I saw a Varian messenger arrive earlier and followed him. He met with Mother and Father."

"So." I looked sideways at him. "Messages come and go from here all the time."

He shook his head. "Not like this one. Trust me. I got close enough to hear what he had to say. There's a price on our heads."

I know I didn't hear him right. "What?" I screamed.

"Shh. I heard him say a group in Varia is upset with how Father handled Satra. Seems they have been gathering power and influence in secret for years. They may have infiltrated Kurt's people, too."

"When did you hear this?"

He glanced toward the window. "Not long after Mother cut your hair. It looks nice, by the way."

"Thank you," I replied out of habit, then shook my head. "But Mother told me she had meetings until midday or later. How could she know about the messenger if she was with me, in my room, when he arrived?"

"They were talking with the heads of the local merchant guild about a growing dispute between them and traders bringing goods from Satra. That meeting was cut short."

I didn't want to believe it, but I had heard murmurs about such complaints before we left for Varia. "Assuming that's the case, why would we leave? Isn't it safer here? We have guards around us all the time," I said.

"We also have Varians around us—some closer than the guards. No one knows who all is involved. Uncle Crum is doing what he can, so is Kurt, but they just don't know anything for certain."

I shivered. "Why now?"

"That's what Father asked. Their best guess is our trip to Varia angered someone. Or maybe they think they have a big enough force, so they're trying to start a war." He frowned for a moment. "What does it matter? I don't think we're safe here now.

Whoever this is could expect us to have our guard down and strike where we feel least exposed."

I took a deep breath and considered what he'd said. Would someone attack us in our home? "I'm not saying I believe you, but if I did, where would we go? It doesn't sound like Varia is safe."

"I thought about that, too," he said, nodding. "Can your new toy make the trip to Satra?"

"My boat? Of course. Easily."

He closed his eyes. "I hate to ask but...can you get us there in it?"

"I know the way."

"Without anyone seeing us until we reach the Satran capital?"

"Maybe," I considered. "The trade barges keep within sight of the shoreline. We can sail south until we're out of sight, then turn east to Satra. My boat will be faster in the open water, so no one could catch us even if they tried."

"Good. That's where we'll go. And we can visit Rorec and Asfrid."

"We can't just show up," I said. "What would we tell them?"

"That you were testing your new boat, like Kurt asked when he gave it to you. How long would the trip take?"

"Less than a day," I said, after thinking about it for a moment. "Probably."

"Is there room for three days' worth of supplies on the boat?" he asked.

"With room to spare, but why?"

He tapped his finger on the table and groaned. "If you're just testing your boat, Rorec won't expect us to stay long. We'll need to be ready to sail away, then find someplace else to get back on land and camp for a while."

"Sure, that would work. But—"

"What?" he asked, glaring at me.

"It's not that I don't believe you..." I sighed. "None of this makes sense."

"If you don't believe me, ask Mother and Father. But if you start asking questions, they'll wonder where you heard about this, and I'll get in trouble for eavesdropping, and we'll still be in danger. You know you can trust me. We have to take care of each other until the conspirators are found out."

He's right, getting him in trouble wouldn't do either of us any good. "Fine. How are we going to gather three days' worth of supplies and get them to the boat without someone noticing?"

"I'll work on that," he said.

"What can I do?"

"Keep acting like you're recovering from the attack."

"I'm not acting," I snapped. "I'm still hurt."

"I know, but your injuries are keeping Mother distracted. Don't act any differently than you are now. Any change, and she'll suspect something is going on. You know she'd figure out we're planning something long before Father."

Makes sense. "I can do that."

"Good...but start packing so you're ready to leave with little notice. In case things move faster than we expect."

"Are you sure this isn't a trick?"

He reached for my hand. "Meyla, it's not a trick. I would never lie to you—not when your safety is at risk."

"What about your safety? You said the threat was against both of us."

"Right...it was. But you're the only one attacked so far. You're hurt...vulnerable. I'm your brother. If anyone's going to take care of you...it's me."

"But we can trust Mother and Father. They'll protect us," I said, squeezing his hand.

"But they don't know who *they* can trust...and they can't act openly if they want to expose the conspiracy. The guard will be too busy watching everyone around us, trying to figure out who the next attacker might be. We have to take care of each other."

"Look me in the eyes and swear you aren't setting me up to get laughed at," I said, crossing my arms.

He locked his gray-blue eyes on mine. "I swear this is not a joke."

I sighed. "Fine. I believe you. When should I be ready to leave?"

"I have to figure a few things out first but...sooner rather than later."

"As long as you have supplies gathered for the trip, I can pack light. How are we going to get everything to my boat without anyone noticing?"

"Let me worry about that. I'll figure something out."

"You're taking on a lot. How do you know someone's not going to notice?"

"You do your part, and I'll do mine. As long as we're there for each other, no one will beat us," he said, giving me a weak smile.

I nodded. "I'm here for you."

He sighed. "And I'm going to take care of you. I need to get started. Take it easy, don't do anything that would draw undue attention, and rest. I know you need it."

"Don't worry about me...or us. We'll be fine," I said.

He nodded, gathered the plates and cups, and got up from the table. "Yes, we will."

Chapter 19

As Regin's footsteps faded in the hallway, an unease settled in my mind. *Is this real? He swore, but... No, I have to believe him. We've had our jests and plenty of disagreements, but nothing like this. In the end, we always take care of each other.*

"Focus," I said, reminding myself of what my brother needed from me. The best distraction for me was tending my plants while trying to act like nothing was wrong. As I worked, I considered if I should mention any of this in my journal but decided against it before laying down to rest.

It was still raining, with the occasional rumble of thunder, when Regin came to tell me dinner would be ready soon. "Remember," he said, "act normal."

"I'm as steady as an oak," I said. "It's you I'm not sure of."

He looked at me, concern growing on his face.

"Fire flits about at the slightest change," I said, then stuck my tongue out at him and laughed.

He joined in, then said, "Come on, let's go eat."

Bera stood in the dining room alone. "King Fitzeirick and Queen Tindra wanted me to let you know they had unexpected business to attend to. They're sorry you all can't eat together as a family this evening."

"Thank you, Bera," I said. "Will you be joining us?"

She shook her head. "I have to see to my mother. She's been ill and doesn't seem to be getting better."

I nodded. "Best wishes for her recovery, Bera."

"Yes," Regin said. "Let us know if we can do anything to help."

"Thank you, Prince Regin."

I opened my mouth to say something as we sat, but Regin shook his head and put a finger to his lips. I cocked my head and squinted.

Soon, our servants gave us both a plate with roast rabbit and potatoes along with mugs of ale.

Once they left the room, Regin nodded. "Keep your voice down. Never know when someone's lurking close enough to hear us. What were you going to say?"

"I was going to ask if you knew anything about our parents' unexpected business."

"No. I've been looking for good places to hide supplies and figuring out how we might escape the castle without raising too much suspicion."

"I wonder if it's related to our situation," I said.

"Fair guess." He nodded.

"Maybe it's good news. Maybe they found who's after us and we aren't in danger any longer."

He scratched his chin for a moment. "I'm not saying that couldn't be the case, but it would be awfully coincidental for someone to get caught the same day we receive word of the danger. We should stick with our plan until we know for sure. Assumptions could get you killed."

"Or you," I argued.

"Yes, of course. But you were the first one attacked. Maybe you're their main target."

"That does make sense since I'm the oldest." I grinned. "And next in line to rule."

He smirked. "And your death would hurt our parents more."

I shook my head. "They couldn't stand to lose either of us."

"You're right, but you being firstborn would sting more."

"Listen, I said that in jest. I'd rather not consider which of our deaths would hurt Mother and Father worst," I said, feeling a bit strange. "I'm already uneasy with what's going on. This isn't helping."

"Sorry," he said. "I've spent a lot of the day thinking about everything...even this troubling subject."

"There has to be something better we could discuss." I reached for my mug.

He shook his head. "I've had my fill anyway. I'm going to go and keep working on figuring out how we get away."

"I could help," I said, after taking a drink.

"No. The less you know, the better."

"Why?" I demanded.

"It's hard enough for one person to keep a secret," he said, getting out of his chair. "Another tongue can let something slip, and then both are caught."

I frowned again. "You'll have to tell me sooner or later."

"Once everything's in place, I'll tell you the whole plan."

"Fine. I'll wait...because I trust you," I said. "But I don't like being kept in the dark."

"Just remember, it's for our safety," he said, then hurried out of the room.

You keep saying that, but I don't have to like it.

Frustrated, and more than a little afraid, I picked a few more pieces of meat from my rabbit before deciding I should pack a few things for our journey before going to bed.

Mother would notice if I put clothes back in my travel pack, but she might not realize I had placed some of them strategically in my armoire. I sandwiched two dresses between three shirts and pants then moved my boots into the bottom of the wooden closet, on top of my pack. Everything could be thrown in the bag quickly, should the need arise. After making sure I had a quiver full of arrows and my bow was in perfect condition, I blew out the candle and went to sleep.

Chapter 20

Someone pounded on my door.

"Meyla," my brother called, from the hallway. "We're being summoned for breakfast."

My eyes fluttered. It wasn't light out yet. "What?"

The door opened, letting in a sliver of lantern light. "Mother and Father want us in the dining room."

"Why so early?" I groaned.

"I don't know, but hurry."

"Go on ahead," I said. "I'll be there after I change into fresh clothes."

"I'll tell them you're on your way," he said, closing the door and leaving me in darkness.

Striking flint to steel, I lit a lantern and hurried to put on clean clothes. Out of habit, my hand went to check my hair for tangles before I remembered it was short now. I chuckled and hurried to find out what my parents wanted.

Entering the room, I nearly tripped when I noticed my mother and father weren't the only people there. Roi and Grima sat at the far end of the table.

"Meyla, good morning. Tindra told me she'd cut your hair. It looks nice," my father said.

"Easier to take care of, too," Grima added.

"Thank you, Father," I said, and turned to Grima. "Yes, m'lady. Much easier."

She smiled and nodded.

"Sit, please," Father said.

I responded with a shallow bow and hurried to my seat.

"Due to information we received yesterday evening," Father said, "Tindra and I must leave for Varia at first light. Considering the recent attack on Meyla and the nature of our trip, we believe it is best for you and Regin to stay here. Captain Agrim and his company will ride with us. Captain Svan and his men are continuing to search for Zora and Idania as well as watching Deyan's movements. That leaves Captain Sibbi's company to secure the castle grounds."

"And you two are still not leaving the grounds without an escort," Mother added.

Father nodded. "In light of everything, we are leaving Roi and Grima in charge. As far as everyone is concerned, my words come from his mouth."

"Yes, Father," my brother and I said together, without being prompted.

"What's going on?" I asked.

"We don't know enough to discuss it yet," Father said. "Either way, it's nothing for you to worry about."

If it doesn't concern us, why are we meeting like this?

"How long will you be gone?" I asked, hoping he might give something away.

"No more than ten days. Hopefully less," Father said.

"Does this concern us?" Regin asked. I could tell by the look in his eyes that he was having a hard time controlling his excitement.

"Did you hear your father just say we weren't talking about it?" Mother replied.

Regin dipped his chin and slumped his shoulders but didn't argue.

"Roi, Grima, anything you would like to say?" Father offered.

"Meyla and Regin, we are looking forward to spending time with you two," Grima said, smiling. "Something we don't do often enough."

Still unsure of everything, I pressed my lips together and nodded.

Servants entered, carrying platters of warm bread and broiled mutton. Another followed, carrying two pitchers.

"As Einns so often says, 'if you leave the table hungry, it's your own fault,'" Father said, reaching for some meat.

Everyone seemed hesitant to talk while we ate. Regin declared himself full before long and asked to be excused to get dressed.

"Don't take too long, I expect you to ride with us to the southern gate," Father said.

"Of course." Regin grabbed one more strip of meat and left.

I wasn't far behind him.

Chapter 21

Goosebumps stood high on my skin even after I'd put on my hunting clothes. The leather outfit dyed green, gray, and black was the closest thing to armor I had, and it seemed appropriate to wear for seeing my mother and father off. Slinging my bow across my back, I hung my quiver over my shoulder and looked at my new sword. *I need a belt for that.* Reaching for it, I remembered we'd be on our horses and left it.

Regin met me as I turned the corner. He had chosen his hunting clothes, too. Lacking a way to carry his new axes, he held them in his hands.

"How do you plan to ride with your hands full?" I asked.

"I'll tuck them in my belt."

"Then why are you carrying them?"

He frowned. "When I walk, they pull my pants down."

I laughed as a rosy blush colored his cheeks.

"Stop," he said.

I nodded and did my best to quit laughing. "We better get to the stable. It wouldn't do for the princess and prince to delay the king and queen's departure."

"After you," he said, bowing.

My bow bounced against my back, sending little shocks of pain through my body with each step and slowing my pace, but we arrived before Mother and Father.

"Well met and good morning, Princess Meyla," Svinulf called, as we approached through the crowd of people preparing everything for our parents' trip to Varia. "How are you doing?"

The stablehand was about two years older than us, broad-shouldered and well-muscled. His blue eyes were always bright and happy. His hair nearly matched mine in color and was now longer. To tell the truth, if I had eyes for any of the young men working around the castle, Svinulf was the one.

"Well enough, I suppose. Thank you for asking."

He nodded and wrung his hands together. "I was sorry to hear you were attacked. I never liked Runa much anyway."

"She never spoke to me much," I said, frowning.

"I think she was interested in me," he said, looking down. "But the feeling wasn't mutual."

"The heart wants what it wants," I said, trying to cover a smile. "Is Senshi ready?"

"Oh, yes, m'lady. She's saddled and ready to go," he said, pointing to where my horse was tied to a post on the far side of the stable. "A warning—she's been fiery this morning. Not sure why."

"Probably upset I've been gone," I said.

He nodded. "Kroner will be right out, Prince Regin."

"Thank you, Svinulf," I said.

He smiled, bowed, and turned to get my brother's horse.

"Come help me get in the saddle," I said. "I'm sure Svinulf will bring Kroner out soon."

"Anything for a chance to see him again," Regin said, chuckling.

"I can visit the stable anytime I want," I said.

"Right," Regin said, smirking. "Let's go."

My brother knelt next to my buckskin mare. She snorted and stomped her front hoof a couple of times, kicking up some small clumps of mud, and swished her black tail violently. "Shh," I hissed. "It's just me." I let her sniff my palm.

She settled, and I was in the saddle with minimal discomfort.

Svinulf brought Regin's gray mare to him. My brother handed me his axes, brushed a layer of moist dirt from his knee, and practically leapt into the saddle.

I knew they were deadly, effective weapons, but in my hands, they felt heavy and unwieldy.

He asked for them back and tucked them into his belt.

I imagined his pants falling down as we rode through the capital and fought back a giggle.

He glanced at me, and I shrugged before saying, "Let's go."

The king and queen's wagon rolled out as my brother and I rode toward the nearest exit from the courtyard.

"Hold here," Savil said, stepping forward to keep us from leaving. "You two cannot go out unescorted. King's orders."

I sighed. "We know."

"Sorry, Your Majesties. Just doing my job," Savil said, not moving.

"We know," my brother and I replied together.

I turned to face the rising sun, watching the sky turn from the dark purple of twilight to the slowly brightening pink and red of first light.

A chorus of hoofbeats and squeaks of leather on leather let me know a group approached from behind. I turned to see Captain Agrim leading about half of his company our way.

"Princess Meyla, Prince Regin. Good morning," the guard captain said, before calling for a halt.

"Well met this morning," I said.

"How are you doing, Princess?" Agrim asked.

I reached to rub my back. "Still a bit sore but getting better."

He nodded. "Good to hear, but I'm sorry it happened."

"No more so than me," I said.

He nodded and turned to my brother. "And you, my Prince. I hear you've been beating up some of my men with those new axes of yours."

Regin looked at the ground. "Your men give better than they get, Captain."

"Hard-learned lessons are the ones you remember most," Agrim replied.

"Aye, sir. That's true."

"Make way for King Fitzeirick and Queen Tindra,!" someone shouted behind us.

Agrim bowed. "Time for us to go. Be safe."

"Travel safe and swift," I said.

He nodded, called to his men, and poked his horse with his heel.

My brother and I moved to the right side of the path and turned to watch for our parents. Four men rode ahead of the royal wagon. I recognized two of them, Lopt and Ingvar. I'd seen the other two but couldn't remember their names.

As my parents drew closer, Regin lifted his axes across his chest. I held my bow across mine in salute.

"Listen to Roi and Grima," Father said, stopping the wagon next to us.

"And behave," Mother added.

"Travel safe and swift," I said.

"We await your return already," Regin said.

With a nod, Father snapped the reins and guided the wagon through the southern gate. Once they were out of sight, Regin and I rode back to the stable with two of the gate guards holding our reins.

Chapter 22

"What are your plans for the rest of the day?" Roi asked, as I dismounted my horse with a groan.

"I...um...I don't know," I said, pressing my lips together. "Haven't had much time to think about anything except my parents leaving for some reason —"

"That they won't tell us," Reign said, taking my reins and leading our horses to a tie post.

"They will discuss everything with you when the time is right," Roi said, sunlight shining off his bald head when he nodded. "I'm not sure it was absolutely necessary to go now, but I couldn't advise against the trip either...all things considered."

"What things might those be?" I asked, not expecting an answer.

"Not my place to tell," he said, grinning at me. "Trust that all will be explained when they return."

Uncle Roi was hard to trick.

"Where's Aunt Grima?" I asked, tired of this subject. *Especially since no one is saying anything about what's going on, and I'm sure it's about me.*

"She's in the berry patch, helping Einns gather raspberries for lunch," he said, pointing toward the far side of the castle grounds.

I pursed my lips for a moment. "I'll see if they need help."

"You know the rules," Roi said. "I'll trust you to go directly there and not venture off someplace you're not supposed to go."

I scoffed and frowned. "I'm not a child. Don't treat me like one."

He chuckled. "To me, you'll always be the little girl who surprised her mother by being a woodsyth."

I smiled at his jest. "If anything, you need to keep your eyes on Regin. He's the troublemaker."

"Am not," my brother said, as he approached, carrying his axes again.

"As next in line to rule, I declare you Croy's royal troublemaker," I said, laughing.

"Bah," Regin said, and clanged his axes together. "Best me, and I'll accept the title."

"Both of you settle down, or I'll secure you in your rooms until Fitzeirick and Tindra get back," Roi said, putting his hands on his hips.

"Yes, sir," we said.

"Regin, maybe we can find some time today for me to teach you about axe fighting," Roi said.

My brother's face lit up. "First, can you take me to see Thorgault so I can find out when my vest will be ready?"

"Can I go, too?" I asked. "I need a sword belt and a new coin purse."

Roi chuckled. "Have you two heard about the time your father misplaced his coin purse?"

I furrowed my brow. "No."

Regin scratched his chin and shook his head.

"Maybe I'll tell that tale over dinner tonight. It's much too good to use at lunch." He laughed again for a moment.

"I look forward to hearing it," I said. "Are you going to take us to the market?"

"No," Roi said.

I groaned.

He put his hand on my shoulder. "It's too risky, and you know it."

"But—" Regin protested.

Roi raised his eyebrows and turned to him. "No, I won't take you alone either, but here's what I will do...*if* you both stop complaining."

I nodded.

"I'm listening," Regin said.

"After I've worn the prince out and before lunch, I'll go to Thorgault's, check on the vest, and get a belt and purse. Is that a deal?"

"But Thorgault doesn't know how long of a belt I'll need," I said.

"Wait here," Roi said, before going into the barn.

Regin shot me a questioning look, and I shrugged.

Roi returned with a piece of rope. "Raise your arms, Princess."

"What are you going to do to me?" I asked, putting my hands on my hips.

"Measure you," he said. "Arms up."

I did as he asked, and he looped the rope around my waist twice, then tied a knot in it before letting it fall to the ground. "Now, Thorgault will know what length belt you need."

"Oh," I said, not sure how to react.

"Good thinking," Regin said.

Roi put the loop of rope over his shoulder. "Come with me, Prince. Let's see how you handle those axes."

My brother gave a toothy grin and hurried to where he trained with the guard.

"Don't hurt him," I said, half-smiling.

"I won't," Roi said, nodding. "Just want to make sure he isn't going to hurt himself."

"But he's held his own with several of the younger guards," I said.

"They've been playing with him," Roi said. "I don't play."

"Oh," I said, smirking. "In that case, I'll gladly spend my time helping Grima and Einns."

"Enjoy your time in the garden, Meyla."

I nodded and headed for my room to drop off my bow and quiver before making my way to the berry patches.

Chapter 23

Exiting the far side of my home, I nearly ran into Aunt Grima and Einns.

"Guess you two don't need any help?" I said.

They stopped. Grima looked at me for a moment. "What do you mean?"

"I was coming to help pick raspberries," I said,

"Oh," Grima said.

"We have plenty, m'lady," Einns said, "but I appreciate you trying."

I sighed. "Well, there goes another plan for the morning."

"I'm going to go prepare these," Einns said. "See you two at lunch."

"Yes, Einns. Thank you," I said.

"Enjoyed our time together, son," Grima said, then she turned back to me. "Have you changed your bandage?"

"Not yet."

"Let's go to your room, and I'll take care of it."

Grima lit a candle while I laid my treatment out on the table.

The dried, honey-encrusted bandage pulled at my skin, making it itch.

"Close your eyes for a moment," Grima said.

My hand twitched, wanting to scratch the wounds.

"They're healing well, but I think you're going to have faint scars," Grima said. "Doesn't matter—you're still beautiful. Don't worry about it."

I wasn't worried until you said something. "Should we go see Abi?"

"I'm no herbalist, but I've treated enough of Einns' cuts as he was growing up to tell there's nothing anyone can do to change this," she said. "Plus, we'd have to send for her; you're not leaving the castle grounds."

"Will you tell me why?" I asked.

Grima scooped some of Abi's sticky concoction out of the jar and looked me in the eyes. "I trusted your mother with a very important secret years ago. She has kept it. I will not betray her trust."

"I would say I understand, but I don't."

"Trust is hard to earn and easy to break," Grima said. "That's all you need to understand."

"No," I said, clenching my fists. "I know that...believe me. I don't understand what is going on and why it's a secret."

She squeezed my shoulder. "Because it's what's best for everyone involved. Your mother tends to revel in rumors as an odd form of entertainment, but she doesn't often see the potential harm in untruths accepted as fact. A lie repeated often enough might as well be true...because everyone will believe it, regardless."

I nodded and relaxed my hands. "I know you're right but that doesn't mean I have to be happy about it."

"That's a lesson many people don't learn by your age," Grima said. "All I can say is be patient and trust all will be explained when your parents return. Now, hold still and relax your cheek so I can finish applying this treatment."

Once the bandage was soaked, I had to wait for the mixture to skin over before Grima asked what I wanted to do until lunch.

"Honestly, I'm still letting the morning sink in," I said. "I'd love nothing more than to be in my boat out on the water somewhere."

Grima smiled and took my hand. "I can't do that for you, but would you like to help me harvest some jute?"

"Not sure how much work I can do," I said. "My back and side are still tender."

She nodded. "You can keep me company...tell me about your recent trip to Varia. At least you'll be outside, and your stories will make the time pass faster."

Got nothing better to do. "I'd be glad to."

We stopped by the stable where Grima got a small cart, then Svinulf hitched an especially well-behaved, gray donkey to it. "Tronto will listen to you, Princess. He's so good, you won't need a whip."

I smiled and thanked him, then blushed as he helped me onto the seat. When I nodded to thank him for the assistance, I think he blushed a little, too.

Grima covered her mouth, then hooked a finger into Tronto's bridle and led the way to the jute patch.

Chapter 24

Squishing noises rose as we wheeled onto the well-tended soil, soaked from yesterday's rain, in this part of the castle grounds. The fibrous stalks were nearly as tall as Grima and turning from vibrant green to a yellowish tan color.

She pronounced them perfect.

We set into a rhythm of her sything a handful of plants off their roots, even with the ground, and tossing the bundle into the cart while I commanded Tronto to walk or stop as needed. Between directing the donkey and commenting on the harvest, I did my best to entertain Aunt Grima with stories. *Regin's a much better storyteller.*

When the stack behind me grew high enough to feel unstable, I reached back and bound leaves together with my talent so Grima could stack on more before we had to unload the cart. Even with my help, we took three trips to the warehouse before the entire field was harvested. Fortunately, the porters were more than happy to unload the hauls for us.

Sweat dripped from Grima's clothes as we took the last of the harvest to storage. "I'll sleep well tonight," she said, wringing the hem of her dress. "But this may never smell clean again."

I chuckled at her jest. She was a master seamstress and probably knew more about making, repairing, and cleaning clothes than anyone in the rest of Croy. "We both should probably get cleaned up before lunch," I said, pulling a few leaves out of my hair. "You go ahead. I can take the cart back."

"And Svinulf will be more than happy to give you all the help you need," Grima said, smirking.

"And his assistance would be appreciated," I said, hoping she couldn't tell how I really felt.

"I'm sure," she said, nodding. "Thank you for all your help. Roi is good for lifting, but he doesn't understand plants like a fellow woodsyth."

"Glad I could help," I said. "Wish I could have done more."

"You did plenty. See you in the dining room for lunch."

I nodded back. "See you there."

As Aunt Grima predicted, the cute stablehand was eager to take care of the cart and donkey. I may have blushed a little when he bowed and said he looked forward to seeing me again. Truth be told, I floated back to my room...or at least I didn't feel my feet hit the ground, and my back didn't bother me.

I whistled while combing my hair and waiting for the water to warm. Pieces of jute leaves fell to the floor behind me. *Why am I so happy? Because Svinulf said he looked forward to seeing me again? It's not like a date or even a hint of one. He'll see me every time I go to the stable...even if I just walk within sight of it. For all I know, he already has a girlfriend, and she probably isn't wearing a bandage hiding scars underneath. What was it I said to him? The heart wants what it wants.* I sighed. *Why shouldn't I be happy? Other than someone attacking me, and my mother and father are traveling to Varia but won't tell me why, and it might be related to the attack and* —. "Ugh," I groaned, before undressing and getting into the bathing pool.

Not wanting to wet the bandage pasted to my face, I sat with my back against the side of the tub instead of floating in the water. Heat soaked into my body, soothing sore muscles I hadn't noticed and relieving some of the aches in my bruises. Closing my eyes, I breathed slow and steady, letting myself enjoy this simple pleasure.

Once my fingertips turned pale and wrinkled, I set about washing myself.

Drying and combing my hair took no time at all. I pulled on a fresh dress and got out my journal to record my thoughts.

Someone knocked on my door. "Meyla, are you in there?" Grima asked.

"Yes," I said, closing my journal. "Come in, Aunt Grima."

The door opened. She wore a yellow, linen dress with short sleeves. One of her favorites, if I remembered correctly. "Lunch will be on the table soon."

"Thank you. I'll be along shortly," I said.

Grima glanced toward my book. "Should I close the door?"

"No, ma'am, but thank you for asking," I said.

She nodded and turned to walk away.

Chapter 25

Securing my inked thoughts in my trunk, I walked to our dining room as quickly as I comfortably could. Einns had prepared roast duck sandwiches with some kind of paste made from the raspberries to dip them in. A small jug of milk sat next to our plates.

He was eating at the far end of the table. Every time I saw him, he reminded me of Father for some reason. Probably because they had the strong chin common to many Croians. Just like my brother and I, making it obvious we weren't full-blooded Varian.

Grima, chewing, was in her chair. She smiled at me when I entered.

"Enjoy," Einns said, raising his jug and then taking a drink of milk.

Crusty, warm bread crunched when I bit into it before my teeth tore off a piece of juicy, gamey bird. Alone, it tasted good enough, but with the dip, it was delightful. I raised my sandwich in salute to Einns.

He chuckled as Uncle Roi joined us.

"Where's Regin?" I asked.

"Resting," Roi said.

I furrowed my brow in question.

"I told you the guard had been playing with him. I showed him the difference between work and play," Roi said.

"Oh," I said, deciding against asking him for details in case he thought I needed the same lesson.

Grima glared at him. "You didn't hurt him, did you?"

"Nothing he won't recover from," Roi said. "Once he got the hang of what I was trying to teach him, he pressed me pretty good. Worked up quite an appetite," Roi said. "Smells great, son."

Einns nodded while swallowing his last bite. "Thank you, Father. Hope you find it tastes great, too."

"Knowing you, it will be better than that," Roi said, before taking a bite.

"The kitchen isn't going to clean itself," Einns said, getting up from the table.

"You have workers to do that," I said.

"They do tidy, but I insist on doing the final cleaning."

"Oh," I said. "I didn't realize it was so important."

He nodded. "It's important to me. Plus, I have things to prepare for before I start cooking dinner."

"A habit he learned when we worked at the Trader's Cup," Grima said, as her son left the room.

Uncle Roi reached for his wife's hand. "One of the best things to come from there."

"I thought you liked Geri," I said.

"Oh, Geri and I have a good enough history," Roi said. "But he's not the most understanding man in Croy."

"He was fair to us," Grima said. "But meeting you, marrying you, is the best thing anyone could have dreamed of."

By the way they looked at each other, I decided it was a good idea to leave them alone. I took the sandwich from Regin's plate and stood up. "I'm going to check on my brother. It's not like him to miss a meal."

Roi pressed his lips together before looking at me. "I expect you'll find him asleep."

"Thank you for the warning, Uncle," I said.

Chapter 26

Knocking gently on my brother's door, I called his name but got no answer. I knocked harder and called louder. Still no answer.

My hand twitched as I reached for the wooden handle. *I really shouldn't do this.* My heart pounded, not from the effort of sything the latch but from how wrong it was to open my brother's door without his permission.

His room was dark. Originally, the layout was identical to my quarters, but I knew he had rearranged everything at least once. *Another advantage his stonesything talent gives him over me.* My feet scraped across the stone floor, trying to not trip over anything while looking for his table.

"Who's there?" he said sleepily. A lantern flared.

"Me," I said, showing him the sandwich.

"Meyla!" he shouted. All the lanterns lit as he pulled his cover up to his chin. "What are you doing in my room?"

Squealing and closing my eyes against the flash of light, I pointed to the food in my hand. "Checking on you and bringing your lunch."

"What?" he groaned.

"Food," I said. Some juice from the meat flew toward him when I thrust the sandwich in his direction.

"Oh, yeah. I should eat something."

A smell hit me like a blow. Opening my eyes, I saw Regin was out of bed and still wearing his hunting clothes.

"Sit," he said. "We'll talk while I eat."

"Have you bathed?" The stench of a sweaty body grew stronger as he approached.

"No," he said, taking his lunch from me. "I was too tired by the time Uncle Roi decided he'd worn me out enough."

I pinched my nose closed. "I have questions, but I'm not talking to you until *after* you clean yourself. I've smelled more fragrant carcasses."

"But —"

"But nothing," I said. "And you best prepare to beg one of the armorers to help you get the stink out of that leather. Every animal in the forest would smell you and run...except maybe the ravens and the buzzards. They'd come looking for a meal."

"I'm not that —"

"Considering Uncle Roi was involved, Aunt Grima might take pity on you and help you wash your bed cover, but you'd better get fresh straw; otherwise, you're going to stink for days." I turned on my heel.

Regin's protests followed me out of the room, but I didn't stop to argue. *Better warn Aunt Grima.*

I found her not far from the room she and Uncle Roi used when they were staying at the castle. Her hair was disheveled, and she was in a different dress than the one she wore at lunch.

"Regin did what?" she asked, shaking her head as I explained the disaster I'd found in his room.

I frowned and described the scene again.

She sighed. "Thank you for the warning." I thought I saw a grin cross her face when she glanced back toward their quarters. "Roi's resting, but once he's up and about, I'll have him help your brother clean the leather. It's partly his fault."

I opened my mouth, but she raised her hand.

"Yes, Regin knows better, but Roi didn't do him any favors either. You don't work a horse to a sweat and just put it away. Ugh." She put her hands on her hips. "Boys...I swear. Sometimes I think we'd be better off sending them all to the fire. Other times..." With a shrug, she sighed again. "Well...they can be handy to have around."

I nodded. "I'll help clean."

"No. They won't learn their lessons if we do all the work for them. Plus, you're still hurt."

"If you insist, Aunt Grima."

"I do. Now, go find something to do and stay out of trouble. Seems my husband and your brother have given me a reason to run home for a bit."

Wandering through the castle with no destination in mind, my thoughts drifted to being on the water. *Can't get in trouble out there. But I can't go to my boat without getting in trouble.* My feet carried me to my room, but I stopped at the door. "Why sit in this stone box when I could be outside?" I asked no one. With a nod, I set off again, heading for one of our many gardens.

Chapter 27

It's surprisingly easy to lose track of time when all you have to do is sit on a cushioned patch of grass, surrounded by a stand of maple trees, and listen to birds twitter and bees buzz about. The serenity was shattered by my brother yelling my name at the top of his lungs.

"Where are you?" he bellowed.

At least I didn't smell him before I heard him. "Over here!" I yelled back, not wanting to get up.

"Where?" he replied, sounding farther away.

"Ugh," I muttered, pushing myself to my feet. Stomping out of my sanctuary, I yelled at him again and waved my hand over my head to get his attention if he bothered to turn my way.

He turned and shouted, "Stay there!"

Exactly what I wanted to do. I nodded and returned to my comfortable spot on the ground.

"Aunt Grima is expecting you," I said, when he came into sight. "And she's going to make Uncle Roi help you clean your leathers. Have you changed your bedding?"

He shook his head. "I'm not worried about that right now."

"You should be," I said.

He scowled at me and flicked his hand as if dismissing my warning. "I'll take care of everything before I go to bed tonight. We need to talk about the amazing opportunity we have to get to safety."

"What do you mean?"

"Mother and Father have a third of the guard with them. The other third are busy looking for your attackers. We have far fewer men to get past now to leave the capital and ride to your boat."

"Don't forget avoiding stablehands, and we have to get through the southern gate...which is guarded by warriors who aren't members of the royal guard. And won't they find it suspicious we are leaving, with supplies, without notice or an order signed by the king?"

Regin waved his hand at me like he was swatting away flies. "We'll leave at night; no one will be at the stable. You can talk our way past the warriors at the southern gate. You're next in line to rule. They have to listen to you."

"So do the royal guard, but they won't just let us stroll out," I argued.

"Because they have direct orders not to," he said.

"Yet you seem to think we can slip past them without the slightest concern."

"I'm working on it," he said, nodding. "Just like I'm working on having supplies ready."

"And don't you think Mother and Father will hear about us leaving the capital?"

"Mother and Father aren't here. We'll be in and out of the Satran capital and safely camped in a forest somewhere before word reaches them in Varia," he said.

I groaned. "Roi and Grima, then. They'll be told at some point, likely near first light, and send men to find us."

"And by then, we'll be in your boat and away from shore. Our aunt and uncle won't know where we went, so the search won't find us. When they do reach the southern shore, all they'll find is our horses. Assuming the beasts don't wander away on their own."

"First," I said, pointing at him, "Senshi is not a beast. Second, someone will report my boat missing, assuming they don't see us taking it and try to stop us."

He frowned, sighed, and shook his head. "From where I'm standing, it sounds like you would rather stay here and wait for the next attack. How did the firstborn of Fitzeirick, Jarl-killer and Conqueror of Satra, become so passive? Our father is not one to wait for something to happen...he makes things happen."

Branches in the surrounding maple trees shook as I stood. Regin took a step back when I pressed my finger into his chest. "Do not call me a coward for choosing to be careful. I never said anything about waiting for the next attack. I have accepted it's in our best interest to find a safe hiding place, but I also understand that if we are not successful in our first attempt to leave, we won't have a second chance. You talk as if everything will work out in our favor. Haven't you paid any attention to Father's stories of his past? You know how rarely that happens."

He raised his hands and dipped his chin. "I meant no offense, sister. I know you aren't cowardly. I'm sore, and frustrated, after Uncle Roi showed me how little I actually knew about using my axes. I shouldn't have taken that out on you."

"Apology accepted," I said, nodding. "I suspect Mother will do the same to me when she teaches me how to use my sword."

Regin tilted his head. "You'd be right to worry. But that isn't a concern for right now."

I stepped back to lean against the closest tree and quiet the plants around us. "What do I need to know?"

"I should have everything gathered by midday tomorrow," Regin said. "When we leave here, get your saddlebags and hide them in your room. Pack what you can tonight but make sure no one sees them, or they will ask questions. You can finish filling them tomorrow after dinner."

I nodded. "And when do we leave?"

"Light a candle at moonrise. After one finger has burned, go to the stables. I'll meet you there."

"And how do you plan to get us off the castle grounds and out of the southern gate?"

He smiled. "Your cheek is fevered, and we can't spare the time to wait for Abi to come; we have to go to her. I'm going with you to make sure you arrive."

"With bulging saddlebags?" I questioned.

"Father always gives Abi coins. We have none, so I'm bringing payment from the storehouse."

"And if they want to search the bags?"

He glared and stomped his foot. "Who are they to question the Prince of Croy? Especially when the princess is unwell."

"Assuming that works, how do we get out of the southern gate?" I asked, trying not to smile at my brother acting angry.

He snapped his fingers. "That may be the easiest. Abi found a patch of some kind of wild plant in the south, right?"

"Lamb's Ear," I said. "What difference does that make?"

He shook his head. "You want some to grow in your room, but it can only be picked under moonlight. I'm going with you to protect against any wild animals prowling around the woods."

After chewing my lip for a moment, I nodded. "You put a lot of thought into this. I'm impressed."

"Thank you," he said, mock bowing.

"Just one more question," I said, trying to not smirk.

"What?"

"What do we do when none of this works?"

He sputtered for a moment before collecting himself. "What do you mean?"

"You've planned for all of this to work flawlessly. Nothing goes that easily."

He put his hands on his hips. "But if we try to plan for every possible difficulty we may face along the way before even trying, we might as well give up now and save ourselves the trouble. I'm not just going to sit here and wait for another attack."

"I know...I know you're right," I said, nodding. "I'm just...scared."

Regin stepped to me and put his arm around my shoulder. "Meyla, you have nothing to be scared of. I'm here for you. We'll take care of each other—no matter what."

I hugged him. "Thank you, but you weren't attacked. You won't carry scars on your face."

"What scars?" he asked, stepping back.

"Aunt Grima said she thinks the scratches will leave scars," I said, frowning.

He matched my expression. "She's no herbalist... How would she know?"

"Einns practically grew up with a knife in one hand and a cleaver in the other. Our aunt knows a thing or two about cuts and how they heal."

He sighed. "True, so maybe she's right, but they can't be too bad. I mean, Father's scar is only so noticeable because he was branded. A few scratches can't leave much of a mark."

"Thanks," I said, rolling my eyes. "You know exactly how to make a girl feel better about a bad situation."

He nodded. "You're welcome. Glad we could talk out here. I'm going to go get fresh straw for my bed now."

How did he not notice my tone? What was it Grima said about sending boys to the fire?

"Good idea," I said. "I'll see you at dinner."

"Remember, we can't act like anything is going on, or we'll get caught."

I nodded. "Don't worry. Everything's going to go as planned." My words practically dripped with sarcasm.

"Exactly," he said, turning to leave.

Is he just not listening to me? There's no way anyone can be that stoneheaded.

Chapter 28

We'll be lucky to get away from the stables without alarming the entire castle. A walk among the trees did little to reduce my concerns. *It's not that Regin's plan isn't good; he just expects everything to fall into place. I suspect it's more likely everything will fall apart.* "Prepare for the best and expect the worst, I guess," I said, to a gray dove perched in a nearby tree. He didn't even bother to coo in response.

After another meandering trip, I exited the stand of trees and retrieved my saddlebags from the storeroom near the stable before wandering toward the castle, trying to relax before I had to face my aunt and uncle over dinner. After I hid my bags in the straw of my bed, I cleaned up and went to the dining room. It was no surprise I was the first one there.

Uncle Roi entered not long after me, carrying gifts. "A belt for you," he said, dropping the black leather strip in front of me, "and a vest for your brother. I hope it's what he wanted."

I hefted the garment and looked it over. From behind, it seemed like a normal, if somewhat heavy, black, leather vest. On the front were two pockets on either side of the chest to hold the axe's blades, then a complicated-looking arrangement of buckles and straps, meant to secure the handles, hung at several angles. "I think you're right, Uncle Roi," I said, dropping the vest with a rattling thunk.

"Try your belt," Roi said.

It seemed long when I picked it up, almost touching the floor when I held the buckle over my head. Frowning, I looked at my uncle and cocked my head.

"Oh, right. Thorgault said it would go around you twice to help keep it in place," Roi said.

Nodding, I wrapped it around my waist two times and buckled it.

"Too bad you don't have your sword with you," Roi said, "we could fix it in place and get everything adjusted."

While fidgeting with the belt, I looked at him. "I've helped Mother with hers. I'm sure I can figure it out."

He nodded and smiled. "Of course, but I'd be glad to help you if you need it."

"Looks like that fits you well," Grima said, entering ahead of a couple of servants.

"I still need to adjust it and get used to it, but I think it will do nicely," I said.

Regin walked in as cups were being filled. He eyed me on the way to his place at the table.

I had moved his vest to his chair to make room for his plate. His smile glowed when he lifted the heavy leather. Slipping his arms through it, he buckled it closed. "I'm going to go get my axes to make sure —"

"You will sit and eat," Roi said.

Regin froze, his fingers intertwined with the buckles and straps. "Yes, sir," he said, dejection clear in his voice.

"We know you're excited, Regin," Grima said, "but I know your parents wouldn't let you leave the table for something like this. Don't expect us to do any differently."

"Yes, ma'am," he muttered, still fiddling with the vest.

Soon we had steaming bowls of goat stew placed in front of us. It tended toward the bland side. Having recently had my fill of spicy Varian dishes, I wasn't about to complain.

Regin attacked his bowl like a ravenous wolf, barely bothering to chew. I wasn't in much of a hurry and took my time eating. *If we make it to my boat, this will be my last warm dinner for a few days.*

Regin's spoon clanked in the bottom of his empty bowl. "May I be excused?"

Aunt Grima looked at Uncle Roi.

He nodded.

"Yes," she said. "But —"

"Thank you!" Regin shouted, bolting from the room.

"Guess he didn't want raspberry honey rolls for dessert," Grima said, shaking her head.

"His loss," Roi said, before chuckling. "More for us."

I smiled at him and nodded.

Grima smacked him on the arm. "Don't make fun of the boy for being excited. You were like that too, once."

"More than once, I'm sure," Roi replied, grinning. "But I wasn't a prince at the time."

"But look at you now. The top adviser to a king and son of a Skald," Grima said, patting his arm where she'd hit it.

"Would you take your father's title, Uncle Roi?" I asked.

"Young lady, that is a good and complicated question. And one I'm not ready to answer right now."

"That's the same thing you said to Fitzeirick," Grima said.

"Except for the young lady part," Roi said, grinning.

I laughed at his jest.

"I have always done what I thought Croy needed of me," Roi said. "When the time arrives for me to decide, I will take stock of the entire situation, including how my decision would affect you, my dear wife, and do what I can to benefit our great country."

Dessert was placed on the table while Roi spoke. I grabbed a roll and ate while he finished.

"That sounds like something Father would say," I commented.

"Aye, it does," he said. "And that should scare everyone."

"Why?" I questioned.

Grima covered her mouth.

"Because I never wanted to spend enough time around rulers to sound like them," Roi said, smiling.

"I don't understand," I said.

"Because you haven't seen anything else," Roi explained. "Your father is a good man. I did my best to guide him as he grew up. Crum is..."

"Be nice," Grima said.

Roi glanced sideways at her. "Better than most. I believe that was because of your father's influence."

"And what about Skald Rorec?" I asked. "Is he a good governor?"

Aunt Grima took her husband's hand.

Uncle Roi pressed his lips together. "Fitzeirick, your father, felt Rorec was the leader Satra needed. I accept the argument that our king didn't have many other options. While I'm not calling my father a bad person, I'm not sure I would have made the same choices."

"You don't love your father?" I asked, confused.

Roi took a deep breath and then sighed. "I appreciate what he did for me, the lessons I learned about life and how to live. Having said that, by many measures, many would not consider Rorec to be good. That's not to say he was bad to my mother...or me. I would not be who I am or where I am today had Rorec not been my father, but that doesn't mean everything he did was right. If I'd had more faith in my father, I would have never believed he could be a traitor as I once did."

"But he wasn't," I argued.

"No, he wasn't. He was doing what he had to do at the time to keep my mother safe," Roi said.

"Most would say that was good," I said.

Roi nodded. "The best he could do...at the time."

Grima cleared her throat. "Meyla, how about you take a roll to Regin, then get ready for bed?"

I could tell by her expression it wasn't a question. "Yes, ma'am. Good night."

"Perhaps we can continue this discussion when we are both less tired," Roi said, smiling weakly. "Sleep well, my princess."

I paused and looked at him. *He does look weary all of a sudden.* "I would like that, Uncle."

Will I be like that when I'm more grown up? My mind focused on the conversation and what it meant while my feet carried me to Regin's door.

Chapter 29

My brother yelled for me to wait a moment after I knocked.

"What are you doing here?" he asked, poking his head out of the open door.

I held the sweet and tart roll out for him. "Bringing you dessert. You could have had some when it was warm if you hadn't been in such a hurry to play with your axes."

"It was more than that," he said, opening the door a little wider. "Come see."

Not only did he have his axes secured across his chest, but he had his saddlebags packed. "All that's left is for me to clean my hunting clothes. How are you coming with your preparations?"

"I...uh...I have my bags...in my room," I said.

He shook his head. "You can't spend all day inside packing them; Grima and Roi will get curious and come looking."

I waved toward his stuffed bags. "But I can't have everything packed because Aunt Grima will come to my room to change my bandage tomorrow morning."

He frowned for a moment. "Pack what you can and still keep your bags hidden. You'll just have to hurry to get everything else ready after dinner. Remember, one finger of candle after moonrise."

"I'll be there," I said, putting my hands on my hips. "You better be."

"Don't worry. I wouldn't miss this for anything." Sparks shot across his eyes.

"What do you mean?"

"This is going to be the greatest adventure of our lives. Are you telling me you aren't excited by the whole thing?"

"I'm not sure I'd use that exact word. Concerned. Scared...maybe. But I still see the necessity of leaving, so I'll be ready to go when the time comes," I said. "Don't doubt me."

"And don't doubt me. We're in this together."

"Together," I said. "Always."

He nodded. "You best get to your room and get packing. Sleep well, sister. Tomorrow will be a long day."

I closed my eyes and nodded, then left for my room.

Chapter 30

Latching the door behind me, I took about half the clothes I'd set aside and placed them in my saddlebags before hiding them in my armoire. Convinced Grima had no reason to look in there, I put out the lone lantern I'd been using and went to bed. Sleep did not come quickly.

The morning came early. I spent some time seeing to my plants. The butterbur still didn't look exactly right, but it might have been better than before. *Not much I can do about it now.* I'd broken plenty of rules as a child, although not as often as my brother, but I'd never considered running away from home...especially after being commanded to not leave. *They'll understand. Once this is all over, they'll see it was for the best.* A long, hot soak in my bathing pool did little to calm my nerves.

Grima had not come to my room by the time I had dressed and combed my hair, so I went searching and found her talking with Einns in the kitchen.

"Good morning, Princess," Einns said, when he noticed me.

Aunt Grima turned. "Are you feeling well?"

"I'm fine. Didn't sleep much," I said. "I could use your help with my bandage."

"Of course," she said. "Let me finish here, and I'll come to your room."

"Breakfast won't be long," Einns said, as I turned.

I thanked him and returned to my quarters to wait for Grima. I was in the middle of packing a few more things when she knocked.

"One moment," I said, shoving a quickly filling bag back into my armoire.

Opening the door, she looked me over again. "Are you sure you're not getting sick?"

"Just tired," I said, wondering why she would ask such a question.

She stepped closer and put her hand on my forehead. "You don't feel fevered, but you look...worn out."

"Nerves," I said, with a slight chuckle. "I'm worried...about my parents. And when I'll see them again. And scars. And..."

Grima pulled me into a hug. "Everything will be fine. You are safe. Your parents are taking care of everything. As far as the scars, don't worry; you are beautiful. Nothing will change that."

"Thank you, Aunt Grima," I said, wiping a tear from my eye.

"Any time, my princess. Any time. If you need to talk, come see me. You can tell me anything and know it stays with me." She squeezed me one more time, then let go. "Let's treat that wound and get some warm food in our bellies. That'll help you feel better."

I gave her a weak smile and sat down for her to change the bandage.

"Pretty sure this is the last time we'll need to do this," she said. "Would you like for Abi to look at your cheek tomorrow, to be sure?"

"No. I trust your judgment."

She patted my knee. "Let's go eat."

I smiled and nodded. "After you."

Uncle Roi and my brother were already eating boiled grains when we got to the dining room.

"Nice of you to wait for us," Grima said.

"Regin wanted to get an early start practicing with his axes," Roi said.

I hadn't noticed he'd worn that silly vest to breakfast. *I thought the idea was to not attract attention. At least he left the axes in his room.* "You didn't work hard enough yesterday, brother?"

"The best way to get better is to work through the pain," he said, tapping his fist to his chest.

"Can't say I agree," Roi said, "but if you're that enthusiastic, I'm not going to discourage you."

"Someone hurt Meyla, and I want to make sure that never happens again," Regin said, looking at me.

"I probably wouldn't have been attacked if I hadn't been alone," I said. "But thank you for wanting to protect me."

"Always," he said, smiling.

"What are you going to do today, Meyla?" Roi asked.

"I don't know. Maybe go to the stables and spend some time with Senshi. She seemed upset last time I rode her."

Grima smirked. "Spending some time at the stables will probably do you some good."

I felt my cheeks warm. "I hope so,"

"Have fun," Regin said, scooping the last spoonful of grains from his bowl and practically chugging his mug of milk. "I'll meet you outside, uncle."

"Don't hurt yourself getting ready," Roi said.

Grima shook her head as Regin hurried out of the room. "I don't miss having a boy that age."

Roi chuckled. "He's ours for now."

"How long will my parents be away?" I asked. *Maybe he'll slip up and give me a clue.*

Roi shrugged. "They will be back when they get back. Some things take time."

To the fire with his vague answer. I nodded to keep from yelling.

"Meyla, if you get done at the stable quickly, would you mind stopping by the storehouse to help me look over the jute?" Aunt Grima asked. "If it has dried enough, I want to start breaking it down today."

"I'd love to help," I said.

"Thank you. It would be appreciated."

Uncle Roi finished the last of his milk. "I'll see you after I wear the young prince out." He kissed his wife on the top of the head.

"Don't hurt him," Grima said.

"He'll be whole. I'll make sure of that," Roi said, then laughed.

"I'll see you later, Aunt Grima," I said, finishing my breakfast.

"Look forward to working with you again," she replied, smiling.

Chapter 31

My heart beat louder the closer I got to the stables. Svinulf waved when he saw me enter the long, open building.

"What brings you this morning, Princess?" he asked, after jogging to me.

"I thought I would spend some time with my mare. She seemed upset the other day. Just want to make sure she is sound and well."

He glanced back over his shoulder. "She's in her stall eating now. She was moving well when I brought her in from the pasture last night. How are you doing?"

"Well enough," I said, looking toward where he glanced. "But I'm worried. Aunt Grima thinks the scratches on my cheek will leave scars and —"

"And nothing," he said, standing up straighter. "You'll still be beautiful. As a matter of fact, don't call them scars; call them beauty marks. And I can't wait to see them."

I know I blushed. "The bandage should be off tomorrow."

"Then come see me first thing, and I'll tell you how great you look."

I smiled wide enough that the honey pulled at the skin on my cheek. "It's a date." *What did I just say?!?*

He grinned and blushed. "Tomorrow morning. Right here. I wouldn't miss it."

I nodded, hoping I didn't look as awkward as I felt. "I'm going to check on my horse now."

"I can walk you down there," he offered.

"No...No. I'm sure you have duties to see to. I know where her stall is," I said, wanting nothing more than to get away.

"Sure," he said, nodding. "Didn't mean to imply you needed help. All the same, let me know if you do."

"Absolutely," I said, "I will."

"Take care, princess."

"You, too," I said, turning to hurry down the aisle to my mare's stall. When I got there, I noticed mud coating her hooves and legs, so I headed to the storeroom to get grooming tools.

After stomping several times, irritated I had interrupted her feeding time, we came to an understanding. I would let her eat if she would let me clean her legs. Knowing her hooves would need more work but not wanting to push my luck, I brushed her until there was no more grain in her feed bucket. Grabbing her halter, I led her to the hard-packed dirt between the rows of stalls and tied her to a pole with a nearby rope.

My back twinged when I bent over to lift her foot, but the constant ache had faded. Going by her snorts and stomping, Senshi wasn't happy with me paying unwanted attention to her feet. It was necessary, however, because a hoof problem would put our escape plan in jeopardy. That thought made me wonder if Regin had checked his horse for any potential issues. *Of course he hasn't. He expects everything to go right.* Although I wanted to go riding, I knew the safer, wiser, course of action would be to check Kroner for any problems.

Putting Senshi back in her stall, I went to check on my brother's mare. To my surprise, her feet were clean. *Maybe he has taken this more seriously than I thought.* Chuckling at that thought, I put Kroner back in the stall and left to help Grima with her jute. Not that I wanted to work on it, but she asked nicely, and I didn't want to give her a reason to ask questions. Plus, it could be the last time I see her for a while, and I truly loved her like a second mother. In some ways, we were closer than that.

Chapter 32

Next to the storehouse, Grima had laid out about a fourth of the stalks with a small stack of the brownest ones against the closest wall.

"Well met, Aunt Grima," I said, approaching her from behind.

She looked at me through her legs. "All is well with your horse?"

"Yes. She's just got a lot of fire in her," I said. "But we came to an understanding."

"One that involved a fair amount of mud," Grima said, standing up.

"Guess the pasture was still soft from the recent rain," I said, brushing my dress off with little success.

"We'll get plenty of dust on us going through these stalks. We'll just stop in time to clean up before lunch," Grima said, giving me directions on how she wanted the plants sorted.

Shortly after midday, she pronounced the work done. About a fifth of the harvest was dry enough to strip into fibers. The rest was put back in the storehouse, stacked by their stage of readiness, and we walked to the castle to clean ourselves and get something to eat.

Fatigue nearly got the better of me at the dining table. Twice, I nodded off and nearly fell out of my chair. Neither Roi nor Regin came to eat while we were there. *Wonder if he's as worn out as I am.* After a body-shaking yawn, I excused myself and left to take a nap.

A creak from my door woke me. Dim light made it difficult to see who was coming in.

"Who's there?" I demanded, wishing my sword was at hand.

"I need you to come to dinner," Aunt Grima said.

Did she say need? "What?" I asked, before a yawn cut me off.

"Come to dinner. We need to talk," she said.

My eyes flew open, and my heart pounded. *She knows. I'm not sure how she found out, but she knows.* "Oh," I said, trying to keep my voice steady. "Is something wrong? Did something happen to my parents?"

"No. Your parents are fine, as far as I know. Just come to dinner so we don't have to say this twice."

I don't want her to see me shaking. "Oh. Yeah, sure. Give me a moment, and I'll be right there."

When the door closed, I hurried to the bathing tap and splashed cold water onto my face until I feared it would wash the bandage away. Doing everything I could think of to look relaxed, I made my way to our private dining room.

Regin was in his seat. I shot him a questioning glance, and he answered with a quick shake of his head. *If I look as nervous as he does, they'll know we're planning something.*

Roi stood and nodded toward my spot at the table. That's when I noticed Captain Svan standing in the far corner of the room. Ice collected in my stomach.

Under the table, Regin grabbed my leg. I took his hand and squeezed.

"Svan," Roi said, before sitting.

The guard captain stepped forward and saluted. "Princess Meyla, Prince Regin, I'm happy to see you are both well."

I furrowed my brow and saluted. "As we are to see you, Captain."

"I wanted to tell you both what we have found."

Regin squeezed my hand tighter. Blood rushed in my ears and roared loud enough that I almost couldn't hear what Svan said next.

"Deyan and his daughters..."

"What...What did they have to say about the attack?" I asked, voice quivering.

"Nothing," Svan said.

Slapping my hands on the table, I stood. "Make them talk, or bring them to me and I will."

Grima jumped up and came to me. "Meyla, calm yourself. Please. Sit."

I looked at her, not understanding her expression, but returned to my seat.

Svan's face lost a little color. "We found them in their home this evening...dead."

The ice returned to my stomach. "Who..." I couldn't complete the question.

"Who killed them?" Regin asked for me.

"We don't know," Svan said.

"So...do you have any suspects?" Regin asked.

"Not as such, my Prince. At least, not right now. But no one kills three people —"

"Five," I blurted, interrupting him. "It could be the same person who killed Runa and her mother."

"We don't know that, Princess," Svan said. "Regardless, someone will brag. When they do, we'll find out."

"Captain Svan, do you know if there is an ongoing threat to the princess and prince?" Roi asked.

"No, I do not. But I feel it is safest to believe there is until we find proof saying otherwise."

"I agree," Roi said, then he turned to us. "Meyla, Regin, do you have any more questions?"

"I..." Words caught in my mouth.

"I'm sure they do, but they probably need time to let this sink in," Aunt Grima said.

Regin put his arm around me and pulled me close. "We have to leave tonight," he whispered.

I nodded and hugged him.

Roi stood. "Captain, thank you. If anything is found, I want to know as soon as possible."

"Of course. My Princess, my Prince. Don't worry. We're going to get this figured out,"

I thanked him, doing my best to stay calm.

Regin stood and saluted until Svan left.

"Do you need to talk about this?" Grima asked, as Regin sat. "I'm sure you have questions...concerns. We may not have answers, but we can listen. No matter what, we will keep you two safe."

I opened my mouth, but nothing came out. I wanted to ask why this was happening or scream or cry or yell or...something. Maybe do everything all at once. Confusion and fear pulled at me until it was all I could do to keep from lashing out with my talent.

Grima came to me again, pulling me out of my chair and into a tight hug. "Shh," she hissed, rubbing my back gently. "Don't feel bad for being scared. We're all here for you. Whatever you need."

I nodded against her, rubbing the sticky bandage against her shirt. For a moment, we stuck together as I pulled away.

"Dinner is ready...if you feel like eating," Grima said.

I nodded again and collapsed into my chair.

"And rounds of ale for all of us," Roi said. "We could use something to help us relax."

I know I ate because my stomach got full, but nothing had any taste. Finally, Regin tapped my shoulder. "Let me walk you to your room."

I nodded.

"Try to get some sleep," Grima said. "We'll talk in the morning."

I didn't look at her, afraid I'd do or say something to expose our plan.

Uncle Roi wished me a good night and then said something to his wife. I stayed focused on getting to my room and didn't try to hear their conversation.

Chapter 33

"Those girls should have stayed hidden wherever they were. I'm sure whoever killed them got Runa and Thyre, too. It only makes sense. We need to get out of the capital," Regin said, once we were alone in the hall.

"I know. I know. But—"

"Meyla, it's too late for doubt. Listen to me. It's one thing to grab someone, drag them to the central forest, and kill them there. It's another to murder people inside the capital and then fade away."

"But you don't know it's the same person—people," I said. "Maybe they were killed because Runa attacked me."

Regin scoffed and looked at me like I'd sprouted another head. "Like you have some secret avenger? Even you said Runa looked like she'd been hanging with thugs." He smacked his fist into his palm. "You're—we're in danger."

"You're sure?"

He nodded. "I'm positive, and I don't want to stay here while they figure out how to slip inside our home and hit us here."

Our hallways seemed a little tighter as we shuffled to my room. I noticed shadowed corners that I'd never paid attention to before. *Could an attacker hide there?* My eyes flitted back and forth, looking for places threats might come from. Shivers started in my hands and grew stronger, traveling up my arms and into my body. By the time we reached my door, I wondered if my shaky legs would carry me inside.

"Breathe," Regin said, opening my door. "We have a plan, and we have time to finish preparing, but we have to go tonight. Everything will be fine. I'll make sure of it. Trust me."

"I know," I said, wobbling to my table. "I do. Thank you, brother, for everything."

He patted my shoulder. "Take a moment to gather the last of your things but watch for the moon. Remember, make your way to the stable one finger of candle after moonrise."

Grabbing his hand, I squeezed it. "I'll be there."

After one more pat, he left, closing the door.

Like the hall, my room seemed smaller. I hurried to light every lantern, making sure there were no shadows, before gathering my journal and writing supplies. As I reached into my armoire for a saddlebag, someone knocked on my door.

I froze.

"Meyla," Grima's muffled voice came through the door.

"One—" My throat went dry. I swallowed. "One moment!" I hurried to the table and laid out my things to make it look like I was writing in my journal.

"Come in!"

My aunt entered and shaded her eyes. "I wanted to check on you," she said. "I know what it's like to be scared...confused...worried. Don't feel like you're alone. We all love you, and we're all here to keep you safe."

I nodded and wiped at my nose. "Thank you, Aunt Grima. I know I'm not alone. I will be all right. I can take care of myself."

I flinched when she put her hand on my shoulder. "But you don't have to go through this alone. Remember that. Focus on it. Trust me," she said. "It helps, knowing you're not alone."

"I know," I said.

"Does writing about it help?" she asked, nodding at my journal.

"Yes."

"Good." She squeezed my shoulder. "Just know you can tell me anything. A shared burden is easier to carry."

"Thank you, Aunt Grima. I'll keep that in mind."

She kissed the top of my head. "Try to sleep. I know it won't be easy, but you look like you need the rest."

I nodded. "I am tired."

After another squeeze on my shoulder, she left, pulling the door closed behind her. I thought I heard a sniffle before it shut all the way.

Chapter 34

I counted to twenty before hurrying to pack the last of my things and going to look for the moon. It was already above the trees. My heart pounded. *I missed moonrise.* I growled and found the nearest candle. Quickly measuring a finger from the melted top, I pressed my fingernail into the wax about halfway up from one finger width. *Maybe that will be right. Would Regin leave without me? Surely not. But a delay could get him caught. Then what would I do?*

Various situations danced in my head, each worse than the last. By the time the candle melted to the mark I'd made, my mind had the castle guards killing Regin and me because they thought we were the attackers.

I shivered, hurriedly clipped my sword to my new belt, threw my bow across my back, hung the quiver from my shoulder, and then hefted my full saddlebags across my shoulders. As I blew out the lanterns around the room, I decided to leave the candle burning to cover the fact I wasn't in my room.

Each footstep echoed in my ears like a beating drum. I was certain someone would hear me and come running to investigate. The weight of the bags pressed my quiver's strap uncomfortably into my shoulder. Only after I had made it outside did I let myself believe I could reach the stable.

My sword hung awkwardly at my side, bouncing against my leg with every step, making me keep a slower pace than I wanted. The building was dark, and Regin was nowhere in sight. I didn't see the horses either. *He's been caught!* My heart raced. Knees buckling, I fought to stay standing under the weight of my bags. As I turned to retreat to my room, my brother ran toward me.

"You're late," he half-whispered. "I had to hide with the horses. Come on—and hurry."

I wanted to shout with joy but knew I couldn't.

He led me to a stand of young oaks. "Secure your bags but don't mount yet. I need to do something before we go."

"What?" I asked.

He motioned toward my horse. "Bags first."

Once my saddlebags were in place, I turned to him. "What now?"

He lifted his hands. "You trust me, right?"

Wouldn't be here if I didn't. "Of course."

"We need you to look and feel fevered. I'm going to heat my hands and press them to your face. It won't be comfortable, but don't cry out."

I took a deep breath and nodded.

His skin wasn't hot enough to burn mine, but it was hard to stand still as my face became uncomfortably hot.

"Get in the saddle, and remember to act sick when we get close to leaving the courtyard," he said.

My vision was blurry. Sweat trickled down my face. Acting sick wouldn't be hard.

I leaned against Senshi to steady myself while Regin mounted his horse and grabbed my reins, leading me toward the closest gate out of the castle grounds at a fast walk.

"Halt!" someone shouted from ahead.

"Make way," Regin replied. "Princess Meyla is sick. I'm taking her to Abi."

"Sorry, my Prince, but we are under strict orders to keep you on the castle grounds," one of the guards said.

"Skail, my sister is ill. We don't have time to send for Abi. I *am* taking her to get treated. If you want to delay us and risk Princess Meyla's life...I won't be the one answering the queen's questions."

A hand brushed against my face. "She's warm and covered in sweat." I didn't recognize the voice.

"Let us go, Skail," Regin insisted. "You're wasting time holding us here."

"I don't—"

I groaned loudly, cutting him off.

"She's sick, Skail," the guard near me said. "The punishment for letting them leave will be lighter than if she dies."

Skail grunted. "Fine, but if I find out this is a trick, whatever penalty we receive, you best be prepared to serve at our side, my Prince."

"Deal," Regin said. "Make way."

We were on our way, with Regin leading me toward Abi's house until the guards could no longer see us. "Take your reins and head for the southern gate," Regin said.

I can't believe that worked. Wiping stinging sweat from my eyes, I put my heels to Senshi's flanks, took the lead, and we trotted toward our next obstacle.

Regin guessed most of the night watch would be newer recruits, and he was right. I didn't recognize a single man at the southern gate.

"Halt!" one of them ordered.

"Make way for Princess Meyla and Prince Regin," I replied.

Two men stepped into the path and raised their hands. "Halt!"

We stopped a few paces from them. "Make way," I said. "I have important business south of the capital. The timing is critical."

"Forgive us, Princess, but we were not told you or your brother would be leaving this evening," one of them said.

"Not all of our movements and travels are announced," Regin said. "Are you telling me we are not free to come and go from our own capital as we please?"

"No, m'lord."

"Then make way," I said again. "I have not yet asked for your name. If you spoil my harvest, I will find out who you are, and you won't have the opportunity to be in my way again."

"Aye, m'lady," he said, bowing. "May your efforts be fruitful."

"Thank you," I said, saluting before prodding Senshi forward.

We kept our speed to a fast walk until we were well away from the wall surrounding our home. I motioned for Regin to come beside me. "This is going too easy," I said.

"It's working exactly as I planned. Better, really."

"That's what's bothering me," I said.

"Well, we still have to reach your boat and get away without being spotted or stopped. Our best chance for success is to get there before first light. If it makes you feel better, there's plenty that could go wrong between now and then."

"I'd rather not think about it," I said.

He nodded, and we pushed our horses to a near gallop.

The farther south we went, the cloudier the skies became. "Did you plan for rain?" I asked, pointing ahead.

"We won't stay dry on your boat anyway," Regin said.

"We will if the water's smooth," I said, pausing for a moment. "And if it doesn't rain."

"Oh."

I chuckled at him and shook my head.

The number of merchant boats had grown since the last time I'd been here. So had the number of houses. Fortunately, all the windows were dark.

Regin rode close to me and motioned toward the forest. I followed him into the trees.

Chapter 35

"Let's leave our horses here and put on our hunting leathers so it's easier to move about unnoticed and find your boat," he said, dismounting.

I wasn't happy about leaving Senshi behind, but I knew she wouldn't go on the boat. It wasn't made to transport horses anyway. I nodded and dismounted. "My back is bothering me," I said, when my feet hit the ground. "Not sure I can carry my bags."

"Give them to me," Regin said. "It will slow me down, but I can carry the load."

After unlashing my bags, I dropped them at his feet, turned to my horse, and hugged her. "Be a good girl and find your way home."

Regin grunted, hefting the weight of our supplies. "Go ahead. Find your boat. I won't be too far behind."

I nodded and kept to the woods until I had to step out to get to the docks. With the clouds blocking most of the moonlight, each boat was a dark blob shifting up and down on the shallow waves reaching the shore.

A cat yowled and swatted my leg when I stepped on its tail. I almost screamed when a rat ran across my foot as I passed a small storehouse. Twice, I stepped into the cold water, trying to see if I had found my boat. As luck would have it, someone had stored it at the far end of the shore, nearly outside the small bay used by traders.

Before I turned to find my brother, I grabbed the wooden craft and pushed my talent into it. *If there's anything wrong, I need to know now.* The hull was sound. It was ready to sail away.

"How much farther?" Regin asked, when I met him.

"There," I said, pointing.

Closing his eyes for a moment, he squared his shoulders and set off again, walking a bit faster.

I kept looking for some sign of life, a lit lantern or a shadowy person walking about, but nothing appeared. *This is too easy. Something has to go wrong.*

"I can't get in carrying all of this," Regin said, when we reached my boat.

I nodded. "I'll get in first. Hand me one thing at a time."

"Go," he said, looking around, "and be quick about it."

The craft rocked when I stepped in, bringing a smile to my face. *I already feel free.* After putting my bow and quiver into a storage cabinet, I held my arm out and grabbed a pair of bags. Securing them at the far end of the boat, I returned for the next load. Regin clambered aboard as I secured the last of our supplies. With his weight added, the bottom of the boat pressed into the sand.

"We're not floating," he said, a hint of panic in his voice. "We're stuck."

"Let me untie the ropes." I pointed to the bench near the middle of the craft. "Sit there. Get the oars in place and pull when I tell you."

"Didn't you hear me?" he questioned, more panic raising his voice. "I said we're stuck."

"I'm in charge now," I said, untying the closest rope securing my boat to the shore. "Take those long sticks, oars, and lay them in the brackets—"

"The what, where?" he asked. "Speak plainly. I don't know anything about this stuff."

I gritted my teeth. "Put them in the notches on either side of your seat. Grip the ends tightly and, when I tell you to, use all your might and pull the ends to your chest like your life depends on it."

"If you say so," he replied.

I untied the last rope and watched for a wave.

"What's that?" he blurted.

I turned and spotted a lantern heading our way. *Time's up.* "Someone's coming. Pull."

The boat moved back, scraping on the sand.

"It's not working," Regin said.

The lantern was closer, moving faster.

"Lift the oars out of the water, hands forward, then drop the oars and pull again. Now," I ordered.

We moved a bit farther from shore.

"Hey! Stop!" someone yelled.

"Do it again," I said.

Regin grunted. The boat slid more freely.

No sense in being quiet now. "Row again!"

Another grunt and the steering lever moved freely. I held it straight. "Again!"

"Stop! Thieves! They're taking a boat!"

"Again—and don't stop until I say."

As we dragged free of the bottom, footsteps splashed into the water and fingertips gripped the edge of my boat.

"Pull those oars!" I yelled, and smashed my fist onto the fingers.

The poor man screamed and fell into the water.

Several lanterns appeared outside of nearby houses.

"Keep rowing," I said, hurrying back to keep us going straight. The boat picked up speed with every stroke.

Regin breathed heavily as the first lights reached the shore. I steered us into a wide turn. Had my brother learned how to row before now, we could have turned much faster, but this was the best I could do until I had time to train him. Once we were broadside to the shore, I told him to stop.

"Why?" he asked, looking at the lights getting into boats not far from us.

"Just listen to me," I said. "When I say so, do the opposite of what you've been doing. It will push us forward, and I can steer easier. As soon as we get a wind, I'll put up the sail, and then no one can catch us."

He nodded without looking at me.

I pulled the steering lever to turn us away from shore and said, "Row. Now."

Regin strained to move the boat with water dragging against the slab of wood making us turn. My back strained as I fought to keep us going where I wanted.

"They're getting closer," he said.

"You worry about pushing the oars. I'll watch them."

He grunted in response.

Now that the shore was directly behind us, I let the lever go straight, and we surged through the water with every stroke of the oars. "Let's see them keep up with us now,"

I said, looking at the merchant transports falling farther behind in their chase. "Keep going, brother. We're almost free."

He grunted again.

After I'd lost sight of land behind us, I told Regin he could slow his pace. He shook his head and kept working. I looked at the sky and found I couldn't see any stars. The thick clouds hung, unmoving, giving no clue as to which way the wind might come from.

"You can rest for a moment," I said, searching for signs of even a breeze.

The oars slapped the water. "Where's this wind you said we'd find?" he asked, between deep breaths.

"It'll come," I said. *Maybe when the sun rises?*

"Do you know where we're going?" Ragged breaths punctuated each word.

I nodded and pointed ahead. "That's south. Satra is east, to our left. Once we catch the wind, I'll turn us southeast, and we'll reach the shore near the Satran capital in no time."

A cool, stiff breeze crossed from east to west. *Not ideal but I can work with it.* "If this keeps up, we'll be on our way, and you can rest."

He grunted.

Convinced we had a wind, even if it wasn't the one I wanted, I had Regin put the oars away and help me raise the sail.

Chapter 36

The heavy, woven material fluttered for a moment then the breeze filled it, pushing it taut. With the load on the short pole ahead of the rowing seat, the boat tilted to the right and tried to scoot sideways. I heaved against the steering lever to keep us headed in a generally southern direction.

"I thought you said we'd turn left once we had a wind," Regin said.

"It's blowing the wrong way," I said. "We'll have to go farther south, then turn and head northeast. Don't worry—I know what I'm doing. You kept telling me to trust you about your plan; now it's your turn to trust me with the boat."

"Sure," he said, nodding. "Will you teach me how to use the boat before we get to Satra?"

I beamed. If there had been any light, it would have shined off my smile. "Once it's bright enough for you to see what I'm doing, I'd be glad to."

"Good," he said. "I'd feel better if I knew what was going on."

The wind picked up, and several waves sprayed cold water over the side of the boat.

"Good thing our leathers can keep us dry," Regin commented.

I nodded but kept my focus on steering.

Soon, it blew harder, and larger waves hit, rocking the boat. Stinging spray pecked at my face and hands.

Regin held onto the seat, and I gripped the steering tightly.

A bolt of lightning flared in the dark sky far to our southeast.

"There's the rain you were worried about," Regin commented, just before the thunder roared.

The sail pole creaked with the next gust of wind.

Lightning flashed again, and the thunder sounded closer.

Another gust hit and pushed the boat more sideways than forward.

"Umm..." Regin hummed.

Gritting my teeth, I heaved against the lever, turning the boat into the wind. The pole groaned when the sail snapped against it. We moved backward.

"What are you doing?" Regin asked, panic in his voice for the second time today.

"Trying to keep us from being blown over," I said.

A wave hit and washed over us, dropping quite a bit of water into the boat.

"Cup your hands! Throw that water out!" I yelled. *If we sink this far from shore, we'll never swim back.*

Regin threw water over the side as a howling wind turned us westward despite my efforts. The sail billowed, squeaking as the wind punished the fabric for being in its way. The hemp ropes securing the sail vibrated like lyre strings, singing from the air rushing over them.

"We're going to die out here!" Regin wailed.

He may be right, but I'm not giving up. "Not if you help me steer," I said.

The lightning seemed to be on top of us. Thunder rattled my bones.

"What do I do?" he asked.

"Stand facing me and keep this lever straight. If it moves toward me, pull. If it moves toward you, push."

He nodded and put his hands next to mine.

The stiff wind pushed us up a wave taller than some hills. We landed on the other side with a huge splash. My boat groaned under the load.

"I don't want to do that again," Regin said, his face pale.

I nodded.

As if the wind-driven sea spray wasn't enough, large drops of rain pounded us from above. *These leathers don't stand a chance of keeping us dry.*

Another large wave loomed ahead, tall and dark. I didn't want to fall down the other side. "Push!" I yelled.

"You said to hold it straight."

"Push!"

We practically flew across the wave's face as we climbed higher than before.

A long bolt of lightning lit the sky, exposing angry, black clouds. Thunder shook the boat hard enough that I felt it through my boots.

"Now straight," I said, as we reached the top.

Instead of falling, we angled down the other side.

"That worked!" Regin shouted.

But we're not out of danger yet, and I have no idea where we are. "Next time, pull."

"What? Why?"

"Pull!" I screamed.

The wall of water helped us turn east, but I didn't think the angle was right as we reached the top. Regin pushed the lever as we went over.

"No, keep pulling!" I screamed, hoping he would hear me over the storm.

Wind hit like a punch in the face.

The sail pole cracked under the load.

I pushed my talent into the wood around us, focusing on the damaged pole until I found the splintering faults. Pressure from the wailing air threatened to snap the wood, and it felt like it would break me at the same time.

I bellowed, loud and long. Fear and frustration gave me more strength, helping me force the damaged pole back together. Drained from the effort, I sagged against the steering lever as we plummeted down the back of the wave.

Frigid pricks of water hit like stings from a swarm of bees. I took a deep breath, shook my head, and forced myself to stand.

We weren't ready for the next wave.

Instead of angling up the slope, the wind drove us straight to the top. As the water dropped from under my boat, it fell, crashing at the bottom of the wave. The sail pole split. The ropes stood no chance and snapped louder than a whip cracking. The wind tossed the entire mess away like a child throwing a toy.

Oh, no. That's it. We are going to die out here

"I'll use the oars. You steer," Regin said, stepping back.

"No," I said, grabbing his arm. "They'd be ripped out of your hands as soon as they hit the water. I'm going to syth this lever in place to steer us straight. All we can do is ride out the storm and hope we don't get tossed out of the boat."

"But it could sink," Regin said, pulling free of my grip.

"If it sinks, we're dead."

"But—"

"We're at the mercy of the wind and the sea," I said. "Nothing we do will change anything now." *And to think, I used to love being on the water.*

Gripping the lever hard enough to feel the wood's grain biting into my skin, I pushed my talent and bound the rudder to the hull. It couldn't move unless the boat broke around it.

Regin pushed on the lever, then looked at me. "You're sure?"

I nodded and pointed at the space under the seat in the middle of the boat. It held about a hand's depth of cold water, but we huddled together, said that we loved each other, and held on as tight as our frigid fingers could.

Chapter 37

I lost track of time, but the storm had to have lasted more than a day. By the time it passed, the sun was overhead, and my boat carried so much water, it was nearly sunk. While the weather raged, Regin and I had taken turns flinging water out in an effort to stay alive.

At some point, the bandage had washed off my face. A strange, almost tingling, sensation came from the covered area each time the breeze hit my cheek. I did my best to ignore the weird feeling while my brother and I worked together to stay afloat. Calm waves rocked the boat gently as we threw handfuls of water over the side. The movement would have been relaxing had we not come so close to dying.

Once I was confident we weren't going under, I freed the rudder and did what I could to keep the boat going straight while Regin continued to throw water over the side.

"How far are we from Satra?" he asked.

I couldn't see anything but water around us. "I'm not sure. We'll keep going straight until I know which way is east. Once I make the turn, all we can do is hope for the best. One thing's for sure: without the sail, this will be a much longer journey."

Regin grumbled something but kept heaving water.

Soon, our saddlebags were uncovered. A large portion of our supplies, including my journal, had washed away. Everything else, including the food we had left, was soaked. Regin was going to throw it out, but I stopped him. "I have a hook and line. We can use it as bait to catch fish."

"But we can't cook anything," he said, "Unless you have some dry wood and your boat is fireproof."

"Raw fish is better than starving," I said, pushing the lever to turn us east.

"I'll make that decision once I'm starving," Regin said.

He wanted to row, but I wouldn't let him. It was better to conserve our strength since we didn't know when we would have our next meal. We floated along slowly without seeing anything but water until moonrise. After discussing our options, I sythed the rudder again to keep us going straight, and we lay in the bottom of the boat for a restless sleep. Before closing my eyes, I noticed none of the stars looked in the right place.

First light woke us. Salt encrusted my leathers, and they creaked when I got up to look around. I couldn't tell if we had even moved overnight. My stomach growled as Regin rose and sat on the rowing seat.

"I still don't see anything," he said. "Are you sure we're headed for Satra?"

"I'm sure of two things. One, that storm pushed us well away from where we wanted to go, and two, we're alive." My stomach rumbled again. "Make that three things. I need to eat."

He pointed to the somewhat drier sack of food. "There's your bait."

When I opened the small cabinet holding the fishing equipment, water drained out. Unsure of which a fish might like more, water-soaked hard rolls or slimy meat strips, I decided a meat strip would stay on the hook better.

Bait attached, I lowered the hook over the side and watched it sink until I couldn't see it anymore then let the line play out from the wooden spool it was wrapped around until it was about half gone. *Now I wait.*

My heart raced when I felt a small thump. My hands quivered, and then something hit the line hard, pulling more from the spool. "Got something," I said, before sything the wooden spool so it wouldn't spin freely anymore. One hard tug later, I was sure I had a meal on the line.

"What is it?" Regin asked, suddenly interested.

"Something big, I think," I said, struggling to pull the slick line in and wrap it back around the spool.

He moved next to me and helped pull the line. Together, we brought a bright, silver fish close enough to the surface that we could see it was easily as long as my thigh and almost as thick. As we pulled, it jumped out of the water, thrashing about in the air, then tried to swim down when it hit the surface.

"Almost got it!" I yelled.

About two arm spans from the boat, a huge, gray creature with black eyes appeared from the depths and cut my catch in half with a single bite. It had a mouth full of short daggers.

Regin and I both squealed at the sight. I pulled hard on the line, desperate for something to eat. What was left of the silver fish landed in the boat. The gray monster circled us, the tall fin on its back poking up from the surface.

We froze when the beast struck my boat from underneath.

"It's going to eat us," Regin said, the now familiar panic appearing again.

"Where are your axes?" I asked, looking but not moving in case the monster struck again.

"In one of the bags, over there," he said, pointing to the pile of damp saddlebags.

"Crawl over and get them," I said, reaching for my sword, amazed it stayed attached to my belt. I drew it. "I'm not going to die without a fight."

"Just don't hurt yourself...or me," he said, digging through the bags.

"Once you're armed, watch from the other side of the boat. If it comes close, hit it," I said.

"Aye."

I stood as still as an old oak with my sword ready to strike, only my eyes moving, searching for movement in the water. Each breath seemed to take longer and longer.

"Do you see anything?" my brother asked, from behind me.

"No."

"Me either. I think it left," he said.

"Keep your axes nearby just in case. Ready to eat?"

"Aye," he said, easing onto the rowing seat but not looking away from the water.

Blood pinked the shallow water sloshing in the bottom of my boat. What was left of the fish's guts dangled from the jagged wound made by the monster's bite.

"Got a knife handy?" I asked.

Regin searched through the bags and soon found a short dagger. "There should be another one in here but..." He shrugged.

"We'll make do with what we have until we get to Satra," I said, working to slice usable meat from what was left of my catch. I ended up with six pieces about the size of my hand.

"Here." I offered one piece to my brother. "One each every day or until we get to Satra. If we run out, I guess I'll try to catch something else."

"And deal with that thing again?" Regin asked, looking out over the water. "I'll go hungry first."

The chewy, white flesh was salty and more than a little pungent, but we both needed something in our bellies. Fortune had smiled on us, and all our waterskins were still in the boat.

Regin coughed and gagged a couple of times as he choked down the meat.

"Chew longer," I said. "Don't try to eat so fast."

"I'll never get this taste out of my mouth," he said, sticking his tongue out.

"And you'll taste it twice if you get sick," I said.

He nodded but gagged once more before finishing the meal.

"Give me something to wrap the rest of this in," I said.

He frowned. "Everything's wet. Just pick any piece of cloth."

I found one of my dresses, sliced about a forearm's length of cloth from the bottom, and wrapped the meat before storing it in the small space alongside the fishing gear.

"What now? Should I start rowing?" Regin asked, looking at the empty space around us.

"I'd rather you save your strength until we see land," I said.

"So, we do nothing but wait?"

I snickered. "You can go swimming if you'd like."

He shivered hard enough for me to see. "With that thing out there...somewhere? Not on your life."

"Then we wait," I said.

Chapter 38

Clear sky and light breezes made us uncomfortably hot, but we agreed it was an improvement over being soaked in cold water. Since we hadn't slept while the storm raged over us, I let Regin lay on the rowing seat to rest while I kept watch. As the sun touched the water, he tapped me on the shoulder. "Get some sleep. You need it."

Unsure I had the energy to lock the rudder again, I looked him in the eye. "Keep us going straight. Make sure we don't turn."

He nodded. "Don't worry."

Laying on the seat, the rough surface pressed into the tender skin around the still-healing scratches. I tossed and turned, shifting until I found a position comfortable enough for me to drift into sleep.

My dreams were violent, filled with lightning, dark clouds, and huge mouths full of jagged, slicing teeth. Sharp, screeching cries pierced the sights tormenting my mind. Opening my eyes, I found the sky was a pinkish purple of an approaching dawn.

Regin was slumped against the back of the boat, asleep. The steering lever was hard to the left. *So much for going straight. Probably went in a circle all night. Good thing we didn't miss any land.* I wanted to be angry with him, but we were both exhausted.

The strange cries in my dreams sounded again, overhead. I looked for the source but saw nothing against the still, dark sky. Louder and closer, I figured out they were coming from the direction we were headed.

Soon, the sky was light enough for me to pick out large, dark birds. *Birds mean land must be nearby!* Long wings spread wide as they bobbed in the air as if they rode the waves of water below them. At first, I thought they might be ravens or vultures, but these birds were like none I had ever seen before. *Where are we?*

"Regin," I said, shaking my brother. "Wake up. Birds!"

He batted at me. "Lemme sleep."

"We must be near land," I said, shaking him again. "Wake up!"

"Land?" he questioned, blinking before looking up at me. "Where?"

"I don't know, exactly, but..." I pointed ahead. "Birds! They have to land somewhere."

"Yeah," he said, rubbing his eyes. "They can't fly forever. Let's find the land."

"I'll steer. You row," I said, pulling him into a hug.

He squeezed me back, then pushed away and got ready to work the oars.

I heaved against the lever to get us pointed straight and said, "Row!"

Regin grunted, and we surged forward toward the brightening sky and the birds.

"Think you could hit one with your bow?" Regin asked, as a few of the large, soaring birds got closer.

"As wet as everything got, I'd need to dry the bowstring and probably straighten all my arrows," I said, wrestling the steering.

"In other words, we're still eating raw fish."

"You think raw bird would taste better?" I asked.

"Maybe," he replied, shrugging before pulling the oars again.

Ahead, something resembling the tops of trees came into view against the blue sky. I yelled long and loud before telling my brother what I'd spotted.

He pulled harder.

Soon, I heard the dull roar of waves washing against land. My heart pounded. "Hear that?"

"Yeah," he answered, straightening his back.

The trees were strange, tall and thin with clumps of leaves toward the top. *Where are we?*

More trees and yellow sand came into view. "Keep going," I said. "There's land ahead."

Regin whooped and pulled hard.

The waves washed over an unseen obstacle before they reached the land.

Something hit the bottom of the boat.

"What was that?" Regin asked.

Before I could answer, we scraped across it. The steering lever ripped itself from my grip, and we slammed to a stop.

"What happened?" Regin yelled, turning to look at me.

I looked over the side. The blue water was clear enough that I could see some kind of weird rock below the surface.

"We've hit a rock...I think," I said.

"This far from shore? Are you sure?"

The bird calls above sounded like they were laughing at us.

"Look for yourself," I said, pointing into the water.

As Regin stood, a big wave crashed into the back of my boat, lifting it free of the obstacle and carrying us forward before slamming the bottom onto the rocks again. Wood cracked, and Regin fell out, screaming when he hit the weird rock.

I rushed forward to grab him. Blood tinged the water. His leathers were cut, as if he'd been attacked with a sharp blade.

"It burns!" he yelled, nearly pulling me out of the boat while trying to get back in.

"Easy," I said, trying to calm him while helping him out of the water.

"The water burns," he said, pressing his hands together once he was seated in the bottom of the boat. Blood flowed from between his hands as well as from cuts on his face, arms, and chest.

"It's the salt in the water. Let me flush your cuts with fresh water. That will help."

"Hurry," he said. I could tell he was trying to not cry.

After finding a waterskin, I glanced up and froze.

Chapter 39

Two boats made of a dull, tan wood glided across the water toward us. Long and skinny with poles jutting from either side, they were unlike anything I'd ever seen before. *Like everything else here...wherever here is.* Three or four men using short, wide oars were in each boat and they were moving fast.

"Get your axes," I said, dropping the waterskin and reaching for my sword. "Someone's coming."

"Out here? How?" he asked, wincing as he gripped the weapons.

"Look," I said, pointing.

They were nearly to us. I could see them clearly. Shorter than most Croian men and not much taller than me, they were broad shouldered with lean muscles and dark skin. Thick, black hair hung past their shoulders. Everyone wore some kind of coarse, woven, tan or brown skirt to cover their private parts but were otherwise naked. Coasting to a stop, they put the oars away and pulled out some sort of wooden spears.

Regin, blood dripping from his chin, took a couple of shaky steps to stand in front of me. "They'll have to go through me to get to you."

The first man on our right grabbed the front of my boat with one hand, holding his spear about waist high with the other.

Regin stepped forward, axes ready to strike.

The strange man said something in a vowel-heavy language, unlike anything spoken in or around Croy, and made a motion I took to mean, 'No.'

"Regin, stop!" I yelled, my sword half-drawn. "Step back!"

My brother hesitated.

"There are too many, and you're hurt," I said, sliding my sword back into its scabbard and putting my hands above my head. "If they want to kill us, we're dead. Put your axes on the seat and raise your hands."

One of the men in the other boat gestured with his spear.

"But—" he started to argue, turning to face the newest threat.

"Think," I said, stopping him. "We left home to save our lives. There isn't enough room on my boat for us to defend each other. If we fall out, the rocks below will cut us to pieces. There are at least three of them for each of us, and their boats aren't stuck. They could just row away and wait for us to starve. Or circle us, jabbing spears from beyond our reach, opening wounds until we lose enough blood to die. There's no way we win, or even survive, except by letting them take us."

"And that's not winning," he said, dropping his axes and raising his hands.

"Maybe not, but it isn't dying a senseless death this far from home either," I said.

Men from both of the boats tried to pull mine free. I could hear and feel the strange stone grinding into the wooden hull. *Stop tearing up my boat!* After a few hard tugs, they gave up and motioned for Regin to step forward. Their strange language sounded like they were angry at us, but they smiled when my brother moved.

"Watch yourself," I said. "Don't do anything foolish."

The short, sturdy men practically lifted Regin from my boat once they had a firm grip on him. He protested and tried to pull away.

"Stop struggling," I said.

With little effort, the men passed him to the back of their boat where the last one pulled Regin's arms behind his back and held him fast.

The lead stranger in the other boat motioned for me to come to him. Every part of my being said this was madness, but I knew I had no choice. Unclipping my sword from the belt, I dropped it and surrendered.

Each hand that touched me was rough, covered with the calluses of a laborer. I was soon held fast, much like my brother.

As my brother's captors turned for the shore, mine fought to free my boat, further scraping the hull across the stone holding my prized possession fast. With each heave and heavy scrape, I could practically feel the bottom of my boat's hull being ripped open. Tears fell as I realized how much work it would take to fix it. I twisted, trying to get free, but the stranger held my wrists fast. "Stop!" I screamed. "You're just making it worse." Given their lack of reaction, they may as well have been deaf.

Slivers of wood bobbed on the surface and followed us to the shore once they ripped my boat free. As their craft scraped to a stop on the beach, a village came into view about twenty paces from the shore.

Clusters of round, tan-colored buildings looked as if they had grown naturally from the sandy ground under those strange trees I'd spotted earlier. I couldn't identify the wood making up the walls. The roofs seemed to be woven out of the same material as the men's loin covers.

The man holding me curled his free arm around my waist and easily hefted me out of the boat. When my feet hit the ground, I turned back to see the other three men dragging my craft out of the water.

Long gashes down the side confirmed my fear. *It may never float again.*

With a light tug, I was walked backward into the village. My captor yelled something in their strange language. Part of me feared the last thing I might ever see was my wrecked boat, laying on one side on this sandy beach.

Looking down, I spotted drops of blood staining dragged boot prints on the sandy ground to my right. *What have they done with Regin?*

My brother screamed from somewhere in the village. "Stop!" he bellowed. "It burns! Stop!"

I twisted, trying to see where his voice came from.

The man holding my wrists twisted my arms and said something harsh sounding.

"They're hurting my brother!" I yelled, trying to free myself.

He raised my arms and pain shot through my shoulders.

I lifted my heels to walk on my toes and lessen the pain. My feet sank into the sand and didn't give any relief.

He lowered my arms, pulled me, said something else I couldn't understand, and walked a little faster.

"Stop!" Regin yelled again.

"You're hurting him!" I screamed, tears coming to my eyes.

Other dark-skinned people came into view, staring at me. The women stood about the same height as their men and wore similar woven clothes hiding their crotch but leaving their chests bare. Their thick, black hair hung in clumps of rough braids, some well below their waist. The few children I glimpsed wore nothing at all. Everyone chattered, pointed, and stared as I was dragged past them.

More men with spears appeared behind me. I craned my neck, trying to see where they were taking me. All I saw were more people and more small houses.

Regin's screams finally stopped. *Is he dead or just unconscious?* My journey continued, but tears blurred my vision. *Where are they taking me?*

We stopped walking, and my escort wheeled me around to face a wide opening in a flat wall. The building was the same tan color as the rest of the homes, but it was larger and rectangular. It reminded me of a primitive attempt at making a Croian meeting hall.

A small fire pit provided dim light inside the building, showing someone sitting on a chair made of the same tan wood as the building. One of the men behind me pushed on my shoulder. *Is Regin in there? Only one way to find out.*

The door closed behind me. Bright spots of sunlight appeared in the woven roof cover, reminding me of stars. When I reached the edge of the firelight, the flames grew tall. I yelped and stepped back from the heat and bright light.

"O wai oe?" the man in front of me asked. At least it sounded like a question.

"Where is Regin?" I demanded. "Where do you have my brother?"

He repeated his question.

Once my eyes adjusted, I found there were others in the room.

Several men, most armed with spears, and a few women. One woman sat to the left of the man I'd first seen. Like the others, he wore almost no clothes, but I noticed a band of small pebbles or shells around his head. In the center of the band, one of those jagged, dagger-like, monster teeth hung down, almost reaching between his eyes. *He must be a king.* My manners took over, and I bowed low.

The room filled with gasps.

"O wai oe?" he asked again.

"I am Princess Meyla. Firstborn daughter of King Fitzeirick and Queen Tindra of Croy."

"Mikilana," he said.

"I don't understand," I said, bringing my hand to my chest. "Is that your name?"

An elderly woman shuffled forward from somewhere behind the man and leaned against the left side of his chair.

"Where..." She paused, rubbed her jaw, and cleared her throat. "Where...are...you...from?"

Chapter 40

My knees shook for a moment. I fought to keep my balance. Once I'd steadied myself, I studied the woman.

Even hunched from age, she looked about a hand taller than everyone I'd seen so far. Flickering firelight showed some lighter-colored patches on her dark skin. Streaks of gray wove through her black hair, but it looked less coarse than the others. "I am from the nation of Croy," I said. "Who are you?"

She turned to the man I assumed was the king and spoke to him in their strange language.

He nodded.

"I...am Mikilana," she said. "This...is... Ali Ha'upu. Vos...of Aina."

I know that word, vos. It's Satran for a ruler. "My pleasure to meet you, Ali Ha'upu," I said, bowing again.

He dipped his head.

"Ahine Ane...is...his...wife," Mikilana said.

"Your Majesty," I said, bowing again.

The woman studied me for a moment, then brought her right hand to her left shoulder. She wore a similar band around her head except with a long, pointed shell instead of a monster's tooth in the middle.

Ali Ha'upu said something to Mikilana.

"Why...have...you come to...Aina?" she asked.

"We, my brother Regin and I, were going to Satra."

Mikilana's eyes opened wide.

"We were caught in a storm and ended up here. We did not know of this place. Where is my brother?"

Again, words were exchanged between the king and Mikilana.

"Lawe ai ai," Ali Ha'upu said, pointing toward the door behind me.

"Come...with me, Kai Meyla," Mikilana said.

I shivered. "Did I say or do something wrong? I don't understand."

"Come," Mikilana repeated. "All...will...be...told."

"Are you taking me to Regin?" I asked, not sure if I should go.

"Come," she repeated, more firmly this time.

Two men stepped forward from the shadows behind the king's chair, lowering their spears.

Better go with her.

The door opened, letting in blinding sunlight.

I turned to walk beside Mikilana as she passed. I had to shade my eyes, but my guide didn't even flinch.

"I have questions," I said, as we stepped outside.

"All...will...be...told," Mikilana said.

Again, the women and children stood watching us. One of the older-looking women pointed at me, said something, then rubbed her cheek.

My scars. My heart pounded.

Although Mikilana walked slowly, the village wasn't as large as I originally thought, and soon, we arrived at a small, round hut. Four men stood near the door, spears at their sides.

One of them stepped forward and said something to Mikilana.

She gave him a harsh-sounding reply and pointed toward the hall.

He stepped back.

Mikilana nodded and pointed toward the hut's door.

"What's in there?" I asked

"The...boy," she said.

I hurried inside. *To the fire with anyone who thinks they can stop me.*

The roof was open, bathing Regin in sunlight. He lay on a table made of the same wood as the hut. They'd taken his leathers off. Dark green leaves wrapped around his arms, lay across his chest, and covered most of his face. His eyes were closed, and I couldn't tell if he was breathing.

I reached for him, but a dark-skinned hand grabbed my wrist.

I balled my free hand into a fist and drew it back.

"No!" Mikilana barked, behind me.

"What?" I turned, pulling my arm from whoever's grasp. "He's my brother! Is he alive?"

Mikilana said something.

A woman answered. She sounded no older than me.

"Kapahu says...yes...for now. Kimo...needs more noni...for...ko'a'ke'a eha."

I wheeled around to look for Kapahu, my fist still raised. A girl, at least a head shorter than me, stepped out of the shadow.

"What's wrong with my brother?" I demanded.

She backed away.

"Ko'a'ke'a...saz"

Saz means poison. She used another Satran word. Why?

"Noni...helps," Mikilana said.

Regin twitched. I reached for him, and the girl didn't stop me this time. He was cold. I turned to Mikilana. "He's the Prince of Croy. My brother. Whatever it takes to save him." I fell to my knees.

The girl gasped.

Tears came to my eyes. "You can have my sword...my bow...even what's left of my boat. But save him. Please."

She patted her chest. "Kimo will...do...his...best."

Closing my eyes, I wrapped my arms around myself and wailed. *Surrounded by people and alone. Lost. Trapped. We should never have left home. Fools...both of us.*

"Stand," Mikilana ordered. "Come."

I looked up at her and shook my head. "I'm not leaving my brother."

"Come," she said, firmer. "He...will...live. Kimo...will...save."

I looked at him again. He shivered harder. Pulling off my hunting shirt, I got to my feet and laid it on him. *Not much of a blanket but better than nothing.* "Hope it keeps you warm, brother. I will be back for you." Turning to my guide, I nodded. "Where are we going?"

Chapter 41

My bare chest didn't seem to attract any extra attention. At first, I covered my chest with my arms, but then I realized that would probably get more attention, and I dropped my arms to my side. *If I walked outside without a shirt at home, the uproar would be heard across the city.* People still gawked and muttered things I couldn't understand as we passed.

Mikilana led me to a hut on the edge of the village. From the outside, it looked much the same as the others I'd seen, a bit larger, maybe, but nothing remarkable. Inside, however, it held a round table made of old, weathered wood. I guessed it was birch or maple but wouldn't know for sure until I touched it. The three chairs around it wouldn't have been out of place in a Satran home. I was certain I'd seen similar seats when we visited Skald Rorec and Asfrid, his wife. *What does Satra have to do with this place?* Nestled in the far corner, I noticed a woven mat, made from the same material as everyone's clothes, stretched tightly across a large, wooden frame.

My escort nodded toward the chairs.

I took the hint, sat in the closest one, and pushed my talent into it. It was birch. *We have plenty of this in Croy, and I've seen it in Satra, but those strange trees on the beach are not birch. At least, I don't think so.* Resting my hand on the table showed me it was the same wood as the chair.

Mikilana brushed her hand against the wall, and a small hole opened above the table, putting light on it. She put a tall, thin cup in front of me. It was the same tan color as the hut around us. I grabbed it and tried to figure out what it was. *This feels more like grass than wood.*

"Ohe," Mikilana said. "No...word...for...you."

"Where are you from?" I asked.

"Aina." She smiled, carrying a bigger ohe container to the table and pouring something looking like watery milk into my cup. She poured some for herself and took a sip before nodding to me.

It wasn't water or milk. The flavor was an odd combination of sweet and salty with another taste I didn't recognize.

"Wainui," she said, tapping the container. "No...word...for...you."

"If you're from here, how do you understand me? Why do you speak Satran?" I asked.

She tapped a finger on the table. "Waapa." She moved her hand like it was floating on water and pointed at me.

"You came here like me? On a boat?"

She shook her head and pressed her lips together. "Kupuna. Father...older. Boat."

"Your father was Satran and came here on a boat," I said, nodding.

She shook her head again. "Older."

I sighed. "Someone older than your father came here on a boat?"

She nodded then slapped her hand on the table. "Ko'a'ke'a. Boat...like...you."

I scratched my chin and took another drink. "The strange stone in the water broke his boat, like mine?"

"Ko'a'ke'a. Yes."

"That's the word for the strange stone out there?'

"Yes."

"Did it poison your older father?" I asked. *If he survived, then Regin should too.*
She shook her head. "Others...many."

"Did they live?"

"Few."

Not the answer I wanted. Regin has to make it. "Did older father ever leave?"
She shook her head.

I want to go home once Regin heals. "Does *anyone* leave?"
She pressed her lips together again. "Ko'a'ke'a."

"It keeps people from leaving?" I asked. "But those other boats—they didn't hit it."

"Mano," she said, clapping her hands together, then shivering.

"I don't understand."

"No...word...for...you," she said, shrugging. Her eyes opened wide. "Ha'upu." She tapped her forehead.

I stared at her for a moment. *The king's face? He doesn't let them go past the stone?* I shook my head again and shrugged. "Your king keeps you here?"

"No." She said his name again, then traced a triangle on her forehead.

The tooth! "The monster out there keeps you here!" I shouted.

She nodded. "Mano."

They are as afraid of the beast as we were.

The young girl who had been with Regin called for Mikilana, saying something, including the name Kimo, that made her pat my hand and get up. "Come...Kimo...brother."

My heart pounded. "Regin? What about him?"

"Ala...awake. Come."

Jumping to my feet, it was everything I could do to not drag my new friend across the village. Another reason I walked at her pace was I didn't know exactly where to go.

Kapahu hurried ahead.

Following Regin's moans as soon as I heard them, I reached the hut well ahead of Mikilana and hurried inside, almost running into Kimo.

Glaring, he barked something at me.

I bowed. "Apologies, sir." I grabbed my brother's hand. "Regin, are you awake?" Someone had taken my leather off him and covered him with more leaves. *Is that noni?*

He squeezed my hand lightly. "Yes." Even his voice was weak.

My heart jumped into my throat. Tears welled in my eyes, but I smiled wide enough to hurt my cheeks. "I've never been happier to hear you say something," I said, squeezing his hand back.

"Where...where are we?" Regin asked.

"Still trying to figure that out," I said. "It's a land called Aina. I've met the king and queen and Mikilana. She speaks Satran."

He shivered. "We made it to Satra?"

"No," I said. "We're in Aina."

Mikilana and Kimo discussed something behind me. All I understood was my name.

"Listen. You have to heal. I can't make it here alone, and I can't leave without you," I said. *I'm not going to tell him we may not be able to leave at all.* "I'm going to learn as much as I can while you get better, then we'll go home, and..." I paused and sniffled. "Oh, the stories we can tell. Our children's children will regale in the tales of this adventure."

The leaves on his face shifted when he nodded. "Weak," he said. "It hurts."

"The stone out there has some kind of poison," I said. "These leaves will help."

"They put...something...in the cuts. It burns," Regin said. "Not nice, like Abi."

I squeezed his hand again. "Different herbalists have their own treatments...and this place is different from anywhere we've ever been."

"Hey, you don't have a shirt on," he said. "Mother might not be too upset if she finds out, but Father will be furious."

"I know...so we won't tell them. They took your leathers off to treat your cuts. You were shivering, so I put my hunting shirt over you to keep you warm."

"Oh. Wait...I'm naked?" he asked.

"Well," I said, trying not to laugh, "you are covered in leaves."

"Oh. Good."

If you can't tell you don't have pants on, I'm not going to mention it. "You should rest. I think that's the only way you're going to heal."

"Aye," he said. "I am feeling sleepy again."

I bent to kiss the top of his head. "I won't be far away."

He nodded, shifting the leaves on his face around.

I let go of his hand, wiped my eyes, and turned to Mikilana. "How long will he be like this?"

She turned to Kimo and said something.

Chapter 42

I studied the herbalist as they spoke. He was less than a head taller than me and dark skinned like everyone except Mikilana. Along with his woven clothes, he had a pouch slung across his chest. It too was made of that coarse, woven material I saw everywhere. At a glance, they looked like they could have been dried versions of the leaves wrapped around my brother.

"Kimo says...much...saz. Heal...or...not." She shrugged. "Hard...to...tell. Must...wait."

I closed my eyes, squeezing the last of the tears from their corners, and nodded. "All I can do is wait. I understand." *I have to figure out how we get home once Regin is better.* "Will you teach me words?"

The elderly woman smiled wide. "Come."

A large fire burned in a pit. *That wasn't there when we passed.* "What's that?"

"Ahiahi...dinner," Mikilana said.

"A cooking fire?"

"Yes."

Wonder what these people eat. "What is the Aina word for 'yes'?" I asked.

"Ae."

Aye? That can't be right. Did she not understand me? "No," I said, "I want to know the *Aina* word for 'yes.' Both Croy and Satra say 'aye.'"

"Ae," she said, with a little more force.

I furrowed my brow. "So, the three languages use the same word?"

"Ae," she said, and laughed.

"Is 'no' no?" I asked. *If she says 'aye,' I'll know it's a jest.*

"A'ole," she said.

It took a couple of tries before she said I pronounced it right.

By the time we reached her hut, I knew a few more words but not well enough to be confident talking with anyone but Mikilana.

We sat at the table, drinking more wainui, while I tried to learn enough Aina words to be able to speak for myself.

My stomach rumbled. I couldn't remember the last time I'd eaten anything.

Mikilana nodded and shuffled to a small, woven basket near the table. She lifted out a clump of curved, yellow things bigger around than my thumb and a bit longer than my first finger. Setting the bunch on the table, she pulled one off, grabbed the stem and tore it open. The yellow covering split, revealing white flesh inside. "Mai'a," she said. "No...word...for...you." After taking a bite, she tore one off and offered it to me.

My talent told me it was from a plant but one I didn't recognize. Copying her, I tore the skin from the flesh and bit it. Soft, my teeth sank into it easily, and creamy like an almost melted block of butter, but I'd never had anything that tasted like it before. It was sweet but not like honey or ripe fruit. "Mai'a," I said. "This is good."

"Mai'a loa," she said, nodding.

"Loa means good?"

"Ae."

"Where does it come from?" I asked.

"Lu'au," she said, pointing out the door.

I raised my eyebrows. "Outside?"

"A'ole. Come." Mikilana got up, and I followed her out of the hut.

She pointed to the closest tree and moved her hand up and down. "Lu'au."

"Tree," I said. "Lu'au means tree?"

"Ae."

I didn't see anything yellow on the tree she pointed to. "Mai'a lu'au?" I asked.

"A'ole." She pointed to the top. "Nui." She acted like she was drinking something. "Wainui."

"Wainui comes from lu'au?"

She shrugged and pointed toward the top again. "Nui."

A couple of large, green, not exactly round things clung to the tree just below the leaves. Mikilana pressed her hand against the tree and one of them fell to the ground with a noticeable thud. She picked it up and handed it to me.

Nearly the size of my head, it was hard and heavier than I expected. Pushing my talent into it, I found fibers running through the thing, then felt a hard, mostly round surface inside.

"Hamama...open," Mikilana said.

I sythed a split in the fibrous outer shell and peeled it away, revealing a brown, roundish, almost hairy nut inside about the size of my fists put together,

"Nui," Mikilana said, pointing to the thing in my hands. "Lulu...shake."

I heard something sloshing inside. "Wainui?"

"Ae. Hamama...open...top."

I turned the nui over in my hands trying to figure out which part was the top. One side had three small, darker spots with no fibers. Opposite it was somewhat pointed. I circled the point, using my talent to pierce the hard shell. After two rounds, it came free.

Mikilana smiled. "Inu...drink."

A warmer, stronger-flavored wainui flowed into my mouth.

."Ae," she said again, nodding. "Hamama."

I quit drinking and frowned. "It *is* open."

"More," she said, gesturing for me to give the inu to her.

After I handed it to her, she drank the rest of the liquid and then sythed the nui in half, revealing a bright white inside. Peeling a strip off, she bit off a piece and offered me the rest. "I'o nui. No...word...for...you."

The firm flesh crunched when I bit into it. It was sweeter than the wainui, and I understood where the flavor I couldn't identify came from. "Tastes good," I said, smiling.

She returned my smile and gave me half of the nui. "Inside," she said, pointing at her hut.

Once we were back at the table, we continued language lessons until dinner was announced.

Chapter 43

The entire village gathered around the pit we'd passed earlier. The biggest wooden pot I'd ever seen, made from nui lu'au if I could guess by the texture, hung over the fire on a thick, nui lu'au pole with other poles supporting it on each end. It reminded me of a roasting spit, only much larger.

Bowls made from nui shells and spoons made from nui lu'au were handed out, first to the king and queen, then to a young man seated on the queen's left. I guessed he was at least a year older than me. He had a thin band of fiber around his head with only a few shells hanging from it. His hair was pulled into a ponytail, secured with a wide band made of the same material as his headband. *Their son?*

Everyone else stood, waiting their turn to be served. The containers were filled with some kind of soup or stew smelling of fish.

I didn't see Regin. "My brother needs to eat, too."

"Ae," Mikilana said. "Kimo."

I nodded and thanked her before tasting my meal. It was salty and fishy with chunks of white meat I didn't recognize. Edible but unlike anything I had ever eaten.

The young man sitting near the king and queen eyed me as we ate. Several times, he leaned over to the queen and said something. She never responded with anything more than a smile or a nod.

I had no doubt he'd noticed my scars.

About halfway through my meal, he approached. By the way people moved out of his way, he had to be the Prince of Aina. We stood nearly eye-to-eye when he stopped in front of me and spoke. Other than Aina, I didn't understand anything he said and turned to Mikilana.

"Kiek Keoni," she said, dipping her head to him. "Aina prince. He...asks...marking."

I tried my best to introduce myself in his language. By the grin on his face and Mikilana's head shaking, I must not have done a very good job. I bowed, then told him about the attack. Mikilana spoke my words to him in Ainan.

"Wai kamali," he said, reaching toward my face.

I flinched back, glaring at him. "A'ole."

People near me gasped and stepped back.

He returned my look.

I turned to Mikilana as she said something to him.

"I am the Princess of Croy," I said, "No one touches me without my permission."

"Keoni says...water...princess," she said. "He...wanted...honor."

"What?" I asked.

"Your...mark."

"I don't understand," I said.

She spoke to the prince again.

He nodded, said, "Wai kamali," again then brought his right hand to his left shoulder before rubbing his finger across his cheek.

"He wants to feel my scars?" I asked.

"Ae," she said.

Dropping my spoon in the bowl, I held out my hand.

Keoni put his hand in mine, and I brought it to my cheek.

Gentle as a tickle, he ran a finger across my face. As he traced the lines, I realized they felt similar to waves on the water. *Is that why he called me water princess?* After one more touch, he stepped back and touched his hand to his shoulder again before turning to return to his seat.

"What was that?" I asked.

"A'ole," Mikilana said. "Later."

Keoni's mother patted his shoulder after he sat. He leaned toward her and said something. She nodded and looked at me.

I'm going to hold you to that. I hurried to finish my soup, as it was getting cold. "I want to see Regin."

"Hele...go," Mikilana said, gesturing toward Kimo's hut.

Chapter 44

The herbalist was smashing something into a paste when I entered. He nodded when I said his name.

Regin's bed had been moved so he could sit up by leaning against the wall. He held a nui bowl to his mouth, sipping from it. Without the leaves on his face, it was easy to see the cuts were angry and red. It didn't look good.

"Good to see you up, brother," I said,

He sat the bowl in his lap and grimaced. "You still don't have a shirt on."

"My leather shirt is in here and..." I shrugged. "No one else wears a shirt either."

He smirked. "I've noticed. Are you going to continue this when we get home?"

"Most certainly not," I said. "You must be feeling better to be thinking about going home. How do you like the soup?'

"This stuff is terrible. Too salty—and what's in it?"

I shrugged. "Some kind of fish. Better than starving, right?"

"Aye," he said, lifting the bowl slowly again.

"Oh, that's the same word the Ainan use for 'yes,'" I said.

He squinted. "How do you know?"

"I've been learning their language. Remember, I told you about an elderly lady who speaks some Satran?"

"Maybe," he said, furrowing his brow. "Some things are...blurry."

"One of her ancestors was Satran; his boat wrecked here like ours did."

"Can we use his boat to fix yours?"

"It was a long time ago, Regin. There isn't much left of his boat now."

"But they have wood, right? I'm on a wooden table," he said, tapping a finger on the platform holding him.

"It's not like any wood we have back home," I said. "I'm figuring it out. You just need to work on healing."

He nodded and took a sip of his soup.

"Do you want me to stay with you while you finish your meal?"

"No. Spend your time figuring out how we get home. The sooner the better," he said. *He was in a hurry to leave; now he's in a hurry to go back?* "Why?"

"We don't belong here. We were supposed to go to Satra...to someplace safe," he said.

"No one knows we're here. If someone's after us, how much safer could we be?"

"This place doesn't feel very safe to me," he said, patting the leaves on his chest.

"I'll get us home, but you have to heal first. You're not going to leave all the work to me," I said, then stuck my tongue out at him.

He tried to laugh, then groaned. "I'll do what I must."

"Eat and rest," I said. "I'll be back as soon as I can."

He nodded and took another mouthful of soup.

I found Mikilana sitting at the table in her hut. While I was gone, she had taken the rest of the i'o nui out of the hulls and made two more bowls with them.

"Kaikua...brother?" she asked, as I sat across from her.

"Eating," I said.

"Loa."

I smiled. "And feeling well enough to complain about the soup. He doesn't care for fish."

She chuckled. "Cr – Croy...tell?"

"You want me to tell you about where I'm from?"

"Ae."

I told her about my country, our people, and our history. She hung on every word and didn't seem upset when I explained that Croy conquered Satra. The sun was sitting low in the sky by the time I finished talking. "Where will I sleep?"

She pointed toward the bed.

"But...that's your bed," I said.

"Ae."

"Where will you sleep?"

"Hui pu...together," she said.

"We're going to share your bed?"

"Ae...safe."

"Am I not safe sleeping alone?"

She shrugged.

"But I am safe with you?"

"Ae."

Maybe it's time to get my sword. Tomorrow. "Fine...for now."

"Ae."

"I told you about Croy; tell me about Aina."

She nodded and told a tale, mixing the two languages. I had to pay close attention to understand even a small amount of her story. By the time she finished, the sky was filled with stars I didn't recognize. Yawning, I stretched. "I'm ready for bed," I said.

"Ae. Moe," she said, pointing at the bed again.

"Moe means sleep?"

"Ae...and...bed."

"Oh," I said. "Do you know where my other clothes are? I don't want to sleep in my hunting pants."

"A'ole," she said, looking outside.

What difference does it make now? I shrugged, walked to the bed, pulled my boots off, peeled the sword belt from around my waist, removed my leather pants, and lay down.

Mikilana closed the door and the hole in the roof and lay down next to me.

The rough fibers were not as comfortable as my straw bed back home. The weight of everything settled on me. I wrapped my arms around myself and focused on breathing, trying to clear my mind and get some much-needed rest.

Mikilana soon breathed the shallow breath of sleep.

At least she doesn't snore.

Chapter 45

"Meyla...up," Mikilana said.

I opened one eye.

My elderly guide stood at the door. Morning light streamed in.

I sat up, then remembered I was naked.

"Palu'u," she said, pointing toward the table.

"What?" I asked, as my bare feet hit the sand floor.

She shuffled in and lifted a woven skirt from the table. "Palu'u."

"Oh. You made that for me?"

"Ae."

I took it from her and held it toward the light so I could study it. It was the light tan of dried leaves. The outside was rough, but the inside was smooth. A thin rope made of fibers twisted and sythed together ran around the waist. "What is this made of?"

Mikilana smiled, ran her hand down the outside, and said, "Nui lau." Putting her hand inside, she said, "Mai'a lau." Rubbing the rope she said, "Nui lu'au."

I put the skirt on, tied it snug at my waist, and took a few steps. It didn't make much sound as I walked, but since it ended about half a hand above my knee, modesty was not one of its strong points. "Lu'au I know," I said. "What is lau?"

She pointed outside. "Helemai...come. Wash first, then I show you."

She led me west out of the village, through a dense field of ohe, to a small lake fed by a waterfall. More people than I had seen before were gathered on the shore and wading into the water. The steady splashing from the fall made it hard to hear the conversations around us, not that I could understand much of what was said.

I tried to ignore the eyes on me and watch what others were doing to get clean. Several people scrubbed their skin with handfuls of wet sand from the lake bed before dunking themselves to rinse off.

Mikilana motioned for me to go ahead. I slipped out of the skirt and waded in. While not warm, the water was not unpleasant, but I shivered at the unfamiliar sensation of gentle ripples lapping against my bare stomach. Not ready to try rubbing sand on my skin, I splashed water onto myself and scrubbed myself with my bare hands.

"Enough," Mikilana said. "Helemai. Lau." She flicked a hand toward the village.

I nodded and followed her to a group of young boys and girls gathered close enough to the beach to hear waves breaking over the ko'a'ke'a. They called Mikilana's name and smiled at her, then greeted me with calls of 'aloha.' I nodded and said, "Aloha," in return.

They sat around piles of leaves, some deep green, broad, and smooth, others a lighter green, not as wide, and much coarser looking. Mikilana gestured toward the piles. "Lau." She touched the broad leaves and said, "Mai'a lau," then pointed to the other pile. "Nui lau."

"Lau is leaves," I said.

"Ae."

I stepped back and watched the children work. Some split the lau into strips; others used their talent to push the moisture from the strips. The next group joined some of the freshly dried strips together with mai'a lau on one side and nui lau on the other. I ran my hand down the outside of my new skirt. More of the nui lau were sythed into longer strips before a few of the oldest-looking boys and girls wove everything into clothes, bed mats, or even bigger pieces.

"Why here?" I asked. It was obvious the leaves had been carried from elsewhere as there were no trees nearby.

"Family," she said, nodding toward the beach. "Helemai."

When we arrived, the first thing I noticed were boats floating a safe distance from the ko'a'ke'a. Men jabbed their spears into the water and pulled out fish. Then I noticed men and women wading, about knee deep, in the blue water in pairs. One held a woven basket while the other lifted chunks of water and dropped it inside. The water streamed out of holes in the bottoms of the baskets.

Leaning forward, I rubbed my eyes and watched it happen again. "How?" I demanded. "How are they lifting water?"

"Wai hana ana," she said. "Water...workers."

Some Satran refer to sything as working. "Wait. Are you telling me there are people who can syth water?"

"You...me...lu'au hana ana," she said, then pointed to a man lifting more water. "Wai hana ana."

"Why?" I asked. "The basket leaks."

"Helemai," she said, gesturing toward the nearest pair.

Mikilana spoke to the one holding the basket when we got close.

She held it so I could see inside. At least twelve, greenish-gray-blue creatures flopped about in the bottom of her basket. It was hard to get a count with so much movement.

"What are those?" I asked.

"Opae," Mikilana said. "No...word...for...you."

"Food?" I asked.

"Ae," she said. "Last...meal."

"Those were in the soup last night?" I asked.

"Ae. Tonight."

"Ae," I said. My stomach growled.

The woman holding the basket chuckled.

"Mano!"

Everyone turned to look at the sea.

"Mano!" one of the men in a boat yelled again.

The monster? Did it follow me here?

Mikilana grabbed my arm and turned me toward the beach. The waders ran for the shore as those in the boat paddled toward the beast.

Once we were safe on dry ground, I turned to watch the men stab at the monster with their spears. Water splashed. The boatmen yelled and stabbed and paddled around the mano in a way that told me they had done this before. It reminded me of watching our guards engage in mock fights.

Soon the splashing stopped, and two men knelt to reach into the water. They hoisted a gray-skinned fish into the air. *That is smaller than the one Regin and I saw.* Cheers went up from the boats and the people around me.

I turned to find a crowd had formed to watch.

My stomach grumbled again. "Mai'a?" I asked my guide.

She smiled. "Helemai."

While we shared mai'a and i'o nui and drank wainui, Mikilana explained the mano would be cooked for a celebration tonight.

I wondered what an Ainan celebration would be like but didn't ask for details. "I'd like to see Regin now."

"Hele."

I took some i'o nui and a mai'a for him.

Chapter 46

Several paces away from the herbalist's hut, I caught a whiff of something smelling like spoiled milk but worse. Kimo and Kapahu were smearing a foul-smelling paste on Regin's arms. His clenched jaw and wet cheeks told me it wasn't pleasant.

From what I could see, the cuts weren't healing well.

"Aloha, Kimo...Kapahu," I said, letting them know I was there.

They greeted me but kept working.

"Morning...sister," Regin hissed, keeping his eyes closed tightly.

"Noni?" I asked, as they continued his treatment.

"Ae," Kimo said, without looking at me.

"I brought you something to eat, Regin. A mai'a and some i'o nui," I said.

"What?" he asked.

"You'll see," I said.

"Better than soup?" he asked.

"I liked the soup," I said, "but I think you'll like this more. It's sweet."

"Good," he said.

"Oh, the boatmen killed a ma—monster this morning," I said.

"Is that what all the yelling was about earlier?" he asked.

"Ae," I said.

Kimo seemed to finish applying the treatment and said something about lau to Kapahu.

"Ae," she replied, before retrieving a stack of noni leaves from a small table against the far wall of the hut.

Regin shivered. "That stuff burns."

"And stinks," I said, waving my hand in front of my nose. *Wonder why I didn't smell it before.*

"I don't notice it anymore," Regin said.

"Maybe the poison affected your nose," I said. "Should I tell the herbalist to treat it...just in case?"

Regin looked sideways at me again. "Don't you dare."

"As soon as they finish, I'll help you up so you can eat," I said, smiling at his protest.

Kimo and Kapahu had my brother's wounds covered quickly.

The herbalist looked at me and gestured toward Regin.

"Thank you," I said.

Kimo smiled and said something I didn't understand.

I smirked and shrugged. "A'ole... Sorry."

He looked at me with a strange expression. Kapahu tapped his arm and said something. The herbalist nodded and they left the hut.

Once Regin was steady, leaning against the wall, I fed him a piece of i'o nui. He chewed it a long time before swallowing. "Not bad. Tastes like the water they keep giving me to drink but stronger."

"Comes from the same tree," I said, giving him another piece.

"I've been drinking tree water?" he asked, grimacing.

I shook my head and explained how to get wainui.

"It comes in its own container?" he asked.

"I guess you could say that, yes. But you'd need a woodsyth to open it."

"Couldn't a stonesyth crush it with something?"

I nodded. "But you risk losing the wainui if it shatters."

"Good point," he said. "Guess woodsyths are useful."

I held up the yellow fruit and shook it at him. "Keep that up, and you won't get the mai'a I brought. I think it tastes better than the i'o nui."

"What is it?"

"Nothing like anything we have at home," I said. "Watch."

He furrowed his brow as I peeled the yellow skin off.

"Never seen anything like that," he said. "And it tastes good?"

I handed it to him. "Try it for yourself."

His eyes lit up as his teeth sank through the flesh. "That is really good," he said, after swallowing.

"Told you it was better than the i'o nui."

"Tell the truth. You saw them kill the monster?" he asked, before taking another bite.

I shook my head. "This one was smaller, but it was the same kind of fish."

"That was no fish," he said.

"I saw them lift it out of the water. It's a fish."

"And they killed it with those wooden spears?" he asked.

I told him exactly what I witnessed from the beach.

"When are they going out to get the big one?" he asked.

"They don't go beyond the ko'a'ke'a," I said.

"Why?" he asked.

"Because of the monster," I said. "At least that's what Mikilana told me." I snapped my fingers. "Oh, and they have watersyths."

"What do you mean, watersyths?" he asked.

I told him about how they caught the opae.

"You just didn't see the basket the other person was using or something," he said. His arms shifted, like he was going to cross them, but he kept them at his sides. "No one can syth water."

"I'm telling you I watched it happen. As soon as you're well enough to get out of here, you can see for yourself."

"Doesn't matter. None of this matters," he said, sounding frustrated or angry. "We're leaving as soon as I can."

"I don't have my boat," I said, crossing my arms. "And I don't know if I can fix it, even if the Ainans let me have it back. I don't even know where our clothes are."

"Then quit wasting time with the old woman, find our stuff, and work on getting us home," he said.

"I'm not wasting time with Mikilana," I argued. "I'm learning everything I can to figure out how to get our belongings back and how to convince them to let me fix my boat *if* I can. I haven't tried to syth any of the wood around here, and I doubt they'll give us one of their boats."

"Sorry," he said, closing his eyes. "It's just..." He paused. "I constantly hurt. The stuff they're putting in my wounds, on my skin, burns. I feel as weak as a newborn. I'm not sure my legs will support me if I try to stand. I keep thinking Abi could fix all of this."

"She's never dealt with this kind of poison, Regin. These people have. Let them do what they know works. Eat and drink what they give you. Rest, and your strength will come back. Let *me* work on how we get home. I'll have something ready when you are well enough to make the trip." *Assuming I can figure out where home is from here.*

He nodded. "Sorry, Meyla. You're right...as usual."

"It's not about who's right and who's wrong," I said. "It's about doing what we have to do for each other to get through this. If I were in your place, I'd tell you to get to know these people. Learn everything you can so they will help us."

He nodded. "I know."

"Rest. I'll come to see you later. Mikilana says there will be a celebration tonight for killing the monster. Wish you could be there."

"Me too," he said. "Help me lay back down."

Once he was on his back, I left the hut and fought back tears. *Why did he have to get hurt? We were just stupid children—we probably deserve getting stuck here for being so foolish. Do Mother and Father know we're gone? Has word reached them in Varia? Surely Roi sent a messenger on the fastest horse. How long have we been gone anyway?*

"Wai kamali," someone said, bringing me out of my gloomy thoughts.

Chapter 47

"Kiek Keoni," I said, when I saw him. "Aloha." I bowed.

"Aloha," he said, and smiled. "Helemai. Mano."

Another one? "Mano?" I asked, pointing toward the beach.

"A'ole. Laila," he replied, pointing to the far side of the village. "Helemai."

I understand some of that. "Ae."

I felt his eyes on me the entire way. He said some things I didn't understand, but I tried to be polite. Once we reached the far side of the village, he stopped and gestured to an unexpected scene.

The small monster hung, head down, over a pit. Even though I knew it was dead, the black eyes looked just as terrifying as the ones on the huge one Regin and I encountered not long ago.

Three wooden poles sythed together at the top made a sort of frame to keep the kill off the ground. It had been stripped of skin. Stone scraping tools lay on the ground nearby, covered in blood. The beast's belly had been split. Ahine Ane was cleaning the guts out. Ali Ha'upu had most of the monster's jaw removed, cutting it out with a stone knife.

Do they not have metal tools?

I gasped when he pulled it free. "So many teeth," I muttered.

Men and women stepped forward as their king backed away, prize in hand. "Mano ma'kee!" he shouted, raising the jaws above his head.

Blood dripped onto Ha'upu's head as his people cheered.

"Mano ma'kee!" Keoni shouted, raising his fists. People around us joined in.

He turned to look at me, a predator's smile on his face.

"Mano ma'kee!" I yelled, having no idea what 'ma'kee' meant.

"Koko!" Keoni shouted, beckoning his father. "Koko!"

I stepped back as the king approached with the monster's mouth, unsure of what Keoni said, and shifted my weight, getting ready to run.

"Wai kamali, Meyla," Keoni said, scooping some of the creature's blood from the ragged meat clinging to the edge of the mouth in his father's hands.

Before I could say or do anything, he smeared his bloody fingers across the scars on my cheek.

"A'ole!" I screamed, shoving Keoni. "A'ole! Get away from me!"

The crowd went silent.

Ha'upu dropped the jaw and reached for me.

I ran.

Somehow, I reached Mikilana's hut without anyone catching me.

"Help!" I cried, hurrying inside.

Sitting at the table, weaving something, she looked at me and her jaw dropped. "Koko...blood. Are...you...hurt?"

"A'ole," I replied, before explaining what had happened.

Ha'upu arrived, with his wife and son close behind. The king called my name from the door.

"A'ole," I said, backing away.

"Noho...sit," Mikilana said, getting up with a frown on her face. She shuffled to the door and blocked me from seeing outside.

The discussion between her, the king, and Keoni sounded heated. I heard my name a couple of times but didn't know what they were saying. Eventually, Mikilana raised her arm and firmly said, "Hele. Hele."

She stood a while longer before closing the door and returning to the table. In slow Satran, she explained that I would not go to the celebration this evening and would stay in her hut until she told me it was safe to leave.

"I don't care about tonight, but what if I don't agree to stay in here?" I asked.

"Ka hoopai ana," she said. "Kiek Keoni...honor...fight."

I might best him, but what if I don't...or what if I do? "What about Regin?"

Mikilana brought her right hand to her left shoulder. "Me."

"You will check on him for me?"

"Ae."

"And you will bring me food?"

"Ae."

I looked at the door and sighed. *Sit here for who knows how long or fight, and then even if I win, I might lose. And what happens to Regin if I fight? Meyla...you are a princess; people depend on you. Do what is right for them instead of what you want.* "I will stay."

"Loa," Mikilana said. "Lesson."

I furrowed my brow. "What do you mean?"

"Time...to...learn...more," she said.

"Oh."

Although it was difficult for both of us, Mikilana did her best to explain what had happened. She spoke Satran slowly, and I learned Ainan no faster.

Eventually, I learned that anytime one of the monsters from beyond the ko'a'ke'a was killed, it was a cause for celebration. Part of the festivities included marking people with koko—blood—from the fish. Usually, it was done to younger members of the village as a rite of passage, another step toward adulthood. She guessed the prince marked me as a form of welcome, a symbol showing I belonged.

I argued that a ceremony I didn't, couldn't, understand was meaningless and he should have waited, or at least asked permission before touching me. I couldn't tell if Mikilana understood what I meant, but she listened, and we talked until she left to join the celebration.

For the first time since the storm, I missed my journal.

Chapter 48

I passed the time by opening a hole in the roof, watching the sky turn dark, and studying the unfamiliar patterns in the stars.

When Mikilana returned, well after moonrise, she brought i'o mano.

The flaky, white meat didn't taste like any kind of fish I'd had before. The flavor made me wonder if the monster was actually a fish. By the time I finished, I'd decided it didn't matter. I would gladly eat i'o mano again.

"Moe," Mikilana said, after I'd eaten.

I nodded, undressed, and went to bed.

The next morning started a routine that lasted for nearly a moon. Mikilana would wake me, escort me to the bathing pond and back, remind me to stay, bring food, check on Regin, report on how he was doing, then begin my lessons. The learning only stopped for meals or to sleep.

Once I accepted my imprisonment, I appreciated the time with my elderly teacher. The only concern I had was that Regin, still bedridden, did not seem to be healing. More than anything, I wanted to see him.

After I finished breakfast one morning, I turned to Mikilana and asked her what I would learn today.

"Wait," she said.

"For what?"

She closed her eyes. "King Ha'upu."

My heart raced. "Why is he coming?"

"To free you so you can see your brother."

"Is he better?" I asked, my heart pounding harder.

"No, and he's asking for you."

"Then take me there now," I demanded.

"No. You must wait."

"If my brother needs me, King Ha'upu can go to the fire," I said, getting up.

She grabbed my arm in a grip tighter than anyone her age should have been able to. "If you want to see Regin, you will wait for King Ha'upu to arrive."

"And if I don't wait?" I asked, hands on my hips.

"You will be forced to leave the village and live on your own, away from the people and the water. It's a slow, miserable death."

And doesn't get me any closer to going home. "Fine," I said, returning to my seat, "I'll wait."

It seemed to take forever before someone opened the door. King Ha'upu called my name and ordered me to come outside.

At first, I wanted to argue. I wanted to yell back that he had no authority over the Princess of Croy. As I stood, my mother's voice whispered in my ear, "Mind your manners. You are a guest in this nation."

With a nod, I brought my right hand to my left shoulder and dipped my chin as I exited the hut. I heard Mikilana's footsteps in the sand behind me.

Since I had seen him last, the king had added two of the mano teeth to his headband, one on either side of the large tooth in the middle. Ahine Ane stood on his right, and Kiek Keoni was on his left. His son's eyes were cast down. Ha'upu pointed to the sand a few paces in from of him and said, "Kneel."

Again, I wanted to defy him, to stare him in the eyes, and show him I was not someone to be ordered around. *Regin needs me.* My manners asserted themselves, once more. Dropping my arm to my side, I did as I was told and fixed my gaze on the sand between us.

I flinched when he called his son's name and ordered him to kneel also.

What is happening?

"Recently, there was a misunderstanding. I had to speak with many people and spend time among the trees and the water to pick out the truth from everything I was told. I have reached a decision and have called the involved parties here this morning to make right what was wrong."

Get this over with so I can see my brother.

"The killing of a mano is uncommon. A reason for ceremony and celebration. Kiek Keoni let blood madness cloud his judgment. In an attempt to honor one of our guests and make her feel more like one of our people, he upset her. Water Princess Meyla struck my son and fled. I understand she was afraid—both of my son and of what would happen because of her actions."

Tell me what I have to do.

"Princess Meyla of Croy, stand."

I hurried to my feet without looking at the king. My knees trembled as I put my arm across my chest and rested my hand on my shoulder.

"Keoni, speak," the king ordered.

I will not accept judgment from him.

I looked at the boy. His lip quivered when his eyes met mine. He took a deep breath and moved to stand.

"Kneel," Ha'upu barked. "Speak."

What is happening? I fought back a gasp.

"Water Princess Meyla, I intended no harm. Struck by the blood and your beauty, I wanted nothing more than to honor you and make you feel more like one of us. I am sorry for my actions. Please accept my words and forgive my actions." Head bowed, he extended his right hand toward me, palm up.

I looked back at Mikilana.

She nodded and placed her left hand on top of her right, then pointed toward the prince.

This better help me somehow. I took measured steps toward Keoni. His hand swayed as his arm quivered. I placed my hand over his, and his shoulders sagged.

"Thank you, Water Princess," he whispered.

"May we speak of this no more and live together in peace," Ha'upu said.

"Meyla," Ane said.

When I turned to face the queen, she beckoned me to her.

I cocked my head, then walked toward her.

She brought her right hand to her left shoulder then offered it to me, palm up. "I am sorry for my son's actions."

I put my hand on hers. "And I am sorry for mine."

She nodded. "No harm."

"No harm," I echoed.

"You are free to move about as you want," Ane said.

"I'm going to see my brother. I hear he is not doing well," I said.

"Kimo has worked hard to help. He and Kapahu have tried every treatment known to cure the poison. I understand nothing has worked well," Ane said. "May that change before it is too late."

"Thank you, your Majesty. Their efforts are greatly appreciated," I said, turning to run to my brother's bedside before anyone could say or do something to delay me further.

Chapter 49

"Welcome," Kapahu said, when I got close to the herbalist's hut. "Happy to see you."

"Thank you. I'm glad to be able to come. Is Regin awake?"

She frowned. "He was, but he is weak."

"So, I understand," I said. "I'll see if I can do anything to help."

She nodded. "May you be successful where we haven't been."

"Thank you for all you have done," I said. "I know it hasn't been easy."

"I fear the worst is yet to come," she said, frowning again.

What does that mean?

Regin looked worse than the last time I saw him, pale and breathing shallow. I took his hand and squeezed it. "Brother, I'm here." It felt strange to speak Croian after speaking nothing but Ainan for so long.

"Meyla," he said. "What happened? Where have you been?"

I told him about the incident, my imprisonment, and the apology.

"So much for diplomacy," he said.

"He attacked me. There was no time to talk."

He wheezed. "Doesn't matter. I must confess something to you before it's too late."

"What do you mean?"

"I'm not getting better," he said, raising his hand. His arm shook with the effort.

"But you will," I said, taking his hand in mine. "And we'll figure out how to get home."

"You can't go home," he said.

"What do you mean?" I asked, rubbing my thumb on the back of his hand. "We can't stay here."

He closed his eyes. "You were supposed to die on the way to Satra."

"What?" *Surely, I misheard him, or he's confused.* "We fled to Satra to save ourselves."

"Listen to me," Regin said. "You were going to teach me how to use your boat on the way to Satra."

"Right. We discussed that before the storm."

"I was supposed to kill you when Satra was in sight and throw your body over the side. Once I reached the land, I would tell the story of an accident where you fell out of the boat, and I couldn't save you."

I flung his hand away. "Why would you kill me? It was *your* plan to save me."

"It was supposed to be Runa, but she couldn't control herself and messed up. Her mistake put my future at risk. She had to pay for it," he said, then wheezed again.

"You mean you killed her...and her mother...and the others?"

"No. The people I was working with took care of them," he said. "I had to find a way to clean up her mess."

"What people?" I demanded, shaking.

"No one you know. An alliance of those unhappy with the way Father handled Satra. Your death was the first step toward correcting his misjudgment."

"I don't believe you," I said, tears welling in my eyes. "The poison is affecting your mind."

"No, sister. My mind is the only thing that is sound. Listen to me. Stay here. You will die if you go home. Depending on how long we've been gone, there may already be a new king. That storm cost me my rightful chance to rule."

I slapped him across the face. "You sent our parents to Varia to be killed? Who do I take my revenge on? Give me names."

"From what I know, the alliance had nothing to do with their sudden departure," Regin said. "I truly have no idea what prompted their trip or what the expected outcome was. Regardless, it made my job easier."

"I want names," I demanded.

He shook his head. "This was never about you, Meyla, but we knew you wouldn't do what was necessary. Please believe me. It's my dying wish for you to stay here and live."

"Names," I growled.

"It's no one you know," he said, "and no one you would ever be able to find."

"But you say there may be a new king. I'll start with him," I said.

"You'll never reach him."

"If my parents are dead, I will visit their vengeance on him to take my rightful place, and he *will* talk before he breathes his last breath. Who is it?"

"They are shadows fading in sunlight…mists blown away by a breeze. Any name I give you will be meaningless. Honor me by staying here."

"Honor you?" I screamed. "You plotted to kill me! Your treachery may cost our parents their lives. You have no honor, and I have no brother *to* honor!"

Leaving the hut, I almost knocked Kimo down in my haste. Running aimlessly through the village, tears blurred my vision to the point I was a danger to myself and everyone in my path.

Chapter 50

Following the sound of waves crashing over the ko'a'ke'a, I reached the beach and kept walking. When the water reached my stomach, I dove in and swam a short distance before turning over and floating on my back.

Eyes closed, surrounded by water, I did my best to just breathe and ignore everything else around me. *He was going to kill me. Regin. My own brother...my twin. And our mother and father—my mother and father—may already be dead with someone else ruling Croy now. Do I heed Regin's warning and stay? But that's the coward's way out. Following a coward is what led me here.*

My heart pounded. Blood roared in my ears. Anger burned through every part of my body.

Trying to keep myself under control, I focused on breathing and the calming water holding me away from everything else.

Doing everything I could to push my fury out, to clear my mind, I felt something move just beyond my fingertips. *A fish?* I looked where the sensation came from, but nothing was there. *My imagination.* Continuing to relax and clear my thoughts, the sensation of movement returned, this time close to my knee.

Instead of looking, I pushed out with my talent only to find my will was already around me. With little more than a thought, I grabbed the small fish swimming near the ko'a'ke'a and pulled it toward me before letting it go. *I can syth water?*

Testing to see if this was really happening, I pulled my energy back into myself and focused it toward the shore.

Immediately, I knew where everyone stood and could feel opae flitting about before one of the Ainans fixed a pool of water around them and lifted it above the surface. *How am I doing his? What does this mean? Have I always been able to syth water but didn't know it?*

This discovery distracted me from my problems as I played with my new ability. Unlike wood, anything I tried to form in water would dissipate as soon as I stopped focusing on it. *Do firesyths have the same problem with their talent? I guess it doesn't matter, nor does it solve my immediate problem. And I can't float out here forever.*

Slowly swimming back to the beach, Regin's confession dominated my thoughts. The only way to be certain he had told the truth would be to return home—a trip I wasn't sure I could make. If he was truthful, I'd be risking my life traveling to put myself in more danger. If it was another lie and I chose to stay, I'd be safe but live on not knowing what, if anything, had happened to my parents and my homeland.

Mikilana met me on the shore. "I believe we need to talk."

"We do," I said, nodding. "About a few things."

"I have mai'a and wainui waiting at home," she said, offering her hand.

"Good," I said. Playing with my newly discovered talent had left me more than a little hungry. Taking her hand reminded me of what it was like walking with my mother, before we grew apart.

"First," I said, peeling a mai'a, "there's Regin." I broke down again, telling her what my brother had said.

She sighed heavily and took a long drink from her cup. "Help us prepare for your brother's death. No matter what."

"Why?"

"None of us know your customs. You are the only one here who can honor your brother when he dies," she said.

"He is a coward," I said, tapping my finger on the table with each word. "He planned to kill me, his twin sister and conspired against his own blood *and* his nation for personal gain. He has no honor. If I never see him again, I will not regret it."

"Passion brings those words easily now. Believe me, you will feel his loss after he's gone."

"What makes you say such a thing? Did you not hear me? My own brother intended to *kill* me."

"But that will not be the only memory you have of him. One day, your mind will call up good times, and you will miss him. I know of what I speak," Mikilana said, a sad look in her eyes.

"I will think about it," I said. "Do you know any watersyth teachers?"

She gave me a questioning look. "Many but why would you ask? You are a woodsyth."

"I am more than that," I said, and explained what I'd discovered while soaking. "I've always felt at peace in and around water. Maybe this is why. There are no watersyths in Croy...at least no one who knows they are. Even if I am the only one, an untrained talent is dangerous."

"Workers of wood and water are not unheard of in Aina. I will speak with Ha'upu. He can arrange a guide for you."

I nodded. "Knowing I have this gift should make me happy, but with Regin's words about the fate of my family and my people...it seems meaningless. Do I go back and risk my life, or stay here and live the life of a coward?"

"Your brother and I would be the only two who would know," Mikilana said.

"*I* would know," I said.

"Here, you are safe, no matter what." She looked around. "This could be your home."

"Home isn't just being safe. I have obligations, responsibilities... My people expect me to lead them after my parents are gone. If I stay, I fear that burden will be more than I could bear."

"Then I will speak with Ha'upu about what he can do to help you return home. Do not expect a swift answer, and do not expect his help to come without cost should he agree to aid your return."

"The least he can do is agree to not interfere. Any assistance beyond that...I will gladly pay the cost," I said.

"I will make sure he understands," Mikilana said, getting up from the table. "Stay here and prepare yourself to speak with our king. I'm sure he will have questions."

Chapter 51

Being left alone was not what I needed. Instead of focusing my thoughts on meeting with King Ha'upu, I considered my options in dealing with Regin. *Is it better to let him suffer or be merciful? Which choice shows I'm a better person and a stronger leader?*

I had little doubt that my father would choose to end his suffering. King Fitzeirick had a reputation for fairness, compassion, and mercy. My mother, on the other hand, tended to revel in the suffering of others when it suited her goals. She would never admit such a thing to me, but I'd heard stories of her time working for King Ander of Varia.

She was paid well to gather information and solve problems for the crown, regardless of what it took. Varian soldiers spoke of my father with respect, but they feared my mother. Perhaps I could combine the best of both parents.

If I kill Regin...how? I would have to study the plants here to find an effective poison. That will take time I do not have. "His axes," I said out loud. I could not resist the irony of ending my brother's life with his beloved blades.

If I could decide on nothing else, I settled on how my brother would die. I didn't see how Ha'upu could refuse a request to return my belongings. It cost him nothing but the time to tell me where they were. *Unless he fears me being armed.* "We shall see," I said. "And if he refuses, he will see what I am capable of."

Unsure of how long I would have to wait before someone brought me before Ha'upu, I let my thoughts drift to repairing my boat. *I'll have to learn more about the trees here and what might work best.* The wooden table rippled under my hand, its familiar energy comforting. *I could never ask Mikilana to give me her keepsakes. They carry too many memories of her family.* Ohe boats work well in calm water. In the rough seas beyond the ko'a'ke'a, I doubted their ability to get me home.

The door opened, interrupting my thoughts, and Mikilana asked me to come with her.

We walked together to the large hall. The roof was open, bathing the room in sunlight. King Ha'upu sat on his chair with people I didn't recognize seated on either side of him—a man to his right and a woman to his left. Two chairs facing them sat several paces away.

Ha'upu invited us in and gestured toward the empty seats.

"I understand you think you have the skill to work water," Ha'upu said, looking at me.

"To my own surprise, your Highness, yes. I have always held a love for water, more than anyone else in my family, but I never knew anyone could work water like my people and yours work wood, stone, and fire. Earlier, after a troubling conversation with my brother—"

"I understand he is not doing well," Ha'upu said, interrupting me.

"He's dying," I said.

"You have my sympathy and that of my family," he said. The man next to him brought his hand to his shoulder.

Another son? "My brother is not worthy of sympathy," I said, "but that is not what we are discussing at the moment. Taking refuge in the water, I found I could feel a fish swimming near the ko'a'ke'a even though I was no more than a few paces from where the water meets the land. At first, I thought it was my imagination playing tricks to distract me from troubled thoughts. Then, I tried to find other things around me and could easily find opae and the people harvesting them. I could catch a fish and release it with no more effort than bending a tree branch."

"Lika," the king said.

The woman next to him stood.

"She will test your ability," Ha'upu said.

"Thank you," I said, bringing my hand to my shoulder. "I look forward to working with you, m'lady."

"I suspect it will prove interesting, Water Princess," she replied, returning my salute before sitting.

"Mikilana also tells me you want to leave our lands and return to your home," Ha'upu said.

"Yes, your Highness. I believe I must find my way home."

"We do not send people beyond the ko'a'ke'a," he said.

"I understand. The water beyond your barrier carries many dangers. My brother and I didn't expect to find Ania when we set out. A powerful storm blew us far from our intended path and to your shore."

"By your own words, you understand why I hesitate to assist you with such a journey," he said. "Though your presence here has brought problems, you seem to be an honorable and pleasant person. Knowing I contributed to putting your life in danger would trouble me deeply."

I bowed to him. "Your Highness, I do not wish to trouble you. Although any help I receive would be greatly appreciated, all I ask is you return everything that belongs to me and do not forbid my leaving."

He raised his eyebrows. "Ka'imi, my brother and one of our master boatmen, has examined the strange vessel you arrived in, and he wishes to help you."

The man to Ha'upu's right stood. "Working with you would help me improve our boats and provide safe access to more of the water, benefiting our people."

"As far as your belongings," Ha'upu said, "it is my understanding that most of them rotted and are unusable. What is left will be brought to Mikilana's hut while Lika tests you."

"Thank you, Ka'imi," I said, then saluted the king. "Thank you, your Majesty. I do have one more problem to discuss with you, should you have time."

"We are here," he said, smiling.

I stood. "From my own brother's lips, I learned he is a coward who conspired with enemies of my family to harm them for his own gain. He intended to kill me with his own hands on our journey. By his confession, my mother and father are in danger...if not already dead. This is what drives me to leave your lands."

"This is troubling," Ha'upu said, frowning. "However, I do not see what I can do about it."

"I ask for permission to end his life without consequence from your laws and customs. I am a danger to no one else."

"What you ask is...difficult. To kill another on purpose is the worst of our crimes. Such an act, traditionally, carries the penalty of banishment to the badlands—a slow, harsh, and lonely death. I must think on your situation and consult the trees and the water before reaching a decision."

"I understand my request is troubling and puts you in a difficult position, King Ha'upu. This is not something I ask for lightly...but I believe it is necessary."

He nodded as I spoke. "You will have my answer soon. Until then, let Lika and Ka'imi guide you."

"If you will not allow it for my own justice, would you consider it a mercy to end Regin's suffering?"

"I will take that into consideration, but you will wait for my answer," he said.

"Thank you, your Highness," I said, before bowing. "May wisdom guide your thoughts. I look forward to your answer and will honor your decision."

"Go," he said, "and may your way be clear."

"Come with me," Lika said. "I will test you before Ka'imi takes up the rest of your day."

I nodded. "Lead the way, m'lady."

Chapter 52

We walked to a part of the village I had never visited. Three huts stood around a small well. "Wait for me there," Lika said, pointing toward the well. "I won't be long."

Eager to be tested and possibly trained, excitement raised goosebumps on my skin. *My roan is a faint memory, mostly of Mother being upset. This feels much more real.* Looking into the well, I noticed the water's surface was easily within arm's reach. *I wonder if it's fresh or salty. Does it matter?*

Lika emerged from her hut with a nui bowl. She reached into the well with her empty hand and lifted enough to fill the bowl. "Dip one finger in and tell me what you feel."

I closed my eyes and tried to remember what I had done before to feel the fish moving. At first, the only thing I noticed was the cool water around my finger. Slowing my breathing, I pushed my talent out and found a small amount of energy drifting through the bowl.

"Good," she said. "Can you move the water while holding your finger still?"

How can she tell what I felt?

Doing the same thing I had done to grab the fish, the water shifted and hardened around my finger.

"Not what I asked," she said. "Try again. Move the water."

It took much more effort than binding the water, but I managed to shift some of it across the bowl.

"Interesting," she commented. "You've shown you can harden some water... How about all of it? Try to lift out what's in the bowl without spilling any."

My wrist twisted uncomfortably to get my palm under the surface. Pushing out more of my talent than I normally used to syth wood, the water grabbed my hand, and I lifted.

"Look," Lika said.

I opened my eyes to see my hand encased in water. A few small drops fell from the bottom, splatting in the bowl, but most of the liquid stayed in place.

"What can you tell me about it?" she asked.

"What do you mean?" I asked, breaking my concentration. The water dropped from my hand, splashing into the bowl.

"Is it safe to drink or tainted? Is it water or something else?"

I shook my head. "I don't know."

"As a wood worker, you can use your talent to discover those things about wood and plants, yes?"

"And more, of course," I said.

"Most water workers can do the same with liquids."

"What if *I* can't?" I asked.

"Then all I can do is advise you to practice what little you can do," she said, shrugging. "There is little else for me to teach you otherwise."

"Is this not something I can learn?" I asked.

She shook her head. "We are talking about a natural talent, not a skill. If you are sensitive to what makes up the water, you can strengthen that ability with practice. If you do not have it at all...there is nothing to improve."

"I see. So, what can I do with my new ability?" I asked, crossing my arms.

Lika pressed her lips together for a moment. "Water working may enhance your wood-working abilities. Moving the moisture inside a plant while working it directly could give some impressive results. You can push water off things, drying them quickly. You can sense movement in the water at a fair distance going by what you told me. You can trap things, holding them in place. Given how easily you bound the water around your hand, I suspect you can focus well enough to walk on water...but only with quite a bit of practice."

"Walk on water?" I asked, wondering if I heard her correctly.

She nodded. "With practice—lots of practice. You'll spend more time wet than dry, should you decide it's worth the effort."

"Just hearing it's possible..." I breathed, still not sure I believed her.

"I can't do it," she said, "but I have known a few who could. Do you have any more questions?"

"Yes, lots, but..." I scratched my head. "This is all so new."

Lika smiled. "I understand. Find me after you have gathered your thoughts. Until then, see if you can challenge Ka'imi. I believe he thinks too highly of himself."

"Good to know," I said. "Thank you for your time, and I will take you up on the offer to answer my questions once my head is clear."

"I look forward to it," she said, nodding.

"Any idea where I might find the king's brother?"

"Ka'imi will be waiting for you near the shore, probably with a boat ready," she said, nodding toward the beach.

I brought my hand to my shoulder, then turned to find my next test.

Chapter 53

As Lika predicted, Ka'imi had a boat at the water's edge and waved me over when he saw me.

At a glance, it was made from ohe sythed together into a long, narrow, shallow, craft. If not for a couple of ohe poles stretching to either side with bundles of ohe sythed to them, running parallel to the boat, it wouldn't have been stable enough to use.

The craft was fast and maneuverable, but I doubted its ability to survive rough water as well as my boat did. Ohe, being more like rigid grass, was stiff and brittle compared to the way most wood flexed along its grain.

"Come. Paddle with me and show me what you know about boats," Ka'imi said.

"These"—I pointed at his craft—"I've never been in before. My boat, I know almost as well as I know myself. They are not the same, I can tell you that. Your boat is made for the calmer waters here; mine was more rugged."

He nodded as I spoke. "Then let me teach you about this one, and together, we may be able to improve both."

I smiled. "Let's see how this goes."

He held the boat for me. "Sit near the front."

Short, shaky steps brought me to a narrow seat about two paces from the front of the boat. The stabilizing pieces slapped the water in time with my movement.

Ka'imi boarded with almost no movement and shoved us off the beach with ease. "Know how to use a paddle?"

"I've pulled oars," I said. "What's the difference?"

"I don't know what an oar is," he said, "but this"—he held what looked like a short oar out toward me—"is a paddle. Take the one near you and use it twice on the right side, then twice on the left."

Without the long handle of the oar, the paddle was harder to move through the water, but each stroke came quicker and I settled into a rhythm. Splashes behind me let me know my teacher was matching my movement, and we were soon speeding toward the ko'a'ke'a. The wind in my hair reminded me of sailing across the lake in Varia. *That feels like such a long time ago.*

"Turn right!" Ka'imi yelled.

"How?" I screamed back.

"Paddle hard on the left and lean to the right until we turn," he instructed.

Heart racing and arms burning, I did as I was told. The boat slowed when the right stabilizing part hit the water, but we turned tightly, as if I had changed direction while jogging.

"Now straight!" Ka'imi yelled.

Shifting my weight back to the middle, I returned to my rhythm of two right, then two left, and we were soon back up to speed.

"Right again!"

Again, even though my arms burned worse now, we changed direction quicker than I would have thought possible.

"Stop!" he ordered.

"How?"

"Drag your paddle in the water."

The force threatened to yank the paddle out of my hands. I gripped the handle, turning my knuckles white, and willed the boat to stop.

We sat parallel to the shore. Gentle waves rocked the boat and lightly kissed the stabilizers as they passed.

"Stand," he said.

"In this narrow thing? I'll fall out."

He laughed. "Brace your feet against the sides. Move with the boat."

I cheated. Sything the ohe around my feet, I stood up straight.

"Now, take a spear and let's catch some lunch," Ka'imi said. I didn't look at him, but I heard a smile in his voice.

With my feet locked in place, I couldn't easily turn to find the fishing spear. The boat rocked wildly with my movement, smashing the stabilizers into the water.

"That's what I thought," he said, still sitting. "Release your feet and trust your balance."

Freeing my feet, I kept my talent pushed into the wood so I could feel every little movement and did my best to copy it while reaching for the nearest three-pronged spear. "I'm more of an archer," I said. "If you're depending on my skills with this for a meal, we might go hungry."

He chuckled. "Urgency is a great motivator. This is the first lesson in boat fishing, taught to everyone who wants to gather out here. Watch the water. When a fish gets close, strike where you think it is."

"Where I think... What do you mean? I can see all the way to the bottom. Any fish within my reach should be a good target."

"I have a feeling you won't believe it until you experience it," Ka'imi said.

He's trying to trick me...somehow. A light-blue fish about the length of my forearm swam to the left of where I stood. Tensing my muscles for a strike, I watched its movements and plunged the spear into the water when my target paused.

The fish darted away.

"Had to be close," I muttered. "I'll get the next one."

Two more fish approached, both about the same size and color as the first, but I had the same result. Splashes of water and an empty spear. "How am I missing?" I asked, unable to hide my confusion.

Ka'imi laughed. "Now you are ready to listen. Push about half the spear into the water, straight down, and watch what happens."

I did as he said and noticed the spear bent at an odd angle as it went below the surface. Pushing my talent into it, to force it back straight, I found it wasn't bent at all. "What? How?"

"Things below the water are not where they seem," he said. "You must be mindful of this before you strike. Whenever you are ready, try again. Oh, and hurry—I'm getting hungry."

"Don't say I didn't warn you," I replied. It was tempting to stick my tongue out at him, but I didn't because I wasn't sure how the king's brother would take such a thing. I got two of the next five fish that came within striking distance.

"Better," he said. "At least *I* won't starve."

Frustrated, I dropped the spear into the boat, sat, put my hands over the side, and pushed my will into the water. It didn't take long to find some of the larger fish that had darted away from my spearing attempts. Shoving my talent into the water, beads of sweat trickled down my face as I hardened the water around them. Spots floated at the edge of my vision when I pulled my prey to me and lifted a pool of water into the boat. My head swam before the world went black as the fish flopped near my seat.

Chapter 54

The crackle of a nearby fire woke me. I tried to sit up, but someone put their hand on my shoulder. "Lie still," Mikilana said. "Rest."

"What happened?" I asked, groggy.

The smell of cooking fish hung in the air.

"You pulled three fish from the water then dropped like a nui," Ka'imi said, from somewhere outside my sight. I could hear a smile in his voice. "As impressive as it was, I would guess you pushed your new talent too hard, Water Princess. There is a reason most water workers stay close to the shore."

"Lika didn't mention it," I said, sliding Mikilana's hand off me. My head pounded when I sat up. A groan came out of my mouth all by itself.

"Here. Drink," Mikilana said, handing me an ohe cup.

The sweet wainui helped me feel a bit better.

"Hungry?" Ka'imi asked.

I turned to find him holding a nui bowl filled with white meat. As I took it from him, someone yelled my name from toward the village. I turned to see Kapahu running toward the beach.

"Over here!" I yelled back, then flinched at the loud sound coming out of my mouth. It was enough to get her attention.

She nodded and ran faster. Stopping a few paces from me, she brought her hand to her shoulder. "Meyla, are you feeling well?"

"Pushed myself too hard," I said. "I'll be fine. Why are you looking for me?"

Her expression darkened. A frown twisted her lips, and she looked down. "Your brother...he's..." Her hand went to her mouth, muting her last words.

Jumping to my feet, I staggered, still a bit light-headed.

"Oh, no," Mikilana said, taking the bowl from me.

"He's what?" I demanded.

"He's passed on," the herbalist's apprentice said.

My legs, already unsteady, failed me. I would have collapsed to the sand except Ka'imi caught me and lowered me gently to the ground.

Everything went numb. Blood roared in my ears, pumped by heavy thuds in my chest. *My brother. My closest friend and life-long companion... He's gone.* "You're certain?" I asked, unsure where the question came from.

Kapahu sat next to me and took my hands in hers. "We are."

I looked at her, my eyes blinking back tears. *He doesn't deserve them.* "How? I mean...when?"

"He—" Her voice cracked, and she swallowed. "Kimo tried his best—we both did."

"I believe you," I said, squeezing her hands. *Why am I comforting her?*

She nodded, and a tear rolled down her cheek. "His breathing slowed not long ago. You should know, he tried to say something but...there wasn't enough breath to talk, and I don't know your language. Then his body tensed, shaking before he went slack. We tried...but it happened so quickly. I couldn't come for you until after. Meyla, I am so sorry." Sobs shook her body, and she fell against me.

Mikilana grabbed Kapahu's shoulders, pulled her away from me, and hugged the distraught girl.

Ka'imi helped me to my feet. "Let's go tell my brother. Preparations must be made quickly. Whatever you need to honor him, we will give. You have my word, Water Princess."

I bristled. "Honor him? I'm glad he's dead. My brother was a coward and a traitor. If not for his conspiracy, I wouldn't have left my home. My boat would not have wrecked on the ko'a'ke'a. He would not have been poisoned and would, likely, still be alive—assuming no one discovered his plot. In Croy, traitors are beheaded and put into the ground where they fell. There is no honor for them."

Ka'imi shook his head. "But he is your brother, your blood. Surely you feel—"

"Nothing," I said, cutting him off. "I feel nothing. If you insist I must have some emotion, then call it relief. I won't have to wash his blood from my hands. Though I wouldn't have regretted ending his life."

He cocked his head for a moment. "Mikilana, please help Kapahu return to the healing hut and inform Kimo he can prepare Regin's body. Meyla and I will talk with my brother about how to proceed."

"Of course," Mikilana said. "Until I see you, Meyla, be at peace."

"I'm fine," I barked, then added a softer, "thank you."

My elderly friend gave me a look I didn't recognize before I turned to walk away.

"I will go with you to speak with the king, but I will do nothing to give any semblance of honor to my brother," I said.

"I understand, but this situation is not one Ha'upu will handle lightly," Ka'imi said. "Your presence is necessary."

"And it will waste time better spent figuring out how I get home," I said.

"Which will happen when everything is ready," he said. "For now, we deal with your brother's death."

I wanted to say something but decided arguing with Ka'imi would not change anything. *Maybe Ha'upu will see reason.*

Chapter 55

Instead of leading me to the meeting hall, Ka'imi took me down a path I'd never seen before. "Where are we going?" I asked.

"My brother seeks wisdom and guidance among the trees, so we go to him."

"I have spent lots of time among many trees and not once have I gained any wisdom," I commented.

"Perhaps you just don't care to listen to them," Ka'imi said.

Or I know they are just trees. Wood and sap with nothing to say. Given his tone, I didn't give voice to my thoughts.

Passing the mai'a groves, we walked farther than I had ever gone from the village and eased our way down a gentle slope to the edge of the densest forest I had ever seen. Ropey vines, some thicker than my wrist, dangled from squat trees. Wide-leafed plants scattered about, catching sunlight wherever it pierced the roof-like canopy above.

The sight was breathtaking and terrifying at the same time. Loud, hooting howls coming from inside strengthened my fear. *At least I know where those sounds come from now...even if I don't want to meet the creature making them.*

"Is this the place where you banish criminals?" I asked.

"No. The badlands are beyond this place. The jungle serves a different purpose for us. Stay close. Some who wander away don't come back."

"I will." As we passed under a low branch, I looked around and tried to commit our path to memory.

The air cooled and carried smells of life and death. I pushed my talent out through the rough grasses around us and found much of what was under our feet was rotting tree limbs, leaves, and other dead plants. *Nothing about this land is normal.*

A loud, hooting call from somewhere ahead stopped me in my tracks. "What was that?"

"A monkey," he said. "Letting others know we're entering their place."

"The Aian aren't the only people on this land?" I asked, suddenly wishing I had a weapon with me.

He chuckled. "Monkeys aren't people—at least not like you and me. Think of a young child covered in dark fur with a tail and feet that grab as well as hands. They can move through the tree tops faster than you can run on flat ground."

"A child that isn't a person?" I asked.

"They are the size of a child, but they aren't children. Keep an eye on the high branches. When you see one, you'll understand.

"If you insist," I said, fighting the urge to leave this strange forest.

"Let's get moving. The monkeys aren't likely to attack us, but they could get upset if we linger too long."

"What would they do?" I asked, trying to keep fear from my voice.

"At first?" He shrugged. "Throw things at us. Getting hit with their waste is the worst."

These children-things throw their...eww. "Let's hurry," I said. "Where are we going?"

"A clearing not too far in. It's where the king goes to find wisdom."

Or get covered with monkey manure. "Can't wait to see it."

As much as I wanted to investigate the plants and trees around me, I kept my talent bound. *No sense wasting energy when a monkey attack could happen at any time.* More than once, I heard limbs and leaves rustle overhead, but I never saw any furry child-beasts.

Loud howls and hoots in the distance were a frequent reminder that something was out there and knew we were in here. Ka'imi didn't look concerned. I wasn't so confident.

He followed a path I could not pick out. I saw neither bare ground nor footsteps, but my guide walked with a purpose that could only mean he knew exactly where to go. He stopped at an arched passage in the thick undergrowth that couldn't be natural. "Aye! My King. Brother, are you here?"

"Aye! My brother, I am," the king replied.

"May we enter?" Ka'imi asked.

"Yes."

We stepped into a small clearing. Blindingly bright sunlight streamed in from above. Shielding my eyes with my hand, I saw a figure supported above the ground in a tangle of branches and vines. Leaves and flowers concealed King Ha'upu's body; only his face was visible.

Ka'imi dropped to one knee and lowered his gaze.

I knelt beside him but kept my eyes up, both from curiosity and to watch for threats.

"My King. My brother. I am deeply sorry for disturbing your sanctuary, but it is necessary," Ka'imi said.

"As I would expect. What is wrong?"

"Regin, brother of the Water Princess, has passed on," Ka'imi said.

The king's eyes closed for a moment. "Then I have no reason to continue my commune." The plants lowered Ha'upu gently to his feet and then peeled away in layers. Visible spots of blood were raised on his forearms and legs.

Were the plants joined to him?

"Kimo is preparing the body," Ka'imi continued.

"As I would expect. Meyla, how would you have us honor your brother's body?"

I stood and squared my shoulders. "Throw him into the sea beyond the ko'a'ke'a. Let the mano have him."

Ha'upu cocked his head and squinted. "Your brother is a prince, correct?"

"*Was* a prince, as far as I'm concerned," I said, not changing my posture.

"The death of royalty must be honored," the king said. "We do not throw even the worst of our outcasts to the dark and dangerous waters."

Ka'imi grabbed my hand, but I pulled away.

"Regin may have been the second born to the king and queen of Croy, but he deserves no honor." I crossed my arms. The plants and trees around us shook with my outburst. "Would you honor a son who killed his mother, father, and sister simply to feed a selfish lust for power?"

The monkeys had gone quiet.

Ha'upu pulled everything out of my talent's control, stilling our surroundings. "Outsiders have come to Aina twice now. When more arrive, I will not be the king who bears the shame of ignoring long-held customs and disrespecting the dead. If you do not wish your brother to be honored according to your practices, he will be honored in accordance with ours."

I brought my right hand to my left shoulder. "He is not my brother. Do with his body as you see fit. As of now, my only concern is returning to my homeland to see if I still have parents and a home."

Ka'imi got to his feet and put his hand on my shoulder. "You are welcome to stay and make a home here. You speak our language. You are a water worker along with wood. Mikilana sees you as her child. You don't have to leave."

I pushed his hand away. "I am grateful for everything your people have done for me, and for trying to save Regin, but this is not my home. This place is beautiful, but it isn't Croy. Mikilana is nice and would have been a lovely mother, but she's not *my* mother. I will not cower here, wondering if my parents are alive or dead...wondering if Regin's conspirators were successful in taking the throne. My father's throne. I couldn't live with myself if I stayed." Tears I didn't want welled in the corners of my eyes.

Ha'upu stepped toward me and offered me his hand. "You have good reason to cry. No one so young should carry such a burden. It seems offering you a home only adds to your sorrow. I'll admit, I do not understand, but I will say I am sorry. Your brother will return to nature at sunrise tomorrow. You should be there, but I will understand if you choose to stay away. Once the ceremony is complete, Ka'imi will work with you to make preparations for your leaving. No one can be sure you will make it back, but I understand you believe you must try."

After wiping my eyes, I looked into his. "I will return to my homeland, even if it means swimming the entire distance, fighting everything the dark, deep water dares send at me."

"Such determination," Ka'imi said. "You will be a great leader."

"If I live that long," I said. *Mother always said I was as stubborn as my father.*

"None of us know what the next day brings," Ha'upu said. "We must return to the village. There is much to prepare."

Ka'imi brought his hand to his shoulder. "Lead the way, my King."

Ha'upu led us on a more direct path through the jungle, plants and vines cleared the way as he walked. His connection to this place was impressive; even roots moved before his feet touched the ground. Monkey cries filled the air as we left their territory.

"Meyla, you should find Mikilana and let her know all is well with you," Ka'imi said. "Before you go, what was your brother's talent?"

"He was strong with fire and carried a touch of stone," I said. "Why?"

"The king and I have many things to do before morning." Ka'imi ignored my question. "Go, be with your friend."

I nodded and headed to my mentor's hut. *And my home...if I wanted one here.*

Chapter 56

My sword, along with Regin's axes and his silly vest, sat on the table, but I did not see Mikilana. After glancing at my belt, I decided against arming myself just to look for an elderly woman among a group of people who didn't seem to have any aggression toward others. Except, maybe, Keoni...but even then, his only misdeed was not respecting my personal space.

After asking a few people where I could find Mikilana, I was told she was at the healing hut. *The last place I want to go.*

My pace slowed as I considered returning to her hut. *What else can I do? Sit and wait for her? What a waste of time. Regin's dead. His blood is not on my hands, though it should be. I should be sad or angry or...something. Why do I only feel relief? Mother could probably tell me...*

With a heavy sigh, I turned for the healing hut but was in no hurry to get there.

A rhythmic humming filled my ears, growing louder the closer I got to Kimo's hut. Mikilana sat with a circle of women near the door, chanting. Younger Ainans carried sticks of green ohe, adding them to a pile near a group of older men sything them into something I'd never seen before.

Two men stood at the hut's entrance, looking as if they were guarding it. White-gray smoke billowed from a hole in the roof. Kimo and Kapahu's voices came from inside, mixing together in a different chant that seemed to ride on the sounds the circle of women made. It would have been an amazing experience if I wasn't so conflicted.

"What is all this?" I asked, once I reached Mikilana.

She answered by scooting to the right and patting the ground next to her. "Sit," she whispered.

"I don't want—"

"Sit," another woman—Milana I think her name was—barked.

Mikilana smiled at me and patted the ground again.

My manners took over. *Better to not cause trouble.*

I sat and listened to them chant words I didn't know. Soon, I was mimicking the sounds they made, softly at first, then louder as I grew more confident in my imitation. Not long after, emotions I'd pushed down boiled into my mind. Love. Hurt. Relief. Anger. Thankfulness. Fear. Hatred. Hope...so much hope. My body quaked as everything came out.

Mikilana pulled me to her and held me as I wailed. I was lost, but I wasn't alone. Regin was gone, and despite what he'd done to me, I would miss him. I couldn't hate him even though he took everything from me. If I let myself ignore our love, our bond, I would be no better than him. *I'd rather die.*

"Go to him," Mikilana whispered.

Without understanding why, I nodded and rose to my feet. The chants grew louder as I entered the smoke-filled building.

Regin lay on the same table, naked as the day we were born. Torches sythed to the end of ohe poles stood at the four corners and created an eerie glow.

He was visibly thinner than the last time I'd seen him. Not quite skin and bones, but I wouldn't have recognized him if I hadn't known him. Kimo stood at my brother's head, fanning a bundle of smoking leaves. He chanted with each stroke.

Kapahu was at the foot of the table, mirroring Kimo's movements with her own smoking bundle and adding to the chant opposite her mentor. Kimo nodded to me without changing his rhythmic movements.

Reaching for Regin's hand, my fingers quivered. Hazy torchlight made his pale body look even more sickly. The warmth I expected when I touched his skin wasn't there. Although my mind knew my brother was dead, my heart wanted the whole situation to be an elaborate jest. I wanted him to turn, look at me, and laugh. Instead, he lay there, cold and still. I brushed his hair away from his eyes. *Looks like he needs a haircut.*

Everything about this was wrong. His death. The Ainan people honoring him. My feelings...all of them. I wanted to hug him, to scream at him, berate him for what he'd done. I didn't know if I should laugh or continue crying.

Nothing made sense.

I wasn't sure anything ever would again.

Someone put a hand on my shoulder.

I turned and looked Queen Ane in the eyes. Her face was bright red.

"Come with me, please," she said.

I nodded, and she turned. Once we were in the light, I realized she had swirls of red down her back and on her arms.

"Where are we going?" I asked,

"We must prepare you," she said.

Usually, I would question her. Maybe it was shock, or something in the smoke, or my confusion...whatever the reason, I followed her in silence, feeling like I was walking in a fog.

Chapter 57

At the edge of an ohe patch, not far from the village, she motioned for me to go to an elderly couple. Both of their faces were covered in red. They welcomed me by name and asked me to sit. I couldn't remember their names, and wasn't sure I'd met them before, but I accepted their invitation.

The queen sat next to me, and the four of us shared a large bowl of soup in silence. Once the meal was finished, the queen asked, "Are you ready?"

"For what?" I replied.

"For Kau'i and Maluhai to prepare you, as they have me, for tomorrow's ceremony," she said.

"What are they going to do?"

She gestured to her face, then turned her back to me. "As Kimo prepares your brother to join with the land, this shows your sorrow as well as support for his journey."

"What do I need to do?" I asked,

"Close your eyes and be still. Think of your brother, what you have lost, and where you will go from here," Maluhai said.

"Will this come off?" I asked, suddenly doubting my decision to follow the queen.

Ane nodded. "As your sorrow fades, the markings will too."

I nodded, straightened my back, and closed my eyes.

The three chanted in unison and smeared a cool, thick cream on my face. Fingers made tickling loops and lines on my back and down my arms. It took all my will to not giggle.

They continued chanting, and my skin warmed under the smooth concoction. *What is this?*

"Tell us about your brother," Kau'i said.

Keeping my eyes closed, I told them Regin's story...our story. Being twins, we had done so much with each other, and to each other, that we often might as well have been one person.

When I finished my tale, they clapped their hands together once.

The loud noise surprised me. My eyes flew open, and I nearly jumped to my feet, ready to run. The three of them rose and placed their right hands on my head. "The Aina mourn with you. We feel your loss as ours. As we assist your brother in his passing, we also offer our support to your family moving forward."

"A family I may no longer have," I said.

"Then may all of our support benefit you," Queen Ane said.

"If I return home, I may never be able to repay your kindness," I said.

"None among us expects anything in return," she said. The elders nodded their agreement.

I couldn't keep the tears from coming again. This time, I wasn't sure if they were from joy or sadness.

"Come with me," Ane said. "The king and his brother have prepared a place of peace where you will wait."

"A what?" I asked.

"It is our custom for the family of the passed to stay apart from the village from the time they are marked until the body is gone. Your meals will be left outside until we arrive with Regin's body in the morning. Then you will rejoin us in celebration of the passing."

"So, I'm not staying with Mikilana?" I asked.

"Not tonight," she said.

It feels like so long since I've slept alone. Maybe it will do me some good. "I'm ready."

"May peace come to you," Kau'i and Maluhai said together.

I followed the queen through the village. Everyone bowed their heads as we passed. We stopped at the edge of the jungle, not far from where Ka'imi led me earlier, where a small hut had been sythed from green ohe. A woven basket sat open near the door. Inside, I found a nui and several mai'a. A small fire burned in a shallow pit near the middle of the structure, showing it was empty except for a bed. Everything was still and quiet...even the monkeys.

"Rest here. Relax. Let the fire burn your concerns and carry them away on the smoke," Ane said. "Tomorrow is a day of celebration and healing."

"What are you going to do with Regin's body?"

"If you have no objections, his body will be burned according to our tradition."

"That will be fine," I said, bringing my hand to my shoulder. "Thank you, your Majesty."

She returned my salute before leaving.

Taking the small offering, I entered the hut, sat near the fire, and remembered how much Regin enjoyed using his strongest talent. *He couldn't resist making flames dance about or jump from place to place.*

Between the meal I'd had before I was marked and the fruit, my stomach was full, and my eyes grew heavy. Moving to the bed, I lay facing the fire, let my focus go blurry, and tried to empty my mind.

With so many emotions hitting me, I wanted to feel nothing, at least for a little while. The strange chants echoed in my mind. So many words I didn't understand. *How could a language I don't know well affect me so deeply?* As much as I didn't want to think about anything, I couldn't help but ponder what the ceremonies I'd seen and underwent meant. What would the morning bring?

Someone tapped on the door. I opened my eyes to embers in the fire pit. *Is it first light already?*

Chapter 58

After a stretch and a yawn, I went to the door. Prince Keoni stood outside with a basket in his hand. "Are you here for the ceremony?" I asked.

He smiled. "No, Water Princess. The sun has not yet set today. I bring your dinner. May I come in?"

"Are you going to touch me?" I asked, crossing my arms.

He closed his eyes and dipped his chin. "I will not. You have my word."

Sweeping my arm, I stepped away from the door.

"Your fire has died. I'll be right back," he said, dropping the basket just outside the hut.

"I can gather wood myself," I said.

"All of your needs will be met until after tomorrow's ceremony. Wait here," he said, making it clear I was not to help.

He wasn't gone long and returned with a good load of branches about the length of my forearm. Sparks jumped when he dropped them into the pit. He stared at the embers for a moment, flicked his hands, and the fire sprang to life. He smiled again. "Sit. I will serve you."

I picked a spot on the opposite side of the fire where I could watch the sunlight fade and waited for my meal.

Keoni handed me a big nui bowl full of a thick, white stew. Stirring it reminded me of boiled grains. Taking a bite, I found it was sweet and salty and chunky. I could pick out the flavors of nui, mai'a, opae, and several different fish. "What's this?"

"Hoolewa," he said. "Everything is cooked together to remind us of what we have when one of us suffers a loss."

"Interesting," I said, taking another bite.

"May I ask you something?" Keoni asked.

My mouth full, I nodded.

"Why do you want to leave us? Is it me?"

I closed my eyes and tried to keep from chuckling. "No." When I opened my eyes again, he had a look of relief. "This is not my home. I shouldn't be here. I need to find my way back to Croy."

"Would you stay if I asked you to?" he said, cocking his head.

What? I furrowed my brow. "This isn't about you. It's what I must do."

"I understand, but Water Princess, you..."

"What about me?" I asked.

He swallowed. "Meyla, you fascinate me. You're marked as something special. You're strong and brave and beautiful. I'd rather look at you than watch sunlight dance on the water."

I shook my head and brought my fingers to the scars on my cheek. "What you say is flattering, but I'm not marked as something special. These lines are scars. I was wounded in an attack. Someone was supposed to kill me, but they failed. The cuts didn't heal well. That doesn't make me special."

"How can you not be special?" he asked. "Those cuts could have healed and left no mark. You come here and find you are a water worker. The only one of your people, yes?"

"I... We never knew anyone could work water. Am I the only one in all of Croy or Varia? Unlikely, but yes, I am the first from my lands and those of our allies to know how. That only makes me special until I can find others there who can do it, too."

"I know fire workers and wood or water workers do not get along well, but you...If you must leave Aina then I will go with you."

"No. You are the king's son, next to lead your people. I may not even make it back home, and if I do, I'll almost certainly never return to your lands. I cannot ask your parents, your people, to make such a sacrifice."

"What if we agreed to join our lands?" he asked.

I wiped my hand across my face. *Surely, he isn't proposing what I think.* "I may get back to find I don't have a home, Keoni. It's possible my parents, everyone I love, are captured or dead. I may not be a princess anymore. I'm in no position to consider an allegiance between Croy and Aina, especially when the Croy I left may not be the one I return to."

"But if you return home and all is well...what then?" he asked, a hint of desperation in his voice.

"My father doesn't like boats, and my mother won't go into water deeper than she is tall. Negotiations of an alliance would be...problematic," I said. "But just because you think the best is what's waiting for me doesn't mean that's what I'll find. My brother had no reason to lie to me. I believe he was supposed to kill me, making him next to rule. With my parent's deaths, he would be King of Croy and doing his conspirator's bidding...whatever that may be."

"Then it sounds to me like you need all the help you can get. Joining our kingdom with yours would benefit us both," he said, nodding.

"I did not come here looking for a husband. How could I? I never knew this place existed."

"I did not make such an offer." Keoni smiled and added, "Though I would not be against it, since you brought it up. I would be the envy of everyone having a wife at my side with such beauty and fire as well as being a powerful leader in her own right. Think on what I've said. We can talk again once you're better able to see the value of such an agreement."

Either his tongue is as silver as Uncle Crum's, or I need to get used to the taste of my own foot.

"I'm sorry if I misunderstood your intention, Keoni. You are right, and my head is foggy at the moment. When the time is right, perhaps we should meet with your father and discuss what could be considered."

He nodded and got to his feet. "Meyla, thank you for sharing this meal with me. You *do* fascinate me. I never wanted to upset you."

I grinned at him. "Perhaps we both were a bit hasty in our judgment and actions."

He brought his hand to his shoulder. "May you have a restful sleep this evening."

"Thank you."

When he left, I was alone again, this time with a heavy meal in my stomach. I left the door open when I returned to bed and stared into the deepening darkness beyond the fire. The jungle behind me was filled with the sounds of howling monkeys. Barely audible above their loud calls were high-pitched clicks and chirps. *Never heard any birds like that at home.*

Sleep came quickly, thanks to the food and the exhaustion of the day. However, it was not restful. My dreams were filled with visions of a boat tossed about on storm-driven waves, my brother twitching and shivering on the healing bed, and my parents beckoning me home.

"Meyla," a gentle voice called to me. "It will be light soon; you should eat before the ceremony."

Chapter 59

I sat up and looked toward the door. Mikilana stood silhouetted against a dark sky tinged with streaks of pinkish-red. "When?"

"Soon," she said.

I got up and went to her. "Wait for me here."

She handed me a couple of mai'a and a nui. "What are you going to do?"

"Listen to the trees," I said.

She gave me a questioning look but nodded. "Don't take too long. When the pupu sounds, the ceremony will start."

"I don't know what that means," I said.

"I don't know another word for it, but you'll know it when you hear the sound."

I nodded and hurried into the jungle. Sitting at the base of the largest tree I could find nearby, I ate the small meal and pushed my talent out as far as I could. Nearby trees and plants quivered before twisting and leaning toward me. Not far away, monkeys called, and I felt their weight as they scattered among the branches, away from the unexpected movement.

As I breathed and relaxed. Not only could I feel the energy of the plants and trees around me but also the extra energy from the water in the dirt. It had always been there, I just didn't know the difference.

Warmth from sunlight hitting the highest leaves caught my attention. Roots burrowed slowly, diving deeper into the soil, seeking food and water. *Is this what King Ha'upu meant by communing with the land?* The world around me was alive.

I was alive.

Trees bent in the wind, but they never stop reaching for sunlight and water. Grasses were trampled or chewed, but their roots kept them going.

I was bent but determined to stand tall. I'd been trampled, but my roots, who I was and where I came from, would keep me going. *My mother and father called me in my dreams for a reason. I will answer their call.*

My body tingled when I stood to leave the jungle. I walked with my head held high, my back straight, and my shoulders squared, ready to face any challenge that dared cross my path.

Mikilana smiled when she saw me.

I rushed to her, pulling my guardian into a hug as something like a horn sounded from the village.

"The pupu," she said, squeezing me. "We must be ready to meet the march."

I didn't know what she meant exactly, but I followed her without question. She led me to an opening in the jungle growth. At a glance, I could make out a faint path into the dense forest.

A man came into view. He put a large, white shell to his lips, and the horn sound blared. *So that's a pupu.* Behind him, four men carried the ohe crate I'd seen outside of the healing hut. The king and queen followed closely behind with Keoni and Ka'imi a pace behind. Then the rest of the villagers walked in two lines stretching back as far as I could see.

"We will join behind Ha'upu and Ane," Mikilana said.

I nodded but didn't look away from the procession.

The pupu sounded again as the leader passed into the jungle, then I took my position in line.

Following a straight path, we continued into the woods and emerged into a large, square clearing. Instead of the broad-leaved bushes and spiny grasses, this place reminded me of a small field near my home. We turned right and continued along the border between the jungle and the clearing, but the crate was carried to the middle of the open area.

I followed those in front of me until we turned to look back at the clearing's entrance. King Ha'upu motioned for me to stand next to him, then we waited until the flow of people stopped.

"Tell us about Regin," Ha'upu said, gesturing toward where the crate sat.

"What?"

He nodded. "We do not know him. Help us see him as you did."

I looked at the king for a couple of heartbeats, then walked to the center of the clearing. Placing my hand on the ohe, I pushed my talent into it and felt Regin's weight inside. All eyes were on me as I took a breath, held it for a moment, then released it with a big sigh. I had given speeches before but never like this. My heart sped up. *I can do this.*

Chapter 60

"Prince Regin. The only son to Fitzeirick and Tindra, King and Queen of Croy. My brother...my twin. A fire worker, like my mother, with a small talent for stone, like my father. Strong, smart, mischievous...and my constant companion. We did not always get along, but we were always there for each other. He is the reason I found Aina and the reason I must leave. Ambition got the better of him, clouded his judgment, and turned him against his family. Regin did not deserve to die on his back, but he was no longer worthy of living. I mourn the loss of my brother, but I will not honor him or shed more tears because of his passing."

I slapped both hands on the box in front of me. "Regin, my brother and twin, was a traitor to his country, his people, and his family."

The pupu sounded again as I stepped back. The king and queen were at my side as a chant rose from the people around us.

"Fire," Ha'upu said.

The men who had carried Regin to the clearing stepped forward and placed their hands on the crate, and it burst into flame. Stepping back, they brought their hands to the shoulder in salute.

He doesn't deserve such respect.

"The smoke carries our sorrow to the sky, spreading it among the clouds," Ha'upu said. "When the clouds are full, rain falls to remind us of what we lost, but we will smile because the water brings new life."

The four firesyths raised their hands, and Regin's fire grew.

The unmistakable smell of burning hair and flesh filled my nose.

"The ashes of those who have passed drift on the wind, carrying their memories over our lands. Where they fall, the ground is nourished, again bringing new life."

Once more, those men raised their hands, and the fire grew too bright to look at. Cheers rose from the crowd. I closed my eyes as their joy flowed over me.

The fire workers yelled in unison, and then the flames were gone.

A pile of ash was all that remained of my brother.

"You may return to the village when you feel ready," Ha'upu said quietly.

I stared at the ashes a moment, then said, "There is no reason for me to stay away any longer. I want to start repairs on my boat today. It is past time for me to return home. My people, my family, need me."

"Speak with Ka'imi on the way back. He will help you any way he can."

"Thank you, your Majesty," I said, saluting him.

As the first to arrive in the clearing, we would be the last to leave. While waiting, I asked Ka'imi about how we would repair the cracks in my boat and expressed my concerns about using ohe.

"We must use the proper tree," he said. "Today, we celebrate. Tomorrow, we will harvest what is needed."

"I'd rather not wait," I said.

"It is not about what you want," he said. "The day of burning is a celebration. We do not work today."

"I meant no disrespect," I said.

"Join us in remembrance today. The next step in your journey begins tomorrow."

Grass trampled lives on. "I look forward to it," I said.

Cocking his head, he gave me a questioning look, then smiled. "I'm sure many surprises lay ahead, Water Princess."

"I certainly hope not," I said.

He laughed as we turned to leave the clearing.

At the exit, I turned to look at my brother's remains one last time.

By the time we returned to the village, it was a hive of activity. The fire pit was blazing. A huge, stone pot rested in the flames, cooking what looked like days' worth of stew. Elders and children danced about, chanting and singing. The pupu sounded again when the king and queen arrived. Cheers filled the air.

Before long, I found myself joining the revelry. Dancing from one group to another, shouting words I didn't understand. Soon all my concerns were forgotten as I surrendered to the festivities.

I awoke sore the next morning.

Chapter 61

Mikilana was still asleep when I crawled out of bed. After finishing the last of our wainui, I left to gather more. Everyone I saw greeted me and smiled. A small part of me considered staying.

Aina was almost an ideal place to live. The people were friendly, welcoming, and seemed happy. The food was good and plentiful without the need to tend a garden or keep livestock.

But it's not home. If Regin's confession was true, Croy needed me as much as I needed to be back in my homeland. With that in mind, I gathered an armload of nui and returned to Mikilana's hut.

She stood outside, talking with Ka'imi and Keoni, and grinned when she saw me. "Wondered where you'd gone."

"Making sure you didn't go hungry or thirsty," I said.

"Give me those," she said. "You have more important things to do today."

"You've taken care of me," I said. "No reason I can't return the favor."

"Thank you," she said. "And be careful."

"You're welcome, and I will," I said, then turned to the others. "What's the plan?"

"We'll talk on the way to your boat," Keoni said.

"After you," I said.

"Before we put our hands on your damaged boat, I thought we should discuss what you know about how it was built," Ka'imi said. "No one here has ever seen one like it."

"It came from skilled builders in Varia and was meant to test new ideas. I wasn't there when it was made," I said, "but I know that vessel like I know my own hand."

Ka'imi pressed his lips together.

"I think you have the best idea, Uncle," Keoni said.

I raised my eyebrows, but Ka'imi spoke before I could ask. "We should build some smaller boats, combining ideas from yours and ours. Between us, maybe we can create something better than either."

"How long will we spend working on something new? If we repair the damage to my boat, it is ready to go," I said.

"As long as it takes because my father expects our people to benefit from helping you," Keoni said.

"I don't mind helping Aina as much as I can, but I don't want to delay my leaving any longer than necessary," I said.

"I give you my word that we will not keep you from leaving any longer than we must, Water Princess," Keoni said.

"I will hold you to that," I said.

My boat lay on its side several paces from the waterline with the cracks in the bottom easily visible. The splintered steering shaft, where the paddle had been ripped off, caught my eye. "Oh...I forgot about that," I mumbled.

"What?" Ka'imi asked.

While I tried to explain what I meant, he looked more and more confused. Going by Keoni's expression, he had no idea what I was talking about either. It didn't help that their language didn't have words for some of the parts.

"So, you don't always have to paddle this boat for it to move?" Ka'imi asked.

"No. The wind can push the boat faster than you can row it," I said, afraid I would have to explain everything again.

"But those parts are missing?" Keoni asked.

"Along with other pieces, yes."

"And this big skirt, which is also gone, catches the wind?" Ka'imi asked, again.

"It's like a skirt but you don't have a word for it. And it isn't made like these." I patted the garment covering my waist and thighs. "Ours is made of thinner fibers, woven tighter together. But you don't have a word for what I'm trying to describe either," I said.

"Can you show us?" Keoni asked.

"You don't have any..." I groaned and resorted to speaking Croian, "Flax or wool or hemp." The words felt funny coming out.

"I don't understand," Keoni said.

"Me either," Ka'imi added.

"I need something thin like..." A breeze came off the water, and my hair tickled the back of my neck. "Like hair."

"Hair?" Ka'imi questioned. "You make things from hair? How?"

"Not hair. *Like* hair. Bring me a nui husk. I think I can get some fibers from there and give you an idea of what I'm talking about."

"Go," Ka'imi said, nodding to Keoni and gesturing to one of the nearby nui trees.

"You're sure this will work?" Ka'imi asked, head cocked.

"Won't know until I try," I said, moving to lean against my boat.

The prince returned with two nui. I sythed one husk apart, carefully stripping the thin fibers into a fluffy pile on the sand. *Don't have a loom and these are too short even if I did have one. Going to have to do this by hand.* It took a few tries before I got a feel for manipulating the material. Once I thought of it as hemp fiber, it went together quickly into a thin mat big enough to cover my lap. I held it up and said, "Fabric." It flapped in the breeze.

Ka'imi pursed his lips for a moment, then held out his hand. "May I see it?"

I handed the mat to him, and he ran his hand across it before holding it up like I did. Again, the breeze moved it. "And the *sail* you've been talking about is bigger than this?" he asked, handing the fabric to Keoni.

"Much," I said, holding my arms out to the side. "At least this wide, if not wider, and taller. The bigger it is, the more wind it catches and the faster you can move."

"This is softer than our skirts, but..." Keoni pulled at the edges unraveling several strands. "It's not very strong. This won't do what you say."

"Give it to me," I said, with a sigh. After sything the edges together, I handed it back to him. "Try it now."

He frowned but took the mat and pulled on it again. This time, it held and made creaking sounds as the fibers rubbed against each other.

"To weave a piece as big as you say, we'll need a lot more of this," Ka'imi said.

Keoni kept pulling at it, trying his best to tear the mat, but it held. "We need to make more stuff from this."

"There should be lots of husks around considering how many nui are gathered every day," I said.

"Fire workers use this because it burns easily," Ka'imi said.

"Oh," I replied. "Is there anything else like it?"

"Not really, no," Ka'imi said.

"Then we'll need to gather as much as we can," I said.

"Is this necessary?" Keoni asked. "We paddle our boats and don't need anything like this."

"The sides of my boat are higher than yours; your paddles won't work," I said.

"But you have long paddles in there," Keoni argued.

"Yes, but those don't move as fast as your short paddles," I explained. "Even if they did, you would exhaust yourself trying to move as fast as a sail can take you with the right wind."

"And you came here with this wind catcher?" Ka'imi asked.

"Until the storm ripped it out of my boat, yes," I said. *How many times do I have to explain it?*

The king's brother nodded. "Keoni, go tell your father we need all the nui husk we can get, then take this mat to the skirt makers and let them study it. Tell them if they have any questions, find Meyla. We will need a piece like this but wider than your arm span and taller than you."

"And if Father has questions?" Keoni asked.

"He can come to us, or we'll discuss it this evening," Ka'imi said.

"And what will you be doing while I'm gone?" Keoni asked.

"Learning," Ka'imi said. "Stop asking questions and go."

"Yes," Kenoi said.

"Tell me again about how this sail is on the boat," Ka'imi said.

Chapter 62

I pointed to where the pole had snapped when it was ripped away and described how it was put together. I think he finally understood after seeing the small sail I'd made.

"Your concern about using ohe is right," Ka'imi said. "I'm not sure a nui tree would be strong enough either. We will have to find a tree in the jungle that will stand against the wind you described."

"And what about the body of the boat itself?" I asked.

He nodded and rubbed his chin. "I have some ideas, but we need to make some small boats to see if they are good or not."

"The sooner the better," I said.

He sythed a block as long as my forearm and about half that thick from a nearby nui tree. "Let's see if you can make a small version of your boat," he said, handing me the wood.

Closing my eyes, I fixed the details of my craft in my mind's eye and went to work. Sweat streamed down my face and body by the time I finished. Ka'imi opened three nui, and I drank them as fast as I could and almost finished one more before my thirst was quenched. Except for a sail, I had created a near-perfect copy, including the oars and working steering, of the best gift I had ever received. Cradling it in my arms like a baby, I walked into the water and gently floated the boat.

Ka'imi raised his eyebrows and nodded. "Nice work, Water Princess. Now, how do we improve it?"

"In smooth water, with a favorable wind, there is nothing faster. In big waves, it is hard to steer and threatens to roll over," I said, remembering the terrifying storm that blew us here.

Ka'imi clicked his tongue. "Which is more important?"

"Out there," I said, pointing to the water beyond the stone barrier, "if I can steer, the waves won't roll the boat over."

"But if the boat couldn't roll, steering wouldn't matter."

"We climbed waves much taller than your huts—"

"That sounds terrible," he said, interrupting me.

"It was," I replied, nodding. "Go straight up them and you fall down the back side and slam into the water hard enough to crack wood. I had to work several cracks back together to keep us above the water. But if you can steer across the wave, you ride down the back without risking any damage."

He nodded and rubbed his chin. "And you have to use the long paddles."

"Oars," I said, using the Croian word. "Yes."

"What if we could use paddles more like ours?" he asked.

I shook my head. "The sides would be too low. Many waves beyond the ko'a'ke'a would wash over your ohe boats and fill them with water."

"Let's look at them side by side," Ka'imi said, taking wood from another nui tree.

I pushed the copy of my boat around with my watersything talent while he worked.

"Playing?" Keoni questioned, as he approached.

"No," I said, then explained what we were doing.

"Sounds like a waste of time," he said.

"Because you don't understand what it takes to create something new," Ka'imi said, wiping his forehead before joining me in the water with a tiny ohe boat. "What did your father say?"

"He will make sure you have what you need," Keoni said.

"And the weavers?" Ka'imi asked.

"A few seemed excited to try something new," he said.

"Good," he said, placing the small boat next to mine. "Meyla, make waves."

Some of the red paint washed off my hands when I plunged them into the water. The color reminded me of Regin's blood after he fell onto the ko'a'ke'a. Pushing that memory out of my thoughts, I sythed smaller copies of the calmest waves we had seen on our journey. Both boats bobbed on the surface, the ohe boat rolling far less.

"Bigger," Ka'imi said.

I pushed more of my will out, raising the waves until they touched the top of my boat's side. A little water trickled into mine, but the taller waves lifted one outrigger on the ohe boat dangerously into the air, and it splashed hard against the water as the wave passed. Soon, the little craft was full and dropping below the surface.

"And this is what happened out there?" Ka'imi asked.

"Worse," I said, shivering.

"It can't be done, then," Keoni said. "Our boats won't survive, and Father won't let any of our people risk their lives."

"I'm not asking anyone to come with me," I said, turning to him.

"That has not been decided," Ka'imi said, glaring at Keoni. "We're both learning. Mikilana's ancestor came here in something different from either of these. The stories say the boat was undamaged until it hit the ko'a'ke'a. So, it can be done. This is just the first try."

"I never believed those stories," Keoni said.

"Then how do you explain her knowing a language other than Aina?" I asked. "And the gray on her skin?"

"You're special, Water Princess. Maybe she is, too," Keoni said, crossing his arms.

"Nephew, if you are not going to be helpful here, find someplace else to be," Ka'imi said.

"You can't send me away," the boy stated. "Father wants me here to act as his eyes."

"Eyes don't speak," Ka'imi said. "You know little about rowing and even less about building boats. You can watch and help when asked. Otherwise, keep your mouth closed, pay attention, and learn."

Keoni's face turned red, almost as deep as the dye on mine, but he didn't respond.

The king's brother and I looked at the two boats from all angles, working with our copies and discussing possible improvements without stopping to eat lunch. By the time our shadows grew long in the evening sun, neither of our small boats looked anything like they started but neither were better than the originals when it came to dealing with big waves. Keoni must have gotten bored because he left at some point without either of us noticing.

"Guess we should eat," Ka'imi said, patting his stomach.

I nodded. "I'o nui only goes so far."

"True," he said, laughing. "Would you join me and eat with the king and queen?"

"I'd rather spend some time with Mikilana. Once we have a boat ready, I'll likely never see her again and —"

"Say no more," he said, raising his hands. "But I'm sure Ha'upu will want to talk with you sooner or later. Maybe tomorrow."

"I'll worry about tomorrow when it comes," I said. "I enjoyed working with you."

"And I, you," he said, saluting me. "Tomorrow."

"See you in the morning," I said, before heading to Mikilana's hut.

Chapter 63

"Wasn't sure I would see you this evening," Mikilana said, when I entered. "Thought you might spend the night on the beach. I saw the weavers starting on something different. For you?"

I smiled. "They're making a sail to catch the wind and push the boat so we don't always have to row."

"I see," she said. "How did your building go?"

"We tried several things, but nothing seems to work better than what we started with," I said. "Are there any drawings of the boat your ancestor arrived on?"

"Only the stories passed down from parent to child. It was generations ago...legend now, more than truth, I'm afraid," she said, frowning.

I nodded. "Keoni claims he doesn't believe them anyway. Says you're special, like me."

"He has eyes for you."

My turn to frown. "I know. He visited me in the mourning hut and proposed an...alliance. It sounded more like an awkward attempt at making me his promised, but he insisted it wasn't."

Mikilana chuckled and shook her head. "Most girls here would have been insulted by such a thing happening the day one of their family died. Though, if you did stay, being married to our prince would give you much more authority and secure your future among our people."

"I'm sure it would," I said. "But I'm not staying—I can't. And, as much as it pains me, I'll likely never see this place again. Know this, you have been like another mother to me. I will miss you."

"And I will miss you, greatly, Meyla. You've been like the daughter I was never able to have," she said, taking my hand. "I understand your people need you, and you need them, but you will always have a home here, should you return."

I squeezed her hand. "Were things different, maybe I would stay. Were I not a princess in Croy with obligations to my people, I would love this pace. Truth be told, I do love this place...but not as deeply as my home and my family."

A tear rolled down her wrinkled cheek. "I often wonder if my ancestor felt the same way."

"Did they try to leave?" I asked.

"According to the stories, they were too afraid. The few who survived never got back into the water again," she said.

"Whatever happened to them must have been terrible. Possibly worse than the storm Regin and I faced."

"It is said they were on the water long enough to run out of food and ate the men who died first to stay alive," she said. "I'm not sure I believe that myself."

"Desperate people do what they must to survive," I said, remembering what my father had said about the horrible tunnels under our capital.

"But to do such a thing to the dead? Unthinkable. No one could do such a thing and stay civilized."

"Not everyone honors the dead. Before my father conquered the land, a group of Satran people would dig up graves and steal bones to make moving statues. He made sure those who did such things were executed and has men keeping watch for any such activity."

"Then maybe they ate their fallen," she said, and shuddered. "I don't want to talk about this anymore. What will you do tomorrow?"

"Ka'imi and I will keep working."

"He is a smart man. You two will figure this out," she said, nodding. Her expression showed she wasn't happy about the idea.

"My belly is full, and my eyelids are heavy," I said, before yawning. "I'm ready for bed."

"Go ahead. I'll join you later."

The sun was not yet up when I woke. Mikilana wasn't in bed, and I didn't remember feeling her sleeping next to me. Slipping into my skirt, I left to find her. With most of the village still asleep, I did my best to search quietly.

I found her sitting on the beach, close enough to the water for the gentle waves to tickle the bottoms of her feet when they reached the shore.

"What are you doing?" I asked, sitting next to her. "Did you sleep at all?"

She looked at me and blinked. Tears came from the corners of her eyes. "I couldn't get the thoughts of you leaving out of my head. Everything we talked about, especially eating dead men to survive, wouldn't leave me in peace."

I put my arm across her shoulders and pulled her to me. "Don't worry. Nothing like that will happen to me. I'll be fine. I made it here alive, and I'll return to Croy safely and in good health."

"How can you say that?" She pointed toward the barrier in the water. "Those stones killed your brother...killed some of my ancestors. I can't bear the thought of you starving on the water, dying for no reason. Stay. You're safe here."

"I *am* safe here, but this is not where I *need* to be," I said, squeezing her tighter. "If my brother, may the fire take him, told the truth, my family is in trouble...or worse. I have to know. Mikilana, I will miss you dearly, but I must go home."

"Then promise you will return, as soon as you can," she said.

"If only I could," I replied. "Know I will carry you in my heart, all my life."

She nodded and sniffled before wiping her face. "As I will you, Meyla."

"Ready for an early start?" Ka'imi asked. He carried a load of mai'a in his arms. His eyes got big when we turned to face him. "Oh. What's wrong? Are you sick, Mikilana?"

"Only my heart," she said. "I fear I will be lonely when she leaves."

"You were not lonely before. Her coming here does not change that," he said, putting the fruit on the ground and sitting beside her.

"But my hut was empty, and it will be again," she said. "Losing Kalaheo without a child was hard. I survived then, but now..."

"I swear you will not be alone," Ka'imi said, saluting her.

"Having people around, checking on me, is not the same as not being alone," she said, shaking her finger at him.

"She's right," I added, knowing how I felt before I understood the Ainan language.

"I understand," he said, nodding, "and I will make sure you have the company you deserve."

"I'm not sure you do understand, Ka'imi, but we can talk later; I know you two have work to do," Mikilana said, pointing toward the small boats we left on the shore yesterday.

"I meant what I said," he said, getting to his feet. "Meyla, I had a thought...something I want to try. Ready?"

I squeezed Mikilana one more time, then got up and followed Ka'imi.

Chapter 64

"Is Keoni no longer the king's eyes?" I asked, looking around.

"The prince decided our work was not interesting enough to continue watching," Ka'imi said.

I laughed. "Are we going to do anything interesting today?"

"Yes; I have an idea. In order to be safest from the waves you described, it seems we need to raise the boat," he said.

"But it has to be on the water," I said. "This isn't a bird."

He smiled and picked up the small ohe boat copy. "Watch." With little effort, he sythed the poles holding the outriggers until they were pointing down, putting them under the boat itself.

Placing it on the water, the boat stood far above the surface, but the slightest ripple knocked it over and it quickly sank.

"That's even worse," I said, trying to not laugh.

He frowned. "Just the first test. I think I know how to improve it. Watch."

Removing the poles from his model, he grabbed my small boat and worked it until it was flat and wide. It reminded me of the merchant barges that traveled from Croy to Satra and back. Before I could say anything, he attached the poles to the bottom of the flattened boat and put his new creation in the water.

The outriggers kept it above the surface.

I watched it for a moment, waiting to see if it sank, then made waves. Small ones didn't seem to upset this new boat, at least no worse than it had either of the other examples. With larger waves, the craft stayed upright but water washed over the body. "Better but it's still getting wet inside, and now, the oars need to be even longer to reach the water," I said.

"Not my only idea. I'll need more material to try some things," he said. "You get the mai'a and I'll gather ohe."

"I thought we agreed ohe would not work on this boat," I said.

"Ohe won't work on *your* boat. I think it has a place on this one," he said, smiling.

I gathered the fruit he'd left on the sand and returned to our worksite before Ka'imi had come back. Eating a mai'a, I studied the craft he'd made, trying to understand how ohe could make it better. Nothing came to mind.

When he returned, he wasn't carrying a load of long ohe poles, instead, he had a handful of small shoots. Twigs would be the best description except ohe didn't have branches or twigs. It grew straight, getting taller and bigger around the longer it was alive.

He quickly ate then went to work, adding the ohe to his new boat until a small building stood on the platform between the outriggers. "What do you think?" he asked, placing it in the water.

"You've made a floating hut," I said.

"Ours keep the heaviest of rains out, this should stand up to your waves," he said. "Try it."

The outriggers ran a little deeper in the water, but the flat part of the boat was still above the surface. Starting with little more than ripples, everything seemed fine. I kept adding energy until the waves struck the craft about halfway up the side of the hut. It rocked, and turned, but stayed upright. "Not perfect," I said, "but better than anything else we've tried."

"Every journey starts with small steps. What do you see that needs work first?"

"Steering and paddling," I said. "And where do we put the sail now?"

He laughed. "One thing at a time. Which of those is most important?"

"Paddling," I said.

"Fine," he said. "How?"

"I don't know," I said, crossing my arms. "Not from inside the hut, that would take holes in the floor or the sides. Rowing from the platform would require long oars and the outriggers would be in the way."

"If the sail is catching wind, you don't need to paddle, right?" he asked. "What if the outriggers were made like ohe boats where men could paddle from them?"

"It would take...what six or eight people to move a boat that size. I was planning to return home alone," I said. "My boat only needed one or two people."

"What you plan and what happens may be two different things," Ka'imi said. "This isn't just to get you home. I'm working on this to help my people, including finding other lands."

"But I got here by accident," I argued. "I might not be able to find my way back. I won't take others with me to die."

"It will not be your choice to make, Meyla," Ka'imi said, his hands on his hips. "Ha'upu will choose who goes with you...*if* I tell him we have a better boat."

"Then help me fix my boat and let me go alone," I said. "Why risk your people?"

"Your arrival proves there are others out there taking to the water. Ha'upu wants Aina to join them or be ready to face them. He gave me this task to prepare our people for what may come."

Is this what Keoni meant by an alliance with Croy? "Your king doesn't understand what your people will face. You have no real weapons, no army...your worst enemy is mano and they rarely wash over the ko'a'ke'a. One armed and armored warrior could conquer your land."

"Talk with him about your concerns this evening. For now, let's keep working," he said.

"There isn't enough wood nearby to make what you want," I said. "Unless you plan to take down most of these nui trees."

"No, we'll have to go to the jungle to get what we need," he said, grabbing what was left of our breakfast. We ate the last of the mai'a on the way.

Chapter 65

The monkeys were louder than usual when we arrived at the edge of the dense growth.

My mourning hut was gone. I paused where it had stood, remembering my brother's ashes were now scattered about.

"What do you have in mind?" I asked, forcing uncomfortable memories out of my thoughts.

"Two trees I can put my arms around, or one big enough for us to join hands around together."

"Those will be too heavy for us to move by ourselves," I said, envisioning the size of the tree he described.

"I'll gather help to carry them after we find what we need," he explained, before entering the jungle.

Our entrance disturbed the animals above us and soon, manure flew in our direction. Two wads splattered against Ka'imi's chest, and one hit my shoulder before I ducked behind him. Another barely missed my head after he jumped behind a tree.

Foul odor filled my nose. Wiping the gray-brown mess off my shoulder just smeared it and dirtied my hand.

I dove behind the nearest tree and looked for our attackers. Their dark fur hid them well in the shadow of the canopy over our heads. I only caught glimpses of them when they moved.

Twice more their waste hit the ground near me. "What do we do?" I asked, scooting around the tree to get out of their line of sight.

"We have to scare them," he said.

"I think I'm more afraid of them, right now, than they are of me."

Ka'imi yelled.

I don't think that's going to scare them.

The tree he hid behind shook hard enough for leaves to fall. Monkeys screamed as they hurried away through the treetops.

Oh. I shoved my will into the tree behind me, causing it to shake. Soon the monkey's calls faded as they fled.

"Should keep them clear for a little while," Ka'imi said, offering me a leaf about twice the size of my hand. "Use this to wipe off your shoulder."

Cleaner, but no less smelly, we searched for the trees needed to test Ka'imi's idea. It didn't take long before we found two that were about a hand more than his arm span around.

"Help me get them down, and you can strip the branches while I get men to carry them to the beach," he said.

I nodded, and we pressed our hands against the smooth, gray-brown bark. I wasn't sure what kind of tree it was, but it didn't take much energy for us to separate it from its roots. With a shove, it crashed to the ground. A couple of paces away, the second was down with similar ease.

"Keep an eye out, in case the monkeys return before I do," Ka'imi said, glancing up.

I nodded and went to work taking the branches off our future boats, occasionally checking to see if those horrible tree-dwelling creatures came back.

Ka'imi was still gone by the time I had cleaned the logs, making a sizable pile of branches in the process. A few beads of sweat dripped from my nose. I wiped my face and sat to wait for him.

"Split up and carry these to the beach. Place them near her broken boat," Ka'imi said, behind me.

He'd brought about a dozen men to move the logs. They lifted together and turned toward the beach. I followed close behind, admiring their strength.

"Everyone who works wood, stay nearby," Ka'imi said, as they dropped the logs onto the sand. "The rest can go back to what you were doing. Thank you for the help."

Four men nodded, the rest saluted and walked away.

"What do we do first?" I asked.

"Let's work the outside into the correct shape. Then we can make the inside fit what we need."

"Sounds like a good plan. I'll follow your lead," I said.

Sitting on the sand, at the base of the first log, Ka'imi placed both hands on the wood and closed his eyes. I knelt, touched the smooth bark, and did my best to work with his talent as it flowed along the material.

Together we shifted the wood's grain, moving it as we needed, until the outside resembled an ohe boat, flat on the bottom, a steeper curve than the natural roundness on the sides, and pinched in on each end so the boat cut through the water smoothly.

Ka'imi wiped his forehead, then looked over what we had made. He turned to the group of men watching nearby. "Makoa," he called, waving one of them to us. "Guide the others in making this into a boat without outriggers."

"It will dump us out as soon as we get in," Makoa said, looking confused.

Ka'imi pointed to the small, floating hut he'd made, still floating near where we tested it. "That will not roll over."

"Oh," Makoa said. "Let's get to work."

While Ka'imi and I worked the second log into a matching shape, the other boat builders finished the first one.

"How are we going to join them?" I asked, as we watched the crew form the inside of the second boat.

"I'll figure something out," he said.

When the men stood, we had a pair of identical craft shaped like ohe boats.

"What next?" Makoa asked.

Ka'imi looked from the boats to me and then down the beach. "Meyla, go there," he said, pointing, "and lay down with your side facing the water."

"Why?" I asked.

"You'll see," he said.

Chapter 66

I did as he asked and he followed me, marking a line in the sand at my feet and head. "Lay down again, your feet here," he ordered, tapping his foot near my head.

Once I was in position, he drew another line at my head.

"One boat here," he said, pointing at the fresh mark, "and one there." He pointed at the farthest line. "Both facing the water."

Oh, he used me as a measure.

He nodded once the boats were where he wanted. "Now, we need thick branches to reach across," he said, before kneeling next to the front of the closest boat. Putting his hand on the sand at the tip, he marked a line at his elbow then moved to the rear and did the same thing. "Enough to cover from this mark to that one."

"Ohe?" Makoa asked.

"Not strong enough," I said.

"Back to the jungle," Ka'imi said. "Let's hope the monkeys aren't still angry."

Ka'imi directed the builders to trees with branches he wanted. None of them were low enough to reach from the ground. The four men rushed from place to place, using their talent to detach the limbs before scattering to keep clear of the falling wood. He told me to clear the smaller limbs off as the workers continued their harvest. Hurrying to keep up with their pace, I left a trail of sticks and leaves behind as I went from one branch to the next.

Again, we worked without stopping to eat a real lunch. Choosing instead to snack on plants and mushrooms the jungle provided. Twice we had to fend off monkey incursions before we finished gathering the wood Ka'imi thought we needed.

Everyone was tired but we all did our part to get the material moved to the beach and tie the two boats together. The energy of six woodsyths flowed into the fibers, joining wood together in ways it never could have naturally. Once the platform was in place, we were all exhausted and hungry.

"Meet here in the morning," Ka'imi said, "and bring paddles. We're going to test this thing."

My heart sped up. *Another step closer to going home.*

"I believe Ha'upu would like for you to eat with him this evening," Ka'imi said.

If not now, when? "Could I bathe first?" I asked.

"Don't take too long," he replied, gesturing toward the sea.

Another thing I miss from home, a warm bath. I smirked at him and waded away from the shore to rinse myself off. The red flowed off my skin into the water around me, again reminding me of my brother bleeding in my boat. *That day seems like so long ago now.* I swam away from the pinkish water and lay back to soak for a few moments.

Like the last time, as I relaxed my talent reached out and found the energy all around me. Pushing my will down, I hardened the water into a bowl shape and lifted a handful of wet sand to scrub the monkey dung from my shoulder. Once the smelly residue was gone, I rinsed once more before swimming back to shore.

Ka'imi was gone.

No one looked in my direction as I got dressed which served as another reminder of how long it had been since I arrived on Aina. I barely got more than a few smiles and nods as I walked through the village to the king's hall.

Chapter 67

"Welcome, Meyla...Water Princess," Ha'upu said. He sat on the far side of a low, round, ohe table near the entrance. He paused and looked toward his brother. "I understand things are going well."

I saluted the king before bowing. "We have learned a few things that do not work. Tomorrow we will find out if his newest idea works. Will the queen and your son be joining us?"

He nodded. "I expect them to arrive soon. Ane thinks this is all unnecessary and Keoni..." Ha'upu trailed off.

"My nephew thinks anyone who goes past the ko'a'ke'a is as good as dead," Ka'imi said.

I frowned. "I can assure him there are more people living beyond that barrier than in all of Aina. In Croy, this village would be little more than a fledgling settlement. We have...um." I wasn't sure if there was an Ainan word, so I switched to my native language for 'trade caravans' then finished the sentence in Ainan, "with nearly as many people as live here."

"I do not know those words," Ha'upu said, rubbing his chin

As I thought of a way to describe what I meant, I realized I'd need to use more Croain words, so I did my best to explain in Ainan. "A group of people riding, um...animals and pulling...hmm...boats that go on land carrying clothes, and food, and other things."

Both men looked confused. "I can't see how a boat would move on land," Ka'imi said.

"Or what kind of animal one would ride," Ha'upu added.

I sighed. "I think I know a way to help you understand but I need some wood. May I leave for a moment?"

The king nodded.

I rushed to the nearest nui tree and sythed enough material to make two small, crude horses and a tiny wagon. "These animals are called 'horses'," I said, handing one to each of the men.

Both had trouble repeating the word, but they studied the figures as I continued.

"We can ride them or use them to pull a 'wagon'." I placed it on the table and gave it a little push, so it rolled toward them. "Which carries people and things."

"So, not a boat at all," Ka'imi said.

"No, but I don't think you have a word for it," I said.

"We do not," Ha'upu said. "Where do you get these...animals?"

"Some are caught from the wilds, our jungle, and tamed. Others are bred and raised by farmers, people who raise food," I explained.

"But where did they come from?" Ha'upu asked. "We have no such thing here."

I shrugged. "Horses have been in Croy, and the surrounding lands, long before I was born." *I better not tell them about donkeys, goats, sheep, and the other animals we have.*

"And they are big enough to sit on?" Ka'imi asked.

"Once they are old enough, yes," I said, standing. "Senshi, my horse, is just over my head at her shoulder."

Ka'imi's eyes got big.

"You have one of these? Could it be brought here?" Ha'upu asked, still looking at the wooden statue in his hands. "I would like to see it."

"Horses don't like traveling by boat. Being of the land, they prefer to stay there," I said.

"Even a young one?" the king asked.

"Even the best-tempered young horses are nearly wild and would be even worse behaved on a boat. I'm sorry, your Majesty, but I do not think there is a way to bring horses to Aina," I said, frowning.

"What do they eat?" Ka'imi asked.

"Grass but not the coarse kind that grows in your jungle," I said. *Though a goat might eat it.*

The king turned to his brother. "You must get a safe boat built. I want to see this animal for myself."

A shiver ran down my back. "Your Majesty, a storm sent me here. I do not know which way to go to get home. I must advise against you coming with me when I leave."

He chuckled. "I had not planned on traveling on the first boat but, if Ka'imi returns safely then he will know the way and I can travel with him. My brother would never put me in danger."

Wish I could say the same about mine. "With all respect, King Ha'upu, I don't want anyone to leave with me. Death may await me on this trip. No one should risk their lives for me."

"They will risk their lives for Aina, and for me," Ha'upu said. "I have come to understand what your arrival means, and I wish for Aina to make friends with the other people out there."

"Not everyone is friendly," I said. "You do not understand the risk such a trip would bring for your people. Had I come here with fighters, we could have easily killed or captured everyone in Aina." *If I had half the fighting skills of my mother, I could conquer these people by myself.*

"You would rather we sit and wait for these unfriendly people to find us?" Ha'upu said, crossing his arms. "Would it not be better if we knew what we might face?"

I can't disagree with him, and I certainly would have done things differently had I known what I had faced. "Knowing there is a threat is always better than being caught unprepared," I said.

"You have told us about the threat and we," Ha'upu smiled and spread his arms, "are preparing."

"You'll need more than one boat and a few men," I said.

"We can't get everything ready all at once," Ka'imi said. "Tell me, again, how many days were you on the water?"

I shrugged. "At least two but, with the storm, I suspect it was four...or more."

Ka'imi nodded. "Then we'll plan for five. Brother, that is a lot of food to gather, and we don't have long if we leave as soon as I know the new boat is ready."

"You do your job, let me do mine," Ha'upu said.

The king looked past me as his brother saluted. I turned to see Ane and Keoni enter the hall. "Your Majesty," I said, standing and bowing before I saluted them.

"May I sit with you, Water Princess?" Keoni asked.

Chapter 68

What happens if I refuse? "Yes," I answered flatly.

The prince smiled and hurried to my side.

"Meyla, are you well?" Queen Ane asked, as she sat next to her husband.

"I feel fine," I said, giving her a weak smile.

She pressed her lips together for a moment then nodded.

"Have you decided to join in a union?" Keoni asked, turning to me. He looked excited.

"We haven't discussed it," Ha'upu answered, before I could say anything.

"Why not?" he asked, not looking away from me.

"Because now is not the time for such a discussion," his father said.

"But if Meyla leaves without an agreement—"

"I'm sitting right here," I said, cutting the prince off. "You're staring at me so don't talk about me like I'm not here." I didn't try to hide my annoyance.

"Sorry, Water Princess," he said, looking down. "I meant no offense."

"Yet, you couldn't have been more offensive," I said.

Queen Ane cleared her throat. "I told you, my son, such things take time. Patience."

I sighed. "I've already told you I did not come here looking for a husband. All I want is to return home, find out if my parents are still alive, and take back my rightful place if they are not."

Ha'upu eyed me as our meal arrived. "I expect an agreement between my family and yours in exchange for our care and aid."

I closed my eyes. "I will do what I can to aid Aina, assuming I return home. If my parents still rule Croy, trade agreements can be reached, and we can create an alliance...in time. If I have no family, I will be too busy raising an army to take back my throne to aid your people. Regardless, I will not marry Keoni."

"As I told my son," Ane said, "such things take time."

"And interest," I snapped. "And I have neither."

"It is understandable for you to be upset," Ka'imi said. "Loss clouds one's vision for a time. We should all discuss this once everyone is seeing things clearly."

"I see one thing clearly," I said, standing, "the open water beyond the ko'a'ke'a. That is where my future waits. Any effort I spend on anything else is wasted. Though I appreciate your invitation to dine with you, your majesties, I must decline."

"Sit," Ha'upu said, firmly. "Eat with us. Many things depend on our friendship...unless you want us to consider you one of the unfriendly people you insist are waiting to attack once our people leave our homeland."

My manners took over. I saluted and sat. "I am friendly. And I do appreciate everything you and your people have done for me. My parents would have done the same for anyone in need. What you ask for is not an agreement I am willing to make." I turned to the prince. "Keoni, you seem to be a nice boy."

He gave me a wide smile.

"Even if you are impatient. Regardless, I do not believe you are my future. I belong in Croy, with my people. My whole life, I have been preparing to lead my country. I cannot do that from Aina."

"Could we not lead both lands, together?" he asked, a hint of hope in his expression.

"Would your people accept your rule while you lived in a land many days away?" I asked.

"No," Ha'upu said.

"And my people would not consider me their queen if I lived here," I said. "Croy has many things to offer this nation and Aina has things never seen in Croy. Beneficial trade between us is possible, maybe even likely, but I am not part of the bargain."

"You have given us much to discuss, Water Princess," Ane said. "Your parents raised you well, giving you more wisdom than one your age should have. I would be proud to call you daughter."

I nodded. "And had we met under different, more pleasant, conditions...there is a chance I could consider joining our families."

Keoni looked at me again.

"But I see no way for such a thing to happen now," I said.

The prince's shoulders drooped.

"I find myself agreeing with my wife and, it seems, my son could learn much from you, Meyla," Ha'upu said. "He will be among those who travel with you, as my voice."

"It is too risky, your Majesty," I said. "I may not find my home. If I do, it may be different than I left it. I ask that you tell Ka'imi to build a boat I can control by myself so none of your people put themselves in danger for me."

"From what you say, we are already at risk," Ha'upu said. "Ka'imi and I will decide who goes and I insist Keoni be one of them. I will not change my mind."

"Then I will not argue, your Highness, but I will caution you on declaring him your voice. I will not take orders from him," I said.

Ka'imi tried to hide his smile.

"I would not expect you to, given your experience and his lack...he has no reason to give commands," Ha'upu said. "He will speak for his people, when there is a need, and nothing more. Is that understood, son?"

"Yes, father," Keoni said, saluting.

The prince thinks we'll die on the water. Does his father share this belief? Surely, he wouldn't sacrifice his only heir. "What happens to your people if he doesn't return?" I asked.

"Since you are not one of us, that is not your concern," Ha'upu said.

"My brother's death, as a result of poor judgment on his part, harms my people deeply. To say nothing of how it will affect my parents. I do not want such sorrow to come here," I said.

"Giving you a good reason to keep Keoni safe," Ane said, taking her husband's hand.

And all but forcing him on me. I pressed my lips together for a moment then turned to the prince. "I will do all I can to make sure you return home safely."

He smiled wide. "You will not regret my presence."

I certainly hope not.

As we ate, the rest of our discussion concerned our progress with the new boat and was much less awkward. Still, I left there with the weight of my responsibility to the

Ainan people weighing on my shoulders. *Am I doing the right thing for these people? Is Ha'upu?*

Chapter 69

My feet dragged in the sand to Mikilana's hut. She greeted me when I entered. I nodded to her and went straight to bed. Visions of Keoni starving to death kept me from resting well. I felt like I hadn't slept at all when Mikilana got out of bed.

I groaned while getting up.

"Are you well, Meyla?" she asked.

"Bad dreams," I said, reaching for a mai'a.

"That's why you were thrashing about. Should I guess at what's troubling you?" she asked.

"I'm sure you already know," I said, smiling weakly. "My return home."

"Then stay," Mikilana said, taking my hand.

"I have already let down my parents. I won't fail my people," I said.

"Young girls shouldn't worry about such things," she said.

"I was born a princess. It's not a worry. It's my duty," I said.

"Children should be carefree and happy, not readying themselves for what happens after their parents are gone," she said.

"I was happy with my life. It was good. Honestly, I have more worries now than I ever did at home."

"Stop thinking about going back and you'll find those concerns fade in time," she said, looking hopeful.

"I have more reasons to go than to stay," I said. "And I'll never be happy living as a coward."

"Then I will not stand in your way," she said, her gaze falling away. "I want nothing more than for you to be happy."

"I know it's not easy for you to say that," I said, squeezing her hand. "Know that I will never forget you or this place."

Frowning, she nodded but didn't say anything.

Ka'imi called for me from outside as I finished another mai'a.

"We have a boat to test," he said, as I walked out of Mikilana's hut.

"The sooner, the better," I said.

Six men stood around the craft we built yesterday.

"First, let's make sure it floats," Ka'imi said. "Get it in the water."

Grunts and groans rose from the group as we hefted the weighty boat into the water. It sat low, the edge of the outriggers not far above the surface.

I'm not sure this is going to work.

"Three men per side—see if you can paddle straight," Ka'imi ordered.

When the first one got in, it took the boat below the surface and the outrigger sank.

"Well, that was not what I expected," Ka'imi said, scratching his chin. "Drag it out and let's see what we can do to fix it."

"It's too heavy," one of the men said.

"I agree," I said.

"And the finished boat will be heavier still," Ka'imi said. "How do we make it carry more weight without sinking? Meyla, the boat you came here is much heavier than this one. How does it float?"

"It's much taller and wider than those outriggers," I said.

Ka'imi looked at my broken boat for a few heartbeats. "We'll need more wood."

After scaring away a large group of monkeys, we had another tree on the beach and set to work, adding its material to the outriggers until they were roughly twice as wide and raising the sides more than twice as high. With the changes, the craft was even heavier, but it rode higher in the water. Now, the six men could sit in place and paddle but going straight was a challenge.

"It needs a way to steer it," I said.

"In due time, Water Princess," Ka'imi said, watching the boat veer left and right as the men tried to work together. "First, we need to put the hut on it and mount the sail."

"If you have the sail up without a way to steer, it will be uncontrollable," I said. "And moving much faster in the wind."

"But I want to be able to steer from inside," he said, crossing his arms. "If a storm hits during the journey, that will be the safest place."

"So, we build the hut, figure out how to steer, then mount the sail," I said, smiling as I crossed my arms to mock him.

"Turn around! Bring it back to land!" Ka'imi yelled, to his men.

The boat weaved its way back to shore as the paddlers fought to control it.

"This will not work," Makoa said, when they reached the shore.

"We're not finished," Ka'imi said. "Gather enough ohe to make a hut and make sure to get one more long piece, at least as big around as your arm."

"Are we going to work on this long enough that we need a hut on the beach?" Makoa asked.

The king's brother chuckled. "We're building a small hut on the platform and the long pole will help steer the boat."

"How will that work?" Makoa asked.

"You'll see," I said, not sure what Ka'imi had in mind but doing what I could to support him.

"And what will you be doing while we're gathering?" one of the other boatmen asked.

"Checking with the weavers to see how they are coming with the sail," Ka'imi said. "Which reminds me, get two more long poles."

"I don't understand how the sail will work either," Makoa said, shaking his head. the

"You'll see," I said again. "And it will make your job easier."

"If you say so," he replied, before turning to lead the crew away.

"Have you not explained any of this to them?" I asked Ka'imi.

"I figured they wouldn't believe me if I did," he said, shrugging.

I laughed. "I've been working on it with you and I'm not sure I believe it will work as well as you do."

He smirked. "Like you said, they'll see once it's finished."

Chapter 70

The weavers greeted us with big smiles and spread out a large, brown rug on the ground in front of us.

"Perfect," Ka'imi said, saluting them.

I bit my lip for a moment. "Umm...it's at least twice the size we need."

"Better to have more, in case we mess something up. Also, maybe the boat will need two," he shrugged. "Who knows?"

I shuddered at the thought of trying to control two sails. "Now, *I'm* not so sure this is going to work."

He chuckled. "Wait and see."

I sighed. "Fine. How are we going to get it back to the boat?"

"Roll it up and carry it," he said, thanking the weavers again.

Though it was stiff and dense, the sail was lighter than I expected. I thought I could probably carry it by myself if it wasn't so big.

Makoa and the others were eating opae soup when we returned.

"After lunch, it's time to build a special hut," Ka'imi said, resting his hand on the wooden platform.

The boatmen laughed.

"This will never work," Makoa said.

"Maybe, maybe not...we won't know until we try," Ka'imi said.

Much like the boatmen, I doubted the king's brother, but if we could make his idea work it was my best option for getting back home.

Our hunger taken care of, we went to work. Since I had never built an ohe hut before, I made myself useful by carrying the green poles to where they were needed. Before they started on the roof, Ka'imi called for me.

"Yes?" I asked.

"Take wood from your broken boat that we can use as a steering paddle," he said, putting his hand on my shoulder.

I frowned and looked at my craft, laying on its side on the beach. "How are you going to put it on this thing we're building?" I asked.

"That's what the biggest ohe pole is for. I think I know how it will work but you have a better idea of what's needed in the water."

I nodded, still unsure of what he had in mind, and hurried to remove a suitable piece of wood from the vessel that brought me here. From the side of my boat, I sythed a piece as wide as my arm span and about a head shorter than my height then worked it flat. Convinced it would do what we needed, I dragged it back to the worksite to find a long pole, nearly as big around as my calf, sticking out from a slot in the hut's back wall. The end I could see rested on the beach about six paces away from the back edge of the platform.

Ka'imi jumped out of a door on the left side of the hut and splashed onto the beach to help carry my burden. "Let's join this with the steering pole."

"The ko'a'ke'a will rip this off as soon as we try to pass over it," I said.

Ka'imi shook his head. "I'm ready for that. After we get this in place, I'll show you."

Working our energies together, we soon had the wood and ohe connected well enough that it wouldn't come apart, at least until it struck something like the poisoned barrier between Aina and the open water.

"Now, come with me," Ka'imi said.

Inside the hut, another thick pole stuck up from the platform, about a hand away from the back wall. The steering pole rested inside a slot in the stand.

"Watch," Ka'imi said, as he put his hands on the steering lever. With a grunt, he pushed down and the lever reaching out of the back of the boat rose. "We can keep it off the ko'a'ke'a as we pass." He pulled the lever, and it swung with a little effort.

I pursed my lips and nodded. "That should work." Turning, I pointed to the two large openings in the front of the boat, giving a nearly unobstructed view of the water ahead of us. "Now, how are you going to keep the inside dry with those there?"

"We'll have covers for them in case we hit a bad storm, like you did coming here," he said.

"I'm starting to think this might work," I said, walking to look out of the windows.

"There's enough room to walk on either side and in front of the hut," Ka'imi said, joining me. "We can fish off the front, too...if our food runs low."

"I tried that," I said, then shivered. "A mano got most of my catch."

"Yes. I recall your story about the monster and its teeth," Ka'imi said, rubbing his hands together. "I think we'll be safe here." He stomped on the platform. "Above the water."

"What about the sail?" I asked.

"We'll work on it after the roof is done," he said, "While we wait, tell me again about how the sail worked on your boat."

I gestured while describing the main pole and cross poles that held the sail once more. Then went into detail about the ropes and how they controlled how much wind the fabric would catch.

"What are *ropes*?" he questioned. You could tell the word felt strange to his mouth.

"Like the strap that holds our skirts tight," I said, patting my waist. "But as big around as my thumb and much stronger."

"If we bring you leaves, can you make what we need?" he asked.

"I can try," I said. "It shouldn't be hard, but it will take time to make enough."

"I'll ask the weavers to help if needed," he said.

The last of the roof was fixed in place as we talked, covering most of the inside in shadow. Ka'imi poked his head out of the window in front of him and yelled for some of the men to gather nui leaves. The rest, with his help, were to work on attaching the main pole for the sail to the platform and the front of the hut.

With nothing to do but wait, I pushed my talent into the wood platform to get familiar with the feel of this new craft. Where the ohe was bound into the platform, energy did not flow as smoothly as I would have liked. Forcing the grasslike fibers into the wood's grain left stresses that didn't exist where the platform joined the boats on each side. There, the wood joined together smoothly so they felt like one piece. *If the sail pole has the same feel, that could be a weakness. I better mention it to Ka'imi.*

Instead of distracting him by yelling through the window, I walked out of the hut and along the edge of the platform to see for myself what they had done. The tall ohe pole reached well above the hut's roof with another pole jointed across the top. "That won't work," I said, deciding this mistake was more important than my other concern.

"Why not?" Ka'imi asked.

Again, I described how the sail had to be fixed to a bottom cross bar then raised with ropes to the top bar. "This pole has no place to hold the bottom of the sail."

He smiled. "It will attach to the hut, taking some of the load off this pole."

I opened my mouth to say something then stopped and considered what he'd said.

"Your boat had no structure like this," he said, patting the hut's front wall. "I think that's why the wind was able to rip your sail away."

I closed my mouth and nodded. "You could be right, but this hut is not well connected to the platform. Check for yourself."

"I have," he said, then nodded to Makoa. "And so has he. This is stronger than your sail pole."

I hope he's right. "Then how are the ropes going to work?"

"You said the sail has to go to the top bar to catch wind. We will work holes in the cross pole, run the rope through them then through openings in the roof so we can pull from inside," Makoa said.

The first two armloads of nui leaves hit the floor inside as we were talking.

"We need another pole for the top of the sail," I said.

"I don't think so," Ka'imi said. "We can join the rope and the sail together, then they'll move as one."

"That's not how my sail was made," I said.

"We can always change it if it doesn't work," Ka'imi said, "but this way it is lighter and should be strong enough."

"We'll try it your way," I said, hopping through the closest window and sitting to weave the coarse strands of leaves into something resembling a rope.

After bringing a second load, the boatmen joined me in the tedious task. To my surprise, they learned quickly, and we had more than enough rope made before the setting sun turned the sky red.

"Good work," Ka'imi said, then groaned as he stood. "Eat and rest well, we have more work to do in the morning before we can test what we have."

His men grunted their agreement before we splashed our way onto the beach and went our separate ways.

Chapter 71

"You look tired," Mikilana said, when I shuffled inside.

"Lots of work and more still to do," I said, nodding.

"That thing you are building... It looks...different," she said, handing me a bowl of food.

I was too tired to pay attention to what I was eating. "I'm not sure everything's going to work, but Ka'imi is confident. We should know more tomorrow."

"So, you'll be leaving soon?" she asked.

I shrugged. "If all goes well, maybe. I'd like to try one more time to convince Ha'upu that sending Keoni with me is a bad idea."

She raised her eyebrows. "I believe the prince would miss you at least as much as I will."

I sighed. "And he'll get over it sooner than you."

"Might there be room for one more?" Mikilana asked.

I looked at her, shadows from the fading sunlight making her wrinkles look deeper than they were. "It's too dangerous. None of us may survive the trip. Even if we do find my homeland, I may be fighting for my life from the moment I get off the boat."

"I know you're right," she said, frowning. "But my heart tells me to go anyway."

I reached for her hand. "And my heart tells me you would regret leaving the only home you've ever known." *I know I do.*

"You are wise beyond your age," she said, patting my hand and smiling with glistening eyes. "Your parents must be proud."

Closing my eyes, I nodded. *Or they were.* "Thank you."

"Finish eating and get some rest," she said, squeezing my hand.

I yawned, slurped the rest of the food from the bowl, and went to bed.

Mikilana was not there when I woke but she left two nui on the table. I took one and headed to the beach where I could eat and enjoy the sunrise while listening to the waves crash against the ko'a'ke'a.

Ka'imi arrived not long after and his men weren't far behind him. He saluted me and hopped onto the boat as I put a strip of i'o nui in my mouth. Soon after stepping inside the hut, he looked out and waved for me to come inside.

Assuming something was wrong, I hurried to see what he'd found.

Mikilana was asleep on the platform, near the steering lever.

"She wants to go with me," I said, quietly.

"I don't think she'd survive the journey," he said, putting his hand on my shoulder.

"Me either," I said. *None of us may make it.*

"Finish eating. I'll talk to her," he said.

I walked to the front of the boat, sat on the platform, and dangled my feet into the cool water while pulling more strips of white flesh out of the nui shell.

Ka'imi and Mikilana spoke in hushed tones. I didn't bother trying to listen to what he told her but she wished me success before a couple of the boatmen helped her back to shore.

"She loves you like a daughter," Ka'imi said, sitting next to me.

"And I appreciate her taking care of me," I said.

"If we get you home, don't come back here," he said, flatly. "She'll survive this broken heart but no more."

"If I knew it would be safe, I'd gladly take her to the Satran lands. She could see where her ancestors came from," I said, wiping my eyes. "Knowing your family is important."

"*We* are her family. This is where she was born," Ka'imi said, then pointed over the water. "Her ancestors are long forgotten by anyone out there."

"You'd be surprised," I said, remembering what my father told me about why the Satran people feared traveling by water. "Her ancestor's disappearance are the reason Satra's people stay on land."

He nodded. "Maybe, but it doesn't matter. We have work to do. Finish your meal and let's get the sail in place."

Eating the last few bites quickly, I hurried to my feet. "Ready. What do you want to do first?"

"I think we should bind the fabric to the hut, then figure out how best to attach the ropes and see how things work from there," Ka'imi said. "Climb onto the roof and I'll hand you the bottom of the sail."

Remembering how the boatmen used their talent to scamper up trees in the jungle, I climbed the hut's wall and reached the roof with ease. "Ready," I said, sitting with my legs dangling over the edge.

Ka'imi hefted the bulky, rolled-up sail over his shoulder and scaled the main pole one-handed. "Here," he said, shoving a corner toward me.

I guided it onto the roof and let it unfurl down to the platform. The far end fell into the water. Ignoring that problem, for now, I started the task of attaching the woven fiber to the hut. Taking the opportunity to strengthen this part of the structure, I wove the fibers of the roof, the top of the wall, and the bottom of the sail together tightly.

"Now this end," he said, before tossing the part of the sail that had been soaking in the water toward me.

Wet fiber slapped me in the face. I growled at him and set about sything the water out of the tight weave before asking him why I was attaching this end too.

"I want to try something," he said. "You'll see."

And I want to go home, so I'm not going to argue...unless it seems like this won't work at all. Joining the woven cloth to itself took almost no time and even less energy.

Makoa and Ka'imi threaded the rope through the far end of the sail while I worked.

"Make a hole to drop these inside," Ka'imi said, tossing the ends of the rope to me.

With little more than a thought, I opened a passage about the size of my palm, directly behind the sail pole, and dropped the rope through.

"Pull," Ka'imi ordered from inside.

As the coarse rope slid through the opening, the ohe frayed and splintered. "Stop!" I yelled, before explaining what was happening.

"Can you fix it?" Ka'imi asked.

"Maybe," I replied, my voice raising in pitch as I considered how to solve the problem now and keep it from happening every time we raised and lowered the sail. Brushing my fingers over the hole's sharp edge, I pressed the splinters back into place then smoothed the repaired section.

"Let the rope loose a little," I called down.

As it moved back up, the roof splintered again. "Stop!"

Putting the splinters back again, I pushed more of my talent into the ohe, curving the edge and packing the grassy fibers tighter together, leaving a harder, smoother surface for the rope to rub against. "Pull it again!"

This time the coarse rope slid easily across the ohe and the sail came to a stop when it hit the cross pole. "Perfect," I said, before letting out a whoop. *One step closer to going home. Let's see how they plan to secure the rope in place.*

Scurrying down the side of the hut, I stepped in to find two of the boatmen holding the rope tight.

"We need a way to secure it so they can let go," I said.

Ka'imi and Makoa looked at me with their brows furrowed.

I sighed and pushed my talent into the floor to raise a loop between the two men. "Tie the ends of the rope there."

Their questioning expression told me they didn't understand either.

"Watch," I said, grabbing the loose ends of the rope. Thicker and stiffer than what was on my boat, they didn't tie as easily but their coarse texture helped keep my knots in place. "Let go."

Hesitantly, they released the rope and stepped back. Stretching against the load, it creaked but held fast. "The sail will stay up until the knots are untied or something breaks," I said.

"Interesting," Ka'imi said, rubbing his chin before turning to Makoa. "Get in the boats. Let's see if this works."

Makoa looked at him for a moment, then gave the rest of the boatmen their assignments.

"Are you sure this is a good idea?" I asked, as the craft gently rocked with their movement.

"No sense in working on anything else until we know we have something useful," Ka'imi said. "Help me steer."

"What about the sail?" I asked.

"The trees block the wind behind us," he said. "From what you've said, any wind from ahead will stop us. So, no worries."

I smirked at his confidence then nodded and hurried to the steering lever. We both pushed down to free the wood panel on the end from the sand and Ka'imi shouted for the boatmen to paddle forward.

Chapter 72

The boat lurched as the men struggled to free it from the beach. The sound of wood sliding over wet sand filled the hut then we moved. Zig-zagging left and right, the men struggled to paddle together without one side being able to see the other.

Ka'imi bent to look through the hole in the hut's back wall, watching for when the steering board was over water. "Let's see if this helps," he said.

Together, we eased the wood down and worked to keep the boat going straight. With the unnecessary motion gone, we picked up speed.

"When are we going to try turning?" I asked.

"Beyond the ko'a'ke'a, where we have more room," he said.

"Then I better drop the sail," I said.

"Leave it," Ka'imi said. "I want to see what happens."

I can open the tie-down loop from here if I have to. Grunting a response, I kept my hand firmly on the steering lever and my eyes fixed on the stone barrier ahead of us.

Makoa yelled for Ka'imi from outside.

"Keep going!" the king's brother bellowed back.

The rope quivered, telling me we were moving fast enough for the sail to work against the men paddling.

"If you want to go faster, we have to let the sail down," I said.

"Leave it and we'll find out what happens," Ka'imi said.

I don't know what he's expecting but this could go wrong, quickly. With a sigh, I did my part to keep us going straight.

"Lift the panel!" he yelled, as the poisonous stone barrier loomed in the shallow water now not far ahead.

Without our help to guide it, the boat twitched from side to side again. A wave crashed over the far side of the ko'a'ke'a, giving us a bigger cushion of safety and we passed over the barrier without touching it.

"Yes!" he bellowed. "Keep going!"

I took my hands off the steering lever. The panel splashed back into the water, jerking the boat straight again but almost ripping the lever out of Ka'imi's hands.

"What are you doing?" I asked. "We have no supplies and no way back if we sink out here."

He glared at me for a moment then nodded. "Right. Sorry, but I haven't had this much fun in a long time. Turn left and we'll go back."

I grabbed the steering to help as he shouted orders.

The boat shuddered as we slowed while fighting to turn. The sail rope went slack for a moment, and we swung left harder than we probably should. Working against the lever, I did what I could to help us turn smoothly.

The rope snapped taut, and the boat surged like a horse going from trot to gallop. Panicked screams came from the boatmen. The long steering pole flexed against our efforts to keep the boat under control. It quivered as Ka'imi shoved energy into it. I felt it crack and lashed out with my talent toward the tie down holding the sail rope in place, splitting it open. With the anchor point gone, the knotted rope flew toward the roof letting the sail go limp and flop over the front windows.

My heart raced as the boat slowed and settled into the water.

"I told you we should drop the sail!" I screamed. Warm prickles irritated my skin from the inside. A shiver I couldn't control shook my body.

Ka'imi dropped to the floor and wiped his hand across his face.

Makoa stomped in. "What were you thinking?" he bellowed.

"Meyla told me what could happen, but I didn't believe her. I wanted to see for myself," the king's brother said, eyes cast down.

"Water Princess, can you get us back to shore by yourself?" Makoa asked. "I'm not sure Ka'imi should be in charge anymore."

"I can hold us straight. If this works at all like my boat did, have your men on the right side paddle until we're facing land. Then both sides paddle, slow and steady, until we hit the beach," I said.

He nodded, glared at Ka'imi a moment, then left to give my directions to his men.

The king's brother stood at the front, holding the sail aside so I could see where we were going and we made our way, safely, back to land.

Makoa and his fellow boatmen left without a word.

Ka'imi looked at me and headed for the door, shoulders slumped.

"Wait," I said.

Chapter 73

"I'll tell Ha'upu to find a worthy leader to help you return home," he said. "I'm sorry I put everyone in danger by not listening to your wisdom."

"Apology accepted," I said. "Will you listen to me now?"

He nodded.

"We learned a lot today, much more than if the sail had been down," I said.

"But we weren't safe. I'm supposed to keep my men safe. I didn't do the most important job I have," he said.

"True," I said, drawing the word out. "But we know the sail works and the rope will hold, and the boat will survive some fairly rough handling.""Make sure you tell all of that to whoever my brother chooses," he said, heading for the door.

"I'm telling the person I'm choosing," I said. "This isn't your king's decision to make."

"If I go, those men won't," he said, pointing toward where the boatmen left.

"Help me make sure the steering lever isn't damaged beyond repair then go apologize to your men. Tell Makoa I'm making you stay if you think it will help," I said.

"Why?" he asked. "I could have killed you."

"Because now you'll listen to me," I said, smiling. "I'm afraid whoever Ha'upu picked to replace you would have to learn this lesson all over again."

"Then let's check that pole. If it is not broken too badly, I still have other damage to mend," Ka'imi said, nodding.

Near the middle of the steering pole, we found three cracks, about as long as my arm. They had let in some water which I drained by opening a small hole while Ka'imi and I considered how to keep the ohe from cracking again.

He wanted to insert wood inside the hollow pole, but I felt that would add too much weight and make it harder to lift from the water when necessary. Together, we closed the cracks and then compromised on a fix wrapping some wood from my boat around the pole from near where it sat in the water to about an arm's length before it passed through the back wall of the hut.

I finished wrapping the wood while Ka'imi took on the task of convincing the boatmen he wasn't going to kill everyone on the trip with his enthusiasm. The sun was past its peak when I finished working but Ka'imi had not returned.

Hunger convinced me I should worry about the king's brother later, so I left to find something to eat. Keoni stopped me on my way to Mikilana's hut.

"My father sent me for you," he said.

"I'll see him after I eat," I said, nodding and rubbing my stomach.

"We have food in the hall," he said.

I tilted my head. "Then I'm ready to talk with Ha'upu."

Lunch was a bowl of roasted opae with chunks of fish and nui. Much to my surprise, Keoni sat next to his father instead of as close to me as he could get away with.

"Do you feel safe on this new boat?" Ha'upu asked.

"I felt safe on my boat," I said, smiling. "Until a storm tore it up and set me adrift to land here."

"Do you believe this craft will get you to your homeland?" he asked, his expression and tone hard to read.

At this point, I'd try to get to Croy on anything that floated. "Yes," I said, trying to hide my desperation.

"I understand my brother put everyone at risk. Do you agree?" he asked.

"Ka'imi was eager to see the results of his hard work. He knows more, now. I expect he will not push his people, or himself, as hard next time," I said, leaving out how I had warned him.

"I'm not sure there should be a next time," Ha'upu said.

No! I'll find a way to take it myself before I stay here. "No need to make a hasty decision, your Majesty. Ka'imi understands he made a mistake." I looked at Keoni and remembered the incident with the mano blood. "Excitement clouded his judgment." I closed my eyes. "You've insisted this boat will benefit your people. Don't let the effort go to waste now."

"I will not go, Father," Keoni said. "You heard Makoa. It's certain death."

I sighed. "Makoa is a hard worker and a good boatman. Doubt clouds his judgment as much as excitement clouded your brother's, your Majesty. Ka'imi is speaking with the men, apologizing for his actions. I will make sure it doesn't happen again."

"How?" Keoni scoffed, crossing his arms. "What makes you think my uncle will listen to you?"

"Because he already has," I said. "As far as you not wanting to go, I think it best for you to stay here anyway, at least until I find out if I have a home to return to. Should you want to visit Croy afterward, you will be welcome. If my family still sits on the throne, I would like to arrange trade between our nations. As I've said before, I believe it would benefit us both."

"Keoni, find your uncle. I will speak with him before making my final decision," Ha'upu said.

"Yes, father."

"Am I part of this conversation?" I asked.

"If you are needed, I will send for you," Ha'upu said. "Thank you for meeting with me."

"Of course, your Majesty," I replied, saluting.

He returned my gesture before I turned to leave.

Chapter 74

Word of our adventure had reached Mikilana's ears. She had paced a track in the sand outside of her hut and hurried to me, wiping her eyes, when she saw me. "Please tell me you've changed your mind." She put her hands on my shoulders.

"I can't stay here," I said, pulling her into a hug. "I don't belong here."

"Then take me with you," she whispered in my ear.

"I know what Ka'imi told you," I said, "and he's right. This is your home."

"It hasn't felt like home since I found out there are still others out there," she said, squeezing me.

I pushed away from her, to look her in the eyes. "Until I can find a way to get you to Satra safely, to see your ancestor's homeland, you must stay here. I can't say when, or if, that might happen...and I'm sorry for that. And for all the trouble I've caused."

"Trouble? No. You've been a joy," Mikilana said. "The only thing troubling was the loss of your brother."

"He caused more than his fair share of problems, that's for sure," I said. "If my parents are still alive, I do not look forward to explaining how he died. My mother... They were close. She'll be devastated both by the loss and his betrayal."

"What about your father?" she asked, taking my hand and leading me into the hut.

I shrugged as I sat. "His half brother betrayed him. My twin brother betrayed me. Guess it's in our blood."

"Then it's up to you to make sure it all ends. Family should always support each other," she said, pouring a cup of wainui for me.

"That's the tragic part. I'm here because my brother disguised treachery as support. His jealousy and greed may have cost both of us everything," I said. My lip quivered, and I hurried to hide it with the ohe cup.

"Do not be ashamed of sadness," she said. "Mourning doesn't mean you forget the ones you lost, it means you learn how to carry them with you."

"Because of what he did, and what he planned to do, to me...I don't want to carry him. How do I leave him behind, spread on the ground where he belongs?"

Mikilana frowned. "I don't know what to tell you. I believe your brother should always have a place in your heart, even though he wronged you."

"Then I'll have to figure it out for myself," I said, taking another sip of the sweet water.

"Meyla, are you here?" Ka'imi called from outside.

Good news or bad? "Yes," I said, getting to my feet.

He met me at the door. "Can you be ready to leave at sunrise?"

Mikilana drew a sharp breath behind me.

"I have almost nothing to take with me," I said, raising my eyebrows. "I could leave now."

Mikilana, stepping to my side, put her arm across my shoulders. "I'm not ready for you to go."

"I know you will carry me with you and I will never forget you," I said, putting my arm around her before turning back to Ka'imi. "Who is going with me?"

"I spoke with the boatmen and gave my word that the sail would be down anytime they were in the outriggers. Makoa got them to agree on the condition that he could throw me off the boat if I don't keep my promise."

I chuckled. "How does King Ha'upu feel about that?"

"I swore to him I would not get thrown off my own boat," he said, smiling.

"And Keoni? Is he coming with us?" I asked.

"He refuses to set foot on the boat," Ka'imi said. "Not sure what my brother will do about his defiance but I'm going as the king's voice now."

"Probably for the best," I said. "My brother was not completely comfortable on my boat, and look at where it got me."

Ka'imi pressed his lips together for a moment then nodded.

"If everyone has agreed to go, why are we waiting for sunrise?" I asked.

"Two reasons: first, the sea will be high, helping us get past the ko'a'ke'a. Also, we need time to gather and load the supplies," he said.

I nodded and stepped away from Mikilana. "Anything I can help with?"

"Gather your things and stay with her," Ka'imi said, tilting his head toward Mikilana. "That's where you are needed."

I reached for her hand. "I can do that."

"Then I will see you on the beach in the morning," he replied, saluting before leaving us standing alone.

Chapter 75

"What would you like to do?" I asked my mentor.

"Enjoy the time I have left with you," Mikilana said, eyes glistening with tears.

"As you wish," I said. "I'll follow your lead."

For a while, we strolled around the village. I listened to her tell stories about growing up and what she had experienced. At one point, we sat near the edge of the jungle and listened to the birds and monkeys as she recalled her husband's funeral. Near the end of the day, we moved to the beach and ate opae soup as the sun sank into the water.

As the last of the day's light faded, Mikilana rose to her feet and held her hand out to help me stand. "I'm sorry I took all of your time today and you didn't get a chance to gather anything of your own before now."

Taking her offered assistance, but using my own strength to rise, I rubbed my thumb across the back of her hand. "This was time well spent, for both of us. I have nothing more than this skirt, my broken bow, my sword, and Regin's axes and vest. Those are in your hut."

"Thank you for understanding," she said, squeezing my hand as we walked side by side.

When we reached the hut, I moved my few things near the door and Mikilana added an ohe cup along with two nui to the small pile.

"Save those for when you get home. Share them with your people and smile when you remember where they came from. There will always be more waiting for you here," she said, before going to bed.

I sat just inside the door and watched the deep, red light of the evening sky give way to darkness before laying next to my mentor and trying to sleep.

Chapter 76

Anticipation, excitement, and fear made themselves known in my dreams. I was back on my boat, wind whipping my hair. Men rowed hard and fast on either side of me as we sped toward a stone wall. No matter which way I turned the boat, we were in constant danger of breaking to pieces against the barrier always looming ahead of us.

I woke exhausted, wondering if it was still night. Looking to the door, I saw Mikilana standing outside, facing east, and saluting the coming day.

Dragging myself out of bed, I fixed my sword belt in place. The now-unfamiliar, leather strap put an unnerving weight on my hips. Its burden grew when I clipped my sword in place.

Mikilana turned when the axes clanged together as I removed them before lifting the black, leather vest.

"I doubt you slept any better than I did," she said. I could hear the smile in her voice.

"I couldn't calm my mind," I said, looking at the bulky garment.

"And I couldn't calm my heart," she replied. "It feels like I'm losing a child I never had."

"And you are like the grandmother I never met," I said, deciding it would be easier to wear Regin's vest than carry it.

If I thought the belt was awkward, the vest was completely uncomfortable. It scraped against the tender skin on my chest and shoulders with every movement. *Obviously, not meant for a woman to wear.* Simply having something covering the top of my body was strange enough, then I strapped the axes in place and their weight nearly pulled me over.

Mikilana got to my side as quickly as she could and offered to carry her gifts while walking me to the beach. I thanked her and we were on our way. I could have sworn all eyes followed me as we passed through the crowd standing between me and the floating hut that would carry me home.

To her credit, she did not cry when the boat came into sight.

I felt the burn of my tears threaten but fought them back, choosing to smile instead.

Someone had turned the vessel around so that the front faced the open water again and the steering pole rested on the beach. King Ha'upu hugged each boatman, then saluted them, before they took their position in the outriggers. Ka'imi saw me and waved, beckoning me to hurry.

Mikilana grunted when I hugged her tight. I kissed her cheek, then brushed a tear from her eye before taking the tall cup and nui from her. "Take care of yourself," I said. "Thank you for everything. Promise me you'll be happy."

"Make it home safely," she said, turning away as I broke our embrace.

My feet dragged as I walked across the sand to King Ha'upu.

"Meyla, Water Princess, be safe," he said. "I look forward to seeing you again."

"Should the wind and water carry me back, I'll smile at seeing Aina again, your Majesty," I said, bowing awkwardly with the unfamiliar weight I carried. "I cannot thank you and your people enough for what they have done for me."

"May we both reap the benefits of the effort," he said, saluting. "Keep my brother on that boat."

"I'll do the best I can," I said, trying to not laugh.

One of the boatmen helped me onto the platform and I stepped inside the hut. Nui and mai'a were stacked against the walls near the front. A pile of rolled-up sleeping mats sat in the rear corner. Ka'imi stood at the steering arm, smiling wide. "Waiting on you, Water Princess."

I placed Mikilana's gifts near the mats and took my position across from the king's brother. "Here's to safe and swift travels," I said.

We pushed down on the lever and Ka'imi ordered the boatmen to paddle. This time, cheers rose outside as the boat lurched forward. My heartbeat sped up along with the craft as we moved away from the beach.

Chapter 78

We dropped the steering pole into the water and kept the boat headed straight toward the stone barrier sitting between Aina and the rest of the world.

With the edge of the ko'a'ke'a in sight, we lifted the steering panel out of the water again, letting it splash back down once we knew we were clear of the danger. Cheers came from both sides as the boatmen celebrated another safe crossing.

The boat slowed when we hit the bigger waves waiting in the open waters.

"When are you going to call them inside?" I asked.

"After you fix the place to tie the rope," he replied, nodding toward the front of the boat.

"Oh, right," I said. "Can you keep us straight until I get back?"

"Don't worry about me," he said.

I hurried forward and worked fast to rebuild the tie down I had sythed apart to get the boat back under control before. After getting the loose ropes in place, I turned and said, "Ready."

"Everyone inside," Ka'imi called.

We slowed, and the boat rocked from side to side, as the men left the outriggers for the safety of the hut.

"Sail up!" I yelled, pulling the rope. The rough fiber tore at my hands when the sail caught some wind. I yelped and several of the men rushed to help me.

"Pull it tight and tie it fast," I ordered. Thin lines of blood rose from minor scrapes across my palms. *Nothing to worry about.* The rope creaked, straining against the wind forcing us forward.

"Where are we going, Meyla?" Ka'imi asked, as we picked up speed.

I peeked out to note where the sun was compared to where we were heading. *North should be good, for now...I hope.* "Keep it straight, as long as this wind holds out," I said.

"It's all up to you now," Ka'imi said.

That's what I'm afraid of.

I kept watch on the sail, and where we were heading, while Ka'imi taught the boatmen how to steer. Near midday, the wind died, and we stopped.

"What do we do now?" Makoa asked.

"Take some time to eat and see if the wind comes back," I said. "I'll drop the sail, so we don't get caught by surprise."

The boat bobbed and rocked under us, riding gentle swells as they passed.

After eating a couple of mai'a, I clumsily scampered to the roof — *Why am I still wearing this stuff? I guess I am carrying Regin home.* — to look around.

Sparse clouds dotted the sky with no threat of a storm. Aina was a dark spot on the water behind us. Ahead, and to both sides, I saw nothing but open water. *Maybe I'll see some familiar stars after sunset.*

Ka'imi didn't look happy with my report. "Should we start rowing?" he asked.
Everyone turned to look at him.

"It wouldn't hurt," I said, "but there's no reason to be in a hurry. If two men per side can get us moving, that's good enough. No sense in wearing ourselves out, in case there's no wind tonight or tomorrow."

"Makoa, put together groups of four, two men per side," Ka'imi said.

The master boatman groaned. "You heard them. Pair up and let's get moving."

Before long, we were underway again, making slow progress. As the day wore on, men took their turns. One group paddled while the other rested. I did my best to keep them supplied with wainui while Ka'imi held us on a mostly northerly course.

With the sun low on the western edge of the water, a stiff breeze blew through the eastern door. "Back inside!" I yelled. "Let's catch that wind!"

The paddlers groaned leaving their seats, rubbing tired muscles as they sat inside the hut.

I raised the sail then helped Ka'imi steer the boat on a northwestern angle with the light wind barely billowing the fibrous fabric. Although I wasn't sure, exactly, how to get back to Croy, I wanted to go more north than west because I was sure the storm Regin and I sailed through had blown us well south of our intended destination.

"Someone watch for storms," I said, seeing the boatmen settling down to eat and sleep.

The man nearest the front nodded and settled into a spot where he could peer at the sky through the big windows. He was the first to fall asleep.

"You should get some rest too," I said.

Ka'imi chuckled. "All I've done is hold us steady. You've worked harder than me. Sleep. I'll wake you when I can't keep my eyes open."

"If you insist," I said, eyeing him and smirking. "Don't do anything to get yourself thrown off the boat."

"You have nothing to worry about," he said, grinning.

"Which makes me more concerned," I said, moving where I could see out the door to the east.

He laughed as I settled and closed my eyes.

Usually, the sounds and smells of being on a boat relaxed me, but now they set me on edge. Unable to relax, I peered across the dark expanse of water. Moonlight danced in sparkles on the ripples of wind-driven waves. Looking into the sky, I gazed at the stars, hoping to find a familiar pattern from the ones I knew at home but afraid I'd forgotten them during my time in Aina.

Chapter 78

"Meyla," someone, a man, called my name in a whisper.

Father?

"Water Princess."

Not my father.

"Your turn to steer. I'm falling asleep on my feet."

My eyes opened as I realized I'd fallen asleep. Heart racing, I looked out and still saw darkness. "Anything I need to know?"

"Nothing has changed," Ka'imi said.

I nodded and rose. "Sleep well."

"Don't do anything that might get me thrown off the boat," he said, laying down.

I chuckled and hurried to the steering lever.

Soon after I took my post, the wind shifted, and I turned us farther to the north to catch it. Several of the men woke when we sped up. "Everything's fine," I said.

They yawned and nodded before looking outside to see if I was telling the truth.

"Call out if you see anything," I said.

"Clouds floating across the moon," someone said.

"Best keep an eye on them," I replied, flicking my eyes toward the western door. "Surprise storms are no fun."

"Aye, Water Princess."

Makoa and Ka'imi woke as the eastern sky brightened and discussed the coming day as they ate together.

"Need a rest?" Ka'imi asked, bringing me a couple of mai'a.

"I'm doing fine, but wouldn't mind a chance to look outside," I said, taking the fruit. "Those clouds have me worried and it would be nice to spot something telling me we're going the right way."

"Makoa and I can take over," he said.

I nodded and kept one hand on the lever until he had a firm grip on it.

Careful not to crush my breakfast, I made my way to the roof and sat where I could look north and west without the sail blocking my sight. Nothing in the darkness looked familiar and the daylight reaching across the sky didn't reveal anything new. Those clouds were already thinning when the sun warmed my back. The only positive was the steady, easterly breeze.

Curiosity satisfied and breakfast finished, I worked my way back down and gave a quick report to Ka'imi.

He nodded but kept his eyes forward.

"All we can do is follow the wind, for now," I said.

"My men appreciate the sail more and more," Makoa said, and laughed. It was the first time I'd heard him make that sound. It reminded me of a choking dog.

"I'm going to look to the east and see if I find anything," I said, turning on my heel.

"Nothing out there, Water Princess," a boatman near the door said.

I nodded and looked anyway. *He's right.*

With nothing interesting to keep our attention, I tried to teach my companions a few useful Croain and Varian words. To give them a break between lessons, I did my best to imitate Uncle Crum and wove tales about my home and Varia, the people I knew and the stories I'd heard from my parents.

"Something's out there!" someone shouted from the front window, interrupting me while I talked about riding horses with the Queen of Varia. Jesca was an amazing rider and a great teacher.

"What?" I shouted back, turning to look.

A dark spot on the water teased us from the northwest. With the sun nearing the water to the west, we would lose sight of the spot against the night sky.

"Turn west until I tell you to stop," I ordered, unsure of who was steering at the time. We slowed a little. The sail relaxed as we turned away from the best angle to catch the wind. "Keep it straight, now!" I yelled, as soon as the spot sat directly in front of the boat.

"What do you think it is?" Ka'imi asked, from my right.

"I don't know," I said. "And there's only one way to find out."

"Keep us steady," he said, over his shoulder.

My eyes stared at the dark spot until it faded into the night sky. Once the sun fully vanished below the water, I walked to the front of the platform and searched the stars. Time crawled as I looked for anything recognizable.

Eventually, I spotted the eight stars that formed a large sword pointing almost perfectly west. It was easier to find when I visited the Varian capital, but I could see it from home too. *Dare I believe I'm near my homeland?*

Calling for Ka'imi, I pointed the form out to him and told him what I thought it meant.

"Are you sure?" he asked.

I shrugged. "As much as I can be. At least, this looks familiar. It must be a good sign."

"I hope so," he said, patting me on the back.

The sail went slack, and we turned to look at it.

"I'd rather not paddle all night," Makoa said, from inside. Several grunts followed his statement.

Ka'imi looked at me. "What do you say?"

I may be almost home. Stepping inside, I looked at the men. "Rest tonight but someone should keep watch. If there's no wind in the morning, we paddle."

"Agreed," Ka'imi and Makoa said together.

"You said you'd been on the water for days before finding Aina," Ka'imi said. "Is it possible we're not where you think we are?"

"I don't know for certain where we are, so yes...we may be lost. If that's what you're asking," I said. "This could be my homeland or, maybe, a new place neither of us knows about."

He sighed. "What does your heart tell you?"

"That I'm closer to home now than I've been since I left," I said, trying to not cry.

"Trust your heart," he said, putting his hand on my shoulder. "It won't steer you wrong."

"It did when I left home with Regin," I said, rubbing one of the straps on the vest between my finger and thumb.

"You were following his heart," Ka'imi said. "From what you've said, none of this would have happened if you had followed yours."

I laughed and shook my head. "Had I stayed home, I would have probably had dinner with a stableboy named Svinulf followed by an argument with my mother about who I fall in love with."

"She wouldn't have approved?" he asked.

I thought about it for a moment and shrugged. "Maybe she would have...she didn't always frown on not doing what was expected. Of course, I may never find out."

"Don't lose hope," Ka'imi said, squeezing my shoulder. "You never know what tomorrow holds for you."

"Right now, I just want that," I pointed to where I'd last seen the dark place ahead of us, "to be home."

"I look forward to finding out with you," he said. "For now, let's eat."

"Go ahead. I'll keep watching."

He nodded and I walked back out, fixing my gaze ahead.

Chapter 81

Except for the murmured conversations inside the hut and the gentle lapping of waves against the outriggers, it was silent. The full moon gave enough light to see the water around me but not enough to pick out the outline of the land we'd spotted against the night sky. I stared at the sword of stars, doing everything I could to convince myself it meant what I thought.

Turning away from the symbol, I looked for clouds; knowing too well that a dangerous storm could be on us with little warning. Fortunately, the sky was clear. *Warm and still is far better than windy, cold, and wet.* With that in mind, I lay on the platform and looked up at the blanket of stars overhead until I fell asleep.

The boat jerked.

Something above me cracked like a whip.

I jumped and looked through blurry eyes. While scratching the crusts out of the corners of my eyes, another gust of wind pushed hard against the hut and the sail strained against the rope. Thunder rolled from the west.

"Get inside!" Makoa yelled.

Dark clouds raced across the moon, flashes lighting their insides.

"Drop the sail!" I cried, clambering through the nearest window.

"No," Ka'imi replied, standing at the steering lever. "We'll catch the wind and stay ahead of the storm."

"Drop it or we may lose it," I said, remembering the destruction the last storm I sailed through brought.

"Not if you help me steer," he said.

"The wind is not blowing the right way and waves are coming," I argued. "Drop the sail so we have one less thing to worry about while we wait for this to pass."

He opened his mouth to say something.

"I will throw you off this boat myself," I said, reaching for the rope.

Makoa grabbed my arm. "I think he's right this time. I've been watching the storm, and it isn't moving this way very fast. Maybe we can stay ahead of it."

"Or we could all die," I said, thunder cracking to make my point.

"If I'm wrong, I'll lower the sail," Makoa said. "Go help steer, Water Princess."

"Fine." I thrust my finger at Ka'imi. "But you do exactly what I say, when I say it, no questions."

"Yes."

"Hard left. That fabric won't take the full force of the wind for long," I said.

The steering pole flexed as we fought to angle the boat. I pushed my talent into the wood and felt Ka'imi do the same.

The gale roared through the hut and pushed the craft sideways, but the rope relaxed enough to stop vibrating.

"Let it back a little," I said. "Ease a little more wind into the sail, and let's see if it will take it."

The rope quivered and creaked but held and we moved more forward than sideways.

"See!" Ka'imi shouted. "We can do this."

"We're not out of danger yet," I said. "Makoa, at the first sign of damage, drop the sail."

"Aye," he said, without looking back at me.

A wind-driven wave crashed against the side of the hut. Water sprayed through the open door hitting everyone like cold pebbles.

"Can we close that?" I yelled.

"We never made doors," Ka'imi bellowed over the gusts.

I groaned. "I guess you never made covers for the windows either."

His frown told me everything I needed to know.

"Use bed pads to cover the openings," I said. "We don't want any more water getting in here than necessary."

The boatmen went to work sealing the hut while Ka'imi and I fought to keep us under some amount of control.

Several times the boat rocked hard to the side. From wind or waves, or both, I wasn't sure.

Twice, the rope went tight enough to hum. Each time we fought to turn the boat, hoping to relieve enough pressure to keep the sail intact.

My arms twitched and burned from pushing and pulling the ohe pole. Several times, it flexed far enough to crack but Ka'imi and I poured our talents into the fibers and kept it together.

As quickly as the wind rose, it went away. The boat settled and stopped moving when the sail rope went slack.

"Open the windows," I said. "I want to see how far we were blown off course."

Across the still water, I could see the land well enough to recognize the man-made cliffs at Croy's far eastern border with Varia. And we were pointed right at them.

Chapter 80

"I know where we are!" I shouted, wanting to jump into the water and swim to my homeland. "There's a Varian outpost not far from the shore. We can get help there." *I hope.*

"Paddle!" Ka'imi ordered.

The boatmen cheered on their way to the outriggers. We surged forward as if the wind had picked up again.

Soon, I could see the trees standing not far from the rocky shore where the sea met Croy.

"We'll need to find a gap in the rocks wide enough to reach the land," I said.

"Paddle slower when we get closer!" Ka'imi yelled.

"Aye," Makoa replied.

Scraping against jagged rocks, the boat lodged within jumping distance of the coarse, gravel beach. Tall, unnatural cliffs loomed large to our right. The Ainan men stared at them in awe. I'd told them the story of how and why they were made but hearing about something and seeing it are two different things.

"Let me lead the way," I said, sything a crude sack from a sleeping mat to carry the cup and nui Mikilana had given me. "Be careful when you jump, we don't have a healer with us."

Everyone nodded, eyes still fixed on the cliffs.

Leaping from the front of the platform, the jagged stones bit into my feet when I landed. "Ouch," I cried. "Land as softly as you can." I turned to wave the crew on, after I got out of the way.

One by one, the men followed my example.

We all sat and checked our feet for cuts.

"Where do we go from here?" Ka'imi asked, after we determined there were no major injuries.

"Follow the cliffs," I said, pointing to the trees ahead of us.

The Ainan men talked among themselves, marveling at everything I saw as common. It was easy to understand how they felt since I had experienced the same thing entering their land.

Fatigue had set in when I noticed a torch flame flickering not far ahead. At first, I thought I was seeing things, then a Varian soldier stepped into view.

"Aloha!" I called out.

He turned. His eyes opened wide, and jaw dropped, then he lowered the spear, pointing it at me. "Who goes there?"

Hearing someone speaking Varian stopped me in my tracks. Ka'imi bumped into me from behind.

"Wilmar. Orvar. Get out here," the soldier said, spear not moving. "There are people here... People I've never seen."

"What?" someone yelled, from behind him.

"I'm...Princess...Meyla." The words came slow as I had to think of the right thing to say. "Daughter of...King Fitzeirick...and Queen...Tindra."

The soldier stared into my eyes. The tip of his spear quivered. "That's not possible. Croian Princess Meyla is dead...along with her brother."

Two more soldiers rushed out of a hidden passage in the stone wall. "What's going on, Guld?" one of them asked.

The man I assumed to be Guld answered, without looking away, "She claims to be Princess Meyla."

"What?" the third soldier exclaimed.

"Can't be," the second one added. "And who's behind her?"

"I don't know. What do we do?"

"I swear," I said, fighting back tears. "I *am* Princess Meyla. Take me to your king. Uncle Crum will recognize me."

"What's wrong?" Ka'imi asked. "You said they would help us."

"What's he saying?" Guld asked, shaking his spear toward Ka'imi.

"They think I'm dead," I said in Ainan, swallowing and having to think how to convince the soldiers I was telling the truth. "We mean no harm. I can explain everything. I swear on my life."

"Don't move," Guld ordered. "Wilmar, go get more men. Orvar, run and tell General Aerison what's happening and to expect prisoners."

I gasped as one of the men turned to leave.

"Yes, take me to General Aerison," I said. "He knows me. He trained my father when he was in Varia, before Fitzeirick was king."

"Is she telling the truth?" the one who was leaving asked.

"Only one way to find out," Guld said. "Orvar, go ahead. Wilmar, stay with me to make sure this isn't some kind of trick. If you know General Aerison, young lady, then you know where we're going. Lead the way, but any wrong moves, and I spill blood."

"Aye," I said, trembling as I stepped onto Varian soil. My best option would be convincing my father's old friend I was alive and needed his help. Hopefully, he'd know if my parents were alive or dead.

No doubt there would be questions about my disappearance, where Regin was, and why I was with these strange men. As long as General Aerison believed me, I had no doubt he would do everything in his power to see I made it back where I belonged.

If Mother and Father were alive, I would return home, and all would be well. However, if my backstabbing brother was right, and they'd been killed by his co-conspirators, they had no idea what was coming their way.

Fitzeirick's blood flowed in my veins. I wouldn't hesitate to remove Regin's allies from the world, stem and root, and send them to the fire...personally.

To the reader:

Thank you for reading this novel. I encourage you to leave a review at your preferred book retailer. If you enjoyed my story, please recommend it to your friends.

You are welcome to follow me on social media at:
www.facebook.com/JAGuynnAuthor
www.twitter.com/JAGuynnAuthor

Also follow my publisher at:
www.facebook.com/3220Group

Other titles by J.A. Guynn

Branded Book 1: Skald
Branded Book 2: King
Branded Book 3: Conqueror